WISHING IN ROME

JENNIFER SKULLY

Redwood Valley Publishing

© 2021 Jennifer Skully

This is copyrighted material. All rights reserved. No part of this publication may be reproduced, stored in a retrieval system, or transmitted in any form or by any means, electronic, mechanical, recording or otherwise, without the prior written permission of the author. This is a work of fiction. The characters, incidents and dialogues in this book are of the author's imagination and are not to be construed as real. Any resemblance to actual events or persons, living or dead, is completely coincidental.

Wishing in Rome
A Once Again Novel
Book 2

🌸

It's never too late for wishes to come true...

Dana and Carol, best friends their whole lives, planned the trip of a lifetime to Rome. They'd plotted every detail, from touring the Colosseum to throwing coins in the Trevi Fountain and making wishes. When Carol dies suddenly, Dana is bereft—even more than when her husband left her for another woman. Then a bequest from Carol arrives, telling her to take the trip to Rome they'd planned together. Dana sets out on the journey, determined to rediscover the woman she used to be and find the woman she wants to become. Carol's final instruction is to make a wish in the Trevi Fountain. But how do you make an impossible wish for the only thing you truly want— to have your best friend back with you?

Marshall Garrison is all business, and so is this trip to Rome. But a chance meeting with Dana Shaw in the Colosseum changes everything. He doesn't believe in forever-after love, but still, there's something exceptional about this brave divorcée, gallantly traveling alone. He sets out to be her guide and her friend, but when he discovers her poignant story, he wants more— to help her believe in wishing for the impossible. And in the process, he might even remember that business is only a substitute for the things he used to wish for...

A later in life holiday romance that will take you away from it all...

Join our newsletter and receive free books, plus learn about new releases, contests, and other freebies:
http://bit.ly/SkullyNews

ACKNOWLEDGMENTS

A special thanks to Bella Andre for this fabulous idea and to both Bella and Nancy Warren for all the brainstorming on our 10-mile walks. Thank you also to my special network of friends who support and encourage me: Shelley Adina, Jenny Andersen, Linda McGinnis, Jackie Yau, Kathy Coatney, and Laurel Jacobson. As always, a huge hug of appreciation for my husband who helps my writing career flourish. And of course, thank you to sweet little Wrigley, who just can't seem to let the Junco birds alone. While their nesting in the atrium, Wriggles is chasing them! Please, Wriggles, please, let the little chicks hatch and fly away! Honestly, the Juncos just don't understand that Wriggles only wants to play!

DEDICATION

To Judy Moffett
Feb 15, 1926 - April 14, 2021

Judy was one of my mother's best friends. They were both ninety-five and they passed within a month of each other. It gives me comfort to know they are together now. Loving friends forever. Afflicted with rheumatoid arthritis in her forties, Judy lived with constant pain for more than half her life. But she never gave up. She never stopped laughing and smiling with my dear wonderful mother. They were both born in England, and that was their first bond. They had lunch together, worked at the church together, went to the movies together, lived their best lives together. I will always remember and love them both, my dear mother, Doris, and her loving friend, Judy.

1

"What you need is an affair." Carol's pace slowed only slightly as they started up the last hill.

"I am *not* going to be like my husband. *Ex*-husband," Dana emphasized, "and have an affair. Besides you have to be married to have an affair."

Best friends, they were as different as vegan versus carnivore, not that either of them was vegan. Dana was taller while Carol was petite. Dana wore her red hair past her shoulders while Carol changed styles and colors like hair was a fashion accessory. This week she was a striking brunette. Next to her, Dana felt frumpy since she hadn't dyed the gray out of her hair in at least three months.

They walked in the park three days a week, a five-mile round trip along the fire road to the ridge. At the top, you could see the Pacific Ocean. Carol also worked out at the gym two days and was in better shape. Dana was winded, mostly because Carol managed to ask enough questions that Dana did all the talking on the way up the hill.

Carol *tsked*. She wasn't even out of breath. "You don't have to be married. An affair just means casual and of short duration. Preferably it's with someone you don't know so you never have to see him again once it's over."

"How on earth am I going to find a man? I'm not in the PTA anymore. And all my clients are female." When her two daughters were in middle school, Dana opened a bookkeeping service she ran out of the house. She hadn't started it thinking she'd need the income if Anthony ever left her; she'd just needed to fill up the time between carpooling and soccer and swim meets.

"Operative phrase here is someone you don't know and don't have to see again," Carol said in a singsong voice.

"So I should troll bars?"

Her best friend always had an answer. That's what Dana loved about her. "What you need is a vacation. Preferably in a foreign country. You always wanted to go to Rome." Carol poked Dana on the shoulder. "That's it, you need a trip to Rome to find a gorgeous, sexy, virile Italian. Somebody younger than you so he's got a lot of stamina." She imitated a manly growl and punched the air. "You'll stay at the best hotels, eat the most delectable food, and have an affair with a scrumptious Italian." She held up her hands as if she were a genie who'd just granted Dana three wishes.

Dana looked around to make sure a jogger wasn't sneaking up behind them, overhearing anything about scrumptious, sexy, virile Italians. But it was only eight o'clock in the morning, and in February, a little too cool and a little too early for most walkers. After climbing the hills, though, Dana had her jacket wrapped around her waist and her gloves in her pocket.

"I know you set me up comfortably in the divorce." Which had been finalized six months ago. Carol had been Dana's divorce attorney, and she was the best in the San Francisco Bay Area.

Dana should have known Anthony was cheating since he

hadn't made love to her in nine months, but she'd told herself that was only natural after almost three decades of marriage.

"But I can't just fly off to Rome and stay in the lap of luxury."

"Of course you can." Carol flapped a hand at her. "You're just afraid."

"I'm not afraid." Dana let her eyes go wide with amazement. "I have the most scathingly brilliant idea." Just like Hayley Mills in *The Trouble with Angels*, one of her and Carol's favorite movies when they were kids. They'd imagined themselves as those mischievous girls. "You have to come with me."

Carol scrunched up her face. "No way. If I go with you, we'll do everything together. And you'll never make the opportunity to find your gorgeous Italian. No." Carol shook her head with determination. "You have to go by yourself."

"But I don't want to go alone." Dana thought of all the things she'd have to take care of. It really was too much effort to even think about it. And who wanted to tour amazing sites like the Colosseum and the Forum and the Vatican all by themselves?

"I can see your mind working. But we can plan this together, I promise. I'll help you book everything. No pressure on you. Then all you have to do is get on the plane, check into your room, and have the best week of your life with a virile young Italian."

"There's no way I'm finding a sexy, virile young Italian."

"You underestimate yourself. You're gorgeous."

Dana snorted. "I'm fifty."

"If sixty is the new forty, that means you're more like thirty."

"Now that's a stretch," she scoffed.

"And while you're there, you have to a make a wish in the Trevi Fountain. Just like in *Three Coins in the Fountain*." Which was another of their favorite movies when they were kids. They'd had so many slumber parties, staying up to watch all the old movies on late night TV.

"I wouldn't know what to wish for."

"Why not wish to be Audrey Hepburn in *Roman Holiday*, riding around on the back of a Vespa with Gregory Peck?" They had definitely loved their old movies.

"Honestly, I don't have any wishes."

Carol rolled her eyes. "Everyone has wishes. Seriously, what do you want the rest of your life to look like?"

They'd had this discussion several times since the divorce. "I just want my girls to get married and give me grandbabies." The girls were both in college now.

"That's what you wish for *their* lives. What about yours?"

"I don't know. I haven't had time to think about it yet." Dana was still sorting out the house, getting rid of things Anthony hadn't taken with him when he left her for a prettier, skinnier, younger woman.

"Wish for what you want most in the world. If you're traveling all the way to Rome and the Trevi Fountain—" Carol spread her hands wide. "—it absolutely has to come true."

Dana didn't know what she wanted most in the world. A husband who didn't cheat? Her life to go back to normal? Though she could say anything to Carol, she didn't want to sound self-pitying. So she laughed and said, "You're crazy."

"I'm not crazy. I just know what my bestie needs. An affair with a sexy young Italian who will worship at your feet and make you feel like a desirable woman in your prime. Which is exactly what you are. I tell you, you'll come back a new woman."

Dana didn't want to be a new woman. She just wanted the security she'd had before the divorce.

Carol stumbled then, grabbed her head, her voice suddenly strained. "Oh my God."

Dana's heart almost stopped. "What's the matter?"

"My head. Oh my God, my head. It hurts so bad. Feels like something popped right here." Carol pointed just behind her right ear. "Oh my God." She held her head in her hands, gasping. "This is bad, really bad."

The pain had come on so quickly, and absolute terror gripped Dana. Was it a stroke? God help her. They were two miles inside the park. How was she supposed to get Carol back down? She didn't have a single bar on her phone. She always lost cell reception on the hill. "Can you make it back down?"

But Carol sank to the ground, still holding her head. "Oh my God. I don't think I can even walk."

"Okay, okay," she soothed, sitting beside Carol, pulling her close. Until finally Carol laid her head in Dana's lap, tears pooling in her eyes, sliding down the side of her nose as she mewled softly like an injured kitten. Dana stroked her arm, up and down, up and down, helpless and useless.

There was no one in either direction who could help, and Dana couldn't just sit there. But if she could get to the flats at the top of this last hill, her phone would work again. It wasn't that far, just around the next corner. "Okay, I'll run up the hill where I can call an ambulance. Then I'll run right back to you, I promise. Okay?"

"Please don't leave me," Carol whispered.

"I have to. I don't know what's wrong, but we need help." They needed it right now. If she didn't move, Carol could die. Or be paralyzed. Or any of the other horrible things that happened if this was a stroke.

As if the heavens opened up and rained a miracle on them, a biker flew around the corner at the top of the hill above them, breaking hard when he saw them slumped in the middle of the road. "Are you all right?"

"My friend needs an ambulance. Right away. Do you have

your cell phone with you?" Her voice was pathetic and pleading and she didn't care. When he nodded, she begged, "Can you get somewhere with reception and call an ambulance?"

"Yeah, sure. I'll blow downhill, faster than going back up."

They saw the guy every day on their walk. He was older, in amazing shape, and the quickest choice. He took off, flying away down the hill.

"Everything will be okay. It'll be okay," she kept repeating to Carol. And herself. "It's just a headache." Dana was terrified it was something far worse. A brain tumor? She tried to tamp down the panic, continuing the soothing caress along Carol's arm.

A middle-aged park ranger arrived first, tall, lanky, glasses a little dirty, his hair a frizzy mass beneath his hat. Dana wanted to throw herself at him, hug him, thank him, beg him to do something.

"I don't know what's wrong." Looking up at him, Carol's head still pillowed in her lap, Dana's heart pounded so loudly she could barely hear her own words. "She just suddenly got this terrible headache."

"And you are?" he asked.

"Dana Shaw. She's my best friend."

Dana was an only child, and Carol had been her best friend since they were eight years old. They'd double-dated through high school, shared every heartache, gone to the same university, shared a dorm room, fallen truly, madly, deeply in love at the same time. They'd worn the same wedding dress because money was tight and they were the same size back then, except for their height. Carol had coached her through the births of her two daughters. She'd held Dana's hand when her mom was dying of cancer ten years ago, and when her dad orphaned her by heart attack only months later. Carol understood her, loved her, always supported her no matter what.

She was going to throw up or pass out.

Dear God, please let everything be okay.

The ranger hunkered down beside Carol, his voice low and deep and oddly comforting. "Can you tell me your name, ma'am?"

"Carol Hunt," she murmured without opening her eyes.

He took out a small spiral pad. "Can you tell me your age?"

"Fifty." Her words were barely audible.

"I can answer all those questions for her," Dana said.

The ranger waved her off. "I know. But we need to see how much she can answer on her own."

Oh God, it *was* a stroke. He asked Carol what day of the week it was, what year, where she was. She knew all the answers.

Dana rubbed Carol's back, even as her panic reached new heights and she was afraid she'd scream. "Can't we just drive her down, get her to a hospital?"

"The ambulance will be here in a minute," the ranger assured her.

Meanwhile, more tears leaked from Carol's eyes. She never cried. Not at weddings or baby christenings, not even at funerals.

Finally Dana heard the shriek of sirens.

She'd never felt such terror and relief in her life.

The paramedics arrived, their sirens splitting the air then cutting off abruptly. They asked all the same questions but wouldn't even speculate on what was wrong with Carol.

Dana could only be thankful they loaded her friend onto the ambulance quickly.

But they wouldn't let Dana ride with her.

The ranger drove Dana down the hill, her heart in her

throat the whole way. He kept to an agonizingly slow speed, mindful of the other hikers now filling up the road. She could have walked it faster.

She climbed into her car in the parking lot, holding onto the steering wheel until her fingers turned white as she stared out the windshield into the dark forest. She opened her mouth, squeezed her eyes shut, and screamed, long and agonizing and soundless in the loneliness of her car. If anyone saw, she didn't care.

Then she called Thomas, Carol's husband.

"Hello?" She heard the worry in his voice, because of course he wondered why Dana would call him on a day when she was supposed to be with Carol.

"Thomas." She swallowed hard before she could get the words out. "Something happened to Carol while we were walking. It could have been a stroke, I don't know. The paramedics are taking her to the hospital. You need to get over there." She told him the location. "I'll come, too. Are you at work?"

Thomas was quiet for so long she thought he'd hung up. Until finally he said, "I don't understand. What happened?"

She didn't know how to explain. He was a lawyer like Carol, and Dana had given him enough details, couldn't he just figure out the rest when he got to the hospital? Why did he have to make her relive it?

But of course he needed to know. You didn't wait for a conveniently dramatic moment at the hospital like they did in the movies. "She got a really bad headache and collapsed right there on the road. A biker called an ambulance. She couldn't even move, Thomas. Something was really wrong. I'm not sure it was a stroke because she could answer all their questions. You just need to get there." She repeated the hospital name.

"Is she alive?" Tension and fear vibrated through his voice.

She would have said that right away, and she wanted to scream at him for asking such a stupid question. But this was his wife, and he couldn't seem to grasp reality. And she was frantic.

"Yes, Thomas, she's alive. I don't know what's wrong. Look, I'll meet you at the hospital. I'm driving over there right now. The doctors will tell us what's going on." She paused a beat, listened. "Are you okay, Thomas?"

She could hear him breathing, too fast. He had high blood pressure. He was on medication. She was suddenly frightened that something would happen to him. "It's okay, Thomas. Everything will be fine. Go straight to the emergency room, and they'll tell you where she is."

"Okay," he said so softly she almost missed it.

Thomas Hunt was an estate lawyer and a quiet man. Sometimes she wondered how he ever got up in front of a judge or pled a case in a courtroom full of people. But he was a good man, he adored Carol, and they had an amazing marriage. They'd met thirty years ago when they were prelaw at university. Thomas and Anthony had been study partners, and Dana was Carol's bestie, so they became a foursome, double-dating.

"She's going be fine, Thomas. It's just a really bad headache, that's all." She said it for herself as much as for him.

He finally croaked out, "Okay, I'll meet you there." Neither of them said goodbye. The line was simply dead.

For a moment she couldn't start the engine. She couldn't even move. She could only hold the steering wheel like it was a lifeline. She should call her daughters. They'd want to know. They adored their Auntie Carol. And while Carol always claimed she wasn't the motherly type, she was the most amazing auntie.

Dana even thought about calling Anthony. He'd known

Carol for thirty years. But then he wasn't too happy with Carol for representing Dana in the divorce. He'd thought they should both use lawyers unconnected to them.

No, she wouldn't call Anthony.

She needed someone, though. But the only person who would really make her feel better was the one person she couldn't call. Carol.

2

"You scared the crap out of me," Dana said, holding Carol's hand. "Don't ever do that again."

Carol laughed softly. It was still hard for her to move even after more than twenty-four hours. She was in ICU, hooked up to beeping monitors. The nurses had allowed Dana in only because Thomas said she was Carol's sister. They were sisters in every meaning of the word except biologically.

She and Thomas had been here all night, and her back was cramped from sleeping in a chair. Thomas had gone home to take a shower while Dana stayed. Neither of them would leave Carol alone.

"I'm only alive because of you." Carol's voice came out croaky.

Dana squeezed her hand. "I panicked. It was that biker we see all the time who rode down the hill and called an ambulance."

"You underestimate yourself." Carol sighed, closing her eyes.

Dana didn't like the smell of hospitals. It was such a

sterile scent, like all the life had been sponged out of everything and all that remained was the pungent aroma of the hand sanitizer everyone used constantly. The food was bad, too, like spaghetti out of a can. At least Carol had a room instead of just a curtain pulled around her bed.

Her head still hurt, she said, but it was bearable, especially with what Carol called "those delightful drugs." She'd had a hemorrhage, essentially a brain bleed. Only half the people with this kind of thing survived. Only five percent of survivors got away without brain damage. It would be a long time, a lot of drugs, and a lot of rest, but Carol would survive. And she still had her beautiful, wonderful mind.

"Darling," Carol said dramatically. "While Thomas is gone, I have to beg you, please, please, please bring me some decent lingerie." She fingered the drab hospital gown. "Look at this, it's horrible." She shuddered. "Thomas is a sweetheart, but his taste in lingerie sucks. He'd probably get me a flannel nightgown and granny panties."

"Not the dreaded granny panties." They laughed together the way they always had. "What else do you want?"

Carol smiled slyly. "Those See's dark chocolate peppermint patties."

Dana shivered with delight. "They're to die for."

"Remember when I gave you a box for Christmas, half dark and half milk, and Anthony ate all the dark chocolate ones you were saving?"

Dana narrowed her eyes. "Bastard."

"That's why I got you that humongous settlement. Payback."

"I bet he wishes he never ate them."

They laughed. It was so good to see Carol like her old self. Her voice was croaky and weak, her movements slow and measured, but she was still Carol.

Dana curled both hands around Carol's fingers. "I was

thinking, that trip to Rome, we're going together when you're better. Wouldn't that be amazing? We could go shopping, stay at your favorite hotels, get massages, like an extended spa day."

"You're supposed to have an affair," Carol said dryly. "I'll cramp your style."

Dana snorted a laugh. "I don't have a style. And I don't need an affair. I'd rather go with you." Her heart still ached with the terror she'd felt. She didn't want Carol out of her sight, and she certainly wasn't taking a holiday without her best friend.

Carol moaned dramatically. "You're so pathetic. I didn't get you that fabulous divorce settlement so you could stay at home and twiddle your thumbs."

"I'm hardly twiddling my thumbs." She squeezed Carol's hand. She couldn't seem to let go of her. Carol was here, she was alive, she was amazing. "I want you to go with me."

Carol let out a long-suffering huff. "All right. We'll go together. But you have to make that wish in the Trevi Fountain. Promise?"

"I promise. I just don't know what I'm going to wish for."

"You can wish for a hot, young sexpot Italian to make love to you all night long."

"Please don't tell me that's what you're wishing for, dearest," Thomas said from the doorway.

"It doesn't mean I don't love you, honey," Carol quipped in a girlish voice.

Thomas still looked tired, his features strained, but he'd shaved and combed his graying hair, which had been sticking out in all directions after twenty-four hours of raking his fingers through it. A tall man, he and Carol made a striking couple with their stark contrast in height. Petite at five foot two, Carol's adversaries in the courtroom underestimated her at their peril. She was a powerhouse.

Except right now.

Carol held out her hand to Thomas. "Now tell my friend here that she needs to go home and get some rest." She turned back to Dana. "I know you were sitting in that chair all night waiting to see if I'd make it. And you smell like it, too." She wrinkled her nose. "Don't look so offended. I'm your friend. I can tell you anything. Go home, get some sleep, and do not, I repeat, do not come back until tomorrow. After ten. I need my beauty sleep."

Dana laughed because this was Carol, always giving her crap.

She prayed her friend would keep on doing it for years to come.

AFTER TEN THE NEXT MORNING, DANA HAD FLOWERS AND See's peppermint patties, all dark chocolate, no milk. She'd stopped at a department store on the way home yesterday and bought a couple of pretty nighties and some lacy underwear. She'd also brought magazines, though Carol had said reading made her head hurt. She could just look at the pictures. Dana had to bring her *something*.

She'd called the girls, told them what was happening, and they'd both be coming on the weekend, driving up from San Luis Obispo where they attended Cal Poly.

The heels of her boots were loud on the linoleum floor. The hallway was pristine, the antiseptic smell suffocating. She avoided glancing in the rooms she passed.

Thomas had called last night to say they'd moved Carol out of ICU. Thank God. It meant she was recovering. Dana turned left down the corridor where nurses flitted in and out of rooms, rolling IV stands, sanitizing their hands, checking monitors. Dana moved out of the way as two orderlies wheeled a man by on a hospital bed.

She came to a complete stop when she saw Thomas in the hallway, facing off with two men and a woman, all three of them in white coats.

He was probably getting an update on Carol's condition.

Yet there was something in the way Thomas shoved his fingers through his hair, turning it into knots. Then he put his hand over his mouth, and one of the white coats held his arm.

Dana felt the wrongness of it deep in her bones.

She dropped the flowers down to her side, petals floating to the floor.

She wanted to turn, wanted to run, just get out before the scent of hand sanitizer choked her. Before Thomas saw her.

Because what you didn't know couldn't hurt you.

Then Thomas turned and there was nowhere to run. Her gut screamed that Carol had taken a turn for the worst. They'd have to operate. *Dear God, please don't let there be brain damage.* Carol was so proud of her brain.

Dana made her feet move, her steps shaky as if she were a drunk trying to walk a straight line, until finally she reached Thomas.

Fresh lines etched his face, and though well over six feet, the stoop of his shoulders diminished him.

"What's going on, Thomas?" She didn't want to ask, but she had to.

She braced herself for bad news. They'd have to do surgery. Carol might never be the same. Or she might not make it through.

"Her blood pressure spiked," Thomas said, his gaze on the pristine linoleum, his face haggard, his skin pallid. "She hemorrhaged again."

That was her worst fear, Carol in screaming, crying agony.

"Is she going back into ICU?" She looked at one of the doctors, the woman, then the man who'd put his hand on Thomas's arm, and finally the last one, all with identical expressions she couldn't read. "Are you taking her into surgery?"

"There wasn't time, Dana." Thomas's voice was so harsh it rubbed her skin raw like a Brillo pad. "She's gone."

"Gone where?" she echoed.

The trio of doctors looked at her with a mixture of sympathy, compassion, and disbelief. Thomas shook his head, closed his eyes, his breath audible in the hallway which had gone terribly, awfully quiet.

She realized how hopeful the question had been. How childlike. How stupid.

Carol was gone, somewhere Dana couldn't go with her. The flowers slipped from her fingers, the bag of chocolates and nighties and magazines dropped to the floor.

Then Thomas put his arms around her and they held each other. Tight. He was all she had left of Carol.

She didn't break down. As badly as she wanted to.

Carol would want her to take care of Thomas.

It was the last thing she could do for her dearest friend.

❦

DANA DIDN'T BREAK DOWN FOR FORTY-EIGHT HOURS. Carol needed her to take care of Thomas. And so she did. It was the only thing that kept her from crumbling.

She got through by repeating it to herself over and over. *Just take care of Thomas.*

She was by his side at the hospital. When it was time, she drove him home, unlocked the front door of the big house, took him inside, made his favorite whiskey sour, helped him upstairs, put him to bed.

She slept in her clothes in the guestroom, pulling a blanket over her.

The next day, she arranged to get Thomas's car since they'd left it at the hospital. When she went home for fresh clothes, she threw out the boxes of lingerie and chocolate, the flowers, the magazines. Some kind nurse had handed everything back to her at some point. The sight of it all made her physically ill.

In the following days, she and Thomas wrote Carol's obituary, she took him to the funeral home, she made phone calls to friends. She helped him with everything.

It wasn't that Thomas was weak, or that he couldn't do it himself, or even that he'd completely lost it. It was that Carol would have wanted Dana to care for him. So Thomas let her. And Dana did it. That was how they survived.

She didn't cry for two days. Not until she was alone in her own home. And then the tears drowned her.

Her daughters arrived home, and once again Dana set about taking care of somebody. She made their favorite meals. She sat in the TV room with them and watched movies they chose. She got out the photo albums, and they went through all the pictures of Carol. She pulled out this one or that one to make a copy for Thomas. They laughed, they cried, they mourned.

The girls helped her write the eulogy. They listened to her practice it. And in the pews of the church on the day of the memorial, they cried as she read it.

She wondered if, looking at the sea of faces gathered to bid Carol farewell, looking at Thomas, her daughters, at Anthony who'd attended with the new wife Carol had never met, she wondered if any of them knew how hollow she was inside.

People always talked about the loss of a husband or wife or child or father or mother or brother or sister. Somehow it was as if losing a friend wasn't as big a deal. They weren't blood. They weren't family. After all, you could always find a new friend, right?

Dana had lost a bigger piece of her heart than she'd lost the day Anthony left her.

Divorce was survivable. But she didn't know how she'd survive losing Carol. She couldn't imagine her life without her best friend. Carol had known her the longest and the best. Carol had been through everything with her, all the messy parts of life that brought out the worst in a person. And Carol had loved her anyway.

How could she go on without the one person who understood her completely?

Dana didn't say any of that in her eulogy. She said all the things people expected to hear, what a wonderful friend Carol was, how much people would miss her, how smart she was, how funny she was, what an asset to the community.

But inside she asked herself where she could possibly go from here without Carol.

3

There'd been few dry eyes during the memorial, and now Thomas's house was filled with all the people who'd loved Carol.

"Oh my God," Natalie hissed. "I can't believe she would show up here looking like *that*."

Dana knew that tone in her eldest daughter's voice. And she knew without looking exactly who Natalie was talking about. "Your father just wants to pay his respects," she said. "He knew Carol a long time, too."

"I'm not talking about *him*." Natalie was glaring daggers. "It's *her*. The nerve."

"We have to get used to her, Nat. She's our stepmother. And she's going to be the mother of our half brother." Olivia was much more tolerant. Natalie hadn't forgiven her father yet.

Anthony had told the girls he'd started seeing the woman after the divorce, but though Dana had never confirmed anything, Natalie was sure he'd been having an affair.

Natalie rolled her eyes, her voice full of disgust. "Yeah, he's finally getting the boy he always wanted."

"Girls, please, it's not the time." She didn't want to fight. Honestly, since Carol's death, Dana had ceased to care about Anthony or the new wife or the new baby.

She and her daughters stood in the living room of Carol and Thomas's beautiful home, watching the comings and goings in the large foyer and the guests milling around the buffet table in the dining room. Thomas had catered the reception, and Dana helped to arrange things. The house was huge, a formal living and dining room, a master chef's kitchen, a family room equipped with a massive flat-screen TV and monolith speakers for the state-of-the-art stereo system. The bedrooms were upstairs along with a home office for each of them.

Today the house was full of Carol's friends, people she'd worked with, clients she'd helped, colleagues she'd had over for cocktail parties, neighbors she'd invited for summer barbecues. Thomas had set Carol's urn next to a flattering picture of her on top of the grand piano. Neither of them played, but they'd hired a pianist for parties.

Dana had spent so many hours in this house, in the kitchen, out by the pool, on the gorgeous wraparound porch, talking for hours, drinking coffee or lemonade or a glass of champagne.

Now, despite all the people cluttering the hardwood floor, the house seemed empty.

"But Mom, it's just so insensitive to you. And she didn't even know Aunt Carol," Natalie said as if she expected Dana to do something about it. Like what, throw the woman out?

After offering their condolences to Thomas, the friends, coworkers, other lawyers, and the multitude of people who'd known Carol had all come to Dana next, hugged her, shook her hand, cupped her shoulder, kissed her cheek as if they understood her loss. She didn't cry. Not while Thomas might still need her.

And she certainly wasn't going to make a scene over her ex-husband's pregnant wife. "Aunt Carol's death has changed me, sweetheart."

She slipped her daughter's gorgeous red hair, so much more brilliant than her own, behind her ear. Both her girls had inherited her red hair and green eyes. Anthony's was an unremarkable brown, though it had gone gray since the divorce. She'd forgotten exactly how genes worked, but it seemed as if the girls should never have gotten her red hair, but both of them had. They were *her* girls.

"It takes something like this to make you realize that you have to move on. Your dad moved on, and I need to as well. He's got a new life. The new baby." She raised a thumb to wipe away the trace of a tear at the corner of Natalie's eye. "That baby bump is going to be your little brother. Just because you're angry with your dad and you're angry with her, you don't want to miss out on that beautiful new baby, do you?"

Natalie fluttered her eyelashes, blinking away a trace of tears. "No, I don't want to miss the baby. I'm just so mad at *him*. She was his paralegal, for God's sake. That's such a cliché. And I really don't like her," she added between gritted teeth.

"That's because she's only six years older than you," Olivia said.

Natalie gaped. "Doesn't it bother you, Liv?"

Olivia shrugged, made a face. "She's not too bad. In a sort of nondescript way. I mean, I don't think she's an airhead or anything, but I do wonder how she got to be a paralegal."

For the first time in days, even weeks, Dana felt like laughing. Just a short snort of laughter. Because Olivia was so laidback. Natalie was the high strung one, while Olivia was just easy. Maybe because she was the second daughter.

"Oh my God," Natalie hissed again. "They're coming over here."

Standing between them, Dana curled her fingers around her daughters' hands. "It's okay, sweetheart. We'll take care of you."

Then Anthony was there. He hugged Natalie, then Olivia, as if he'd chosen to do it in the order of age so no one would be offended. While Nat remained stiff in his arms, she didn't make a nasty comment, thank goodness.

The moment was already awkward enough, because really, how did you introduce the new wife you'd been cheating with to the ex-wife? Although they had met once. It was just that Dana hadn't seen her face since she was hidden by Anthony's pumping buttocks.

But Anthony managed the introductions smoothly, the way he did everything. "Dana, I don't think you've met Kimberly. Kimberly, this is Dana."

As Natalie had said, the girl was a cliché, pretty, blond, tall, and slender. Exactly the kind of woman with whom a middle-aged man would have his midlife crisis.

Carol would have had a field day. Even now, Dana could hear her friend's whisper.

What the hell kind of name is Kimberly? And how can someone be that skinny when they're five months pregnant? She's got to be anorexic. She's probably going to make the baby anorexic. You know what, I think he's getting a bit of paunch, don't you?

Dana smiled. Because Carol was with her. Carol made her laugh. Carol made everything okay.

"So nice to meet you," she said graciously, then turned to her ex-husband. "I'm so glad you could make it, Anthony." Not. "I'm sure that Thomas will be happy to know there's no hard feelings." She smiled, glanced at Kimberly. "I'm sure he would love if you told him a few nice things about Carol." She put her hand on his arm and leaned close, pointing. "He's right over there." Yes, it was a dismissal. She didn't want to be mean, but she simply didn't have the bandwidth to deal with Anthony today. She had nothing left to say to him. And she certainly couldn't think of anything she wanted to say to his wife.

"I'm really sorry about Carol," Anthony said. "I know how much she meant to you."

He leaned forward to hug her, this man with whom she'd lived for almost thirty years and with whom she'd had two children, yet now he was a stranger.

Stepping back, she looked at her ex-husband, his handsome face, his Botoxed forehead, his slight paunch, as he reached back to link hands once again with Kimberly, her baby bump evidence of his affair.

Dana was conscious of her daughters standing beside her, Natalie with her back up, Olivia with her hands behind her, her fingers crossed, hoping this wouldn't degenerate into a brawl.

The one thing she'd sworn to herself, and made Carol swear as well, was that she wouldn't poison her daughters against their father. She'd never told them he was having an affair. She'd never badmouthed him. She'd never tried to make them choose sides. Good parents didn't use their children to get back at each other. When she fought with Anthony after the affair, she never did it in front of them. They were adults, they needed to make up their own minds about their father.

And now she didn't tell Anthony to go screw himself. She didn't tell him the hundreds of things that were suddenly percolating deep down inside her. She didn't even tell him it was classless to bring his pregnant young trophy wife to his ex-wife's best friend's memorial. She'd meant it when she said losing Carol had changed her perspective. She couldn't let Anthony be that important anymore.

She said ever so politely, "Thank you. I really appreciate

that." She gave him a sweet, courteous smile. "Oh, look, Thomas is signaling. You better go see him." She put her hand on his shoulder and gave him a little push in the right direction.

"That was really nice of you, Mom," Olivia said when they were out of earshot. "Thank you for being so polite."

Dana didn't want to be a bitter divorcée. "It's fine, dear. Your father and I are on decent terms, considering the circumstances."

Natalie scowled. "You should have let me tell him that his pregnant bimbo didn't have a place here." She'd always been her father's favorite, which was part of why she was so angry with him now, because he'd left her as well. He had a new wife and soon he'd have a new baby. Natalie would no longer be the favorite. She was afraid she wouldn't get any attention at all. And she was probably right.

Dana put her arm around her shoulders. "It's okay, sweetie. I'm not upset. So you don't need to be upset for me. Okay?" Then she took Olivia's hand in hers, too. "I love you both so much, and in my world, that's the only thing that matters."

"Love you, too, Mom," Olivia said softly. Natalie joined in, and they all hugged.

Her girls were her solace.

Yet even in the midst of that beautiful hug, Dana thought how much she'd miss having Carol watch her girls graduate from college, find fabulous jobs that she and Carol could brag about, get married, have babies.

There would be so many things she would miss going through with Carol. She would never have another friend who could be there with her and understand exactly what she felt.

The reception was winding down, half the guests had already left, including Anthony and his pregnant wife.

Dana didn't want to be bitter. When she looked at everything with hindsight, she recognized that things had been wrong in her marriage. Kimberly wasn't the cause, she was merely a symptom. Dana should have seen this coming years ago. Maybe they would have gone to marriage counseling. They could have done something. Shoulda, woulda, coulda... didn't. If she wanted to take control of her life, she had to admit that she'd let her marriage slip away without even trying. She'd been all about the kids and managing the house and making sure there was a healthy meal on the table and clean clothes in the drawers. She'd forgotten to be a lover as well. That didn't mean the blame was all hers and none of it was Anthony's. But she was the one with the bigger stake in the domesticity of marriage. That was obvious.

And that's what hurt the most. That she was more committed than Anthony.

As if Carol were standing next to her, she knew exactly what her friend would say. *Stop wallowing. Move on.*

The girls had found a group of their own age and were now huddled in a corner, all of them stifling laughter with their hands over their mouths, sidelong glances to make sure no one had seen or heard. For the young, death was only a reality once in a while, when a grandparent died, or an aunt or an uncle. Or their mother's best friend. While their grief was sincere, it was in their nature to move on. If they dwelled on it too long, they'd recognize their own mortality.

A touch on her arm jerked her out of her musings.

Thomas stood beside her, forcing her to look up. When she and Carol had first met him in college, he was on the skinny side. After he and Carol started dating, he'd combatted that with vigorous workouts and long sessions pumping iron. While he'd been angular in his twenties, his face now was full, his body pumped from his daily workout in their home gym. He had grown into his looks, a handsome man, his body toned, filling out the tuxedo he'd worn for the memorial.

The last few weeks, though, had drained the color from his face and leached the joy out of his eyes.

"Can I see you in my office for a moment?" he asked in a soft voice that was natural to him.

"Of course." She glanced over her shoulder at the girls. They didn't notice Thomas leading her up the stairs.

He stopped at the third door on the left along the landing, his inner sanctum.

For a terrible moment, as he opened the door, she was afraid of what she'd see, flashbacks of opening Anthony's office door, his half-naked butt, a pair of legs around his waist, one high heel on, one off.

She always wanted to ask Anthony why he didn't lock the door, why he chose his paralegal. The girls were right, it was such a cliché.

But Thomas's office was unoccupied. The cherrywood bookcases were filled with a conglomeration of law books, financial management texts, hardback mysteries, and paperback thrillers. His desk was a massive old-fashioned wood and leather monstrosity he'd inherited from his father. A few nicks and gouges marred the wood but the leather was pristine. He'd had it redone after his father died fifteen years ago.

Though his office was located in downtown San Francisco, he often invited clients who lived on the Peninsula to meet him here, attested to by the small conference table in the corner next to the window and the leather chairs facing the desk.

The room smelled like freshly polished wood and leather

and Thomas's aftershave. She'd never said it, but she found his scent a little cloying. Carol, however, had chosen it and loved it.

He followed her into the room, closed the door, motioned to a seat, then rounded his desk and took his big leather chair. The desktop was empty except for an envelope. Thomas picked it up, tapped it a few times on the leather, as if tamping down the contents. Or maybe he was nervous. It was hard to tell with Thomas.

He started formally. "I asked you up here to discuss a sensitive matter."

Her stomach dropped.

"It's not bad," Thomas said, sensing her emotions. He laid the letter down and slid it across the desk to her.

Dana wasn't ready to take it.

"Carol didn't think she was dying when she was in the hospital." He held up his hands as if he were warding off a memory. "But there's always those questions running around in your mind afterward." He circled his head with his hand. "All the things you should have done. All the decisions you should have made that would have changed the outcome." He dipped his head, and Dana couldn't tell whether he was looking at the desktop or closing his eyes. Then once more he raised his gaze to hers. "But we didn't know. And she had me write a letter to you that she dictated because her writing was shaky and her eyesight wasn't good." He sighed, so heavily that Dana could see the sorrow weighing his shoulders down.

She realized he'd been putting on a very good act these past weeks. Now he was ready for the house to empty so he could break down without an audience. This, her, the letter, was his last piece of business.

"I don't want you to read it now," he went on. "Take it

home. Don't read it in front of the girls. Wait until you're alone."

He reached down beside the desk and retrieved a bottle of Veuve Clicquot, Carol's favorite champagne.

"Pour yourself a glass of this, settle into a comfortable chair, and sip while you read." He gave her the ghost of a smile, a ghost of the man he'd been before he lost Carol. "That's what she wanted." He paused a long moment, his eyes bleak and futureless. "She prepared for every eventuality. That's what Carol was like. Always thinking ahead, always managing every angle."

"That's what made her such a great divorce attorney," Dana said, wondering if it was the first time she'd opened her mouth since entering the room.

Thomas nodded with that ghost smile again, his voice dropping to a pained note. "I miss her so much."

"So do I."

"But you knew her so much longer. And she knew you. You were the most important thing in the world to her. You and the girls."

"Only next to you."

He tapped the desk twice, sniffed, blinked, as if he kept on talking, he might cry. And Thomas was the type who believed a man never cried in front of anyone else. Even if he'd cried in Dana's arms just a few days ago. He rose, rounded the desk, trailed his hand over her shoulder, then opened the office door. He turned at the last moment. "I need to say goodbye to the last of the guests."

"I'll help clean up." She stood.

"No." Thomas shook his head. "The caterers will do that." Then he added gently, "Thank you for taking care of all the logistics for the memorial. It was a great help."

"We did it together, Thomas."

She wanted to hug him, but he turned down the hall, and she was alone.

Looking back at the letter on the desk, part of her wanted to open it right now. But another part, the bigger part, wanted to hold the letter to her chest and save it for that perfect bottle of champagne just the way Carol wanted her to.

4

With their wistful looks and hugs goodbye after the memorial, Dana knew the girls wanted to hang with their friends. It was duty that made them want to keep their mother company on this difficult day.

Yet, after all the activity, the eulogy, helping Thomas with the details, Dana needed time alone to remember, to truly accept that Carol wasn't here anymore. She couldn't pick up the phone and ask her out for coffee or dinner or a drink after work.

And there was Carol's letter to read.

So she'd waved the girls off for a night out, returned to the kitchen, and opened the bottle of Veuve Clicquot.

Pouring a glass, she saluted her absent-forevermore BFF. "I miss you."

Removing Carol's letter from her purse, she climbed the stairs to her bedroom. After Anthony left, she'd redecorated in soft pastel colors with throw pillows and a flowered eiderdown. When the girls were done with college and out on their own, she might downsize. But for now, she liked them to settle back into their familiar rooms when they came home on holidays and summer break.

She'd created a cozy spot by the bay window with a comfortable chair, using the window seat as a table. Overlooking the pool and the green lawn, it was a tranquil place to read her best friend's letter. Her name was written on the front in Thomas's crisp cursive, though she wished Carol had been able to write it herself.

Slipping out the pages, she allowed herself to hear Carol's voice as she read.

My dearest Dana,

You probably think I'm going to tell you to take care of Thomas. Because we all know he'll be pathetic without me.

She could see Carol and Thomas laughing over that, both afraid that the worst would happen but not willing to face it.

But we're going to talk about you. You don't deserve the dirty deal you got. Which was why I made Anthony pay through the nose. It wasn't just the dark chocolate peppermint patties he ate. I don't want you to have to work another day in your life if you don't want to. I've always told you I'm leaving some money for the girls. I don't want them to move back in with you, especially since you don't have a basement.

That had been their joke, about the kids moving back when they were thirty, living in the basement or a converted garage. Dana wouldn't have minded, but the money Carol wanted them to have would help the girls focus on their bright futures rather than money troubles.

They're like my own girls, you know, without all the diaper changing, sleepless nights, terrible twos, and those pesky teenage years when they hated your guts. I can only say I'm glad I was there to help you through it. Now they just hate Anthony's guts, which is much better in my opinion.

Now I come to you, my dear friend. I'm leaving you some money, too. Of course, I'll get through this and we'll take this trip together.

But just in case— Thomas is giving me a look, but I want all the bases covered. I'm not jinxing my recovery. I intend to get better. But something like this puts the fear of God in you, and you realize you have to say everything now in case you don't get a chance later. So I'm telling you that you deserve to be treated well. You deserve happiness. You deserve the best life has to offer.

Tears welled up then, for all the things Carol believed Dana should have. For the fact that Carol wrote this letter even though she believed she'd get well. Her heart ached with unbearable loss.

I got you the settlement you deserved. And now I want you to have the vacation you deserve. When I'm well, I'm going to pay for it. And if I can't be there, I'm leaving you the money to make sure you do it. I want you to stay at the best hotels, eat the richest food, and buy designer clothes and bags and shoes. Then I want you to find the sexiest Italian lover, a young man who will treat you the way you deserve, to wine and dine you, to be your tour guide as well as your lover. Thomas is giving me that look again. And I can see you screaming that he knows everything you're going to do. Do not freak out, my friend. Thomas has sworn to support you in this endeavor. And if you don't do this yourself, he'll make the reservations for you.

If the worst happens, and I can't go on this trip with you, you must go on your own. And you must throw a coin in the Trevi Fountain and make that wish. Which means you better know what your wish is!

I see you rolling your eyes at me and saying you don't want to do it on your own. But you need to do something that's only for you, Dana. You always do everything for everyone else. So make a wish, take a lover, treat yourself right. To start, I want you to fly first class and stay in my favorite hotel in Rome, the Palazzo Roma. Then you're going to buy a whole new wardrobe. And finally you will find the perfect lover. Thomas just did a quick calc on the back of an envelope for me, and we think $50,000 will be a good start. So that's how much I'm giving you. I love you. You have to do this for me.

Her hand dropped to her lap, the letter fluttering to the floor.

Fifty thousand dollars! It was nuts. She wouldn't even know how to start spending that kind of money. Carol stayed at the best hotels, went to the best restaurants. With no children, Carol and Thomas had been able to afford the best. Despite the big money Anthony made as lawyer for all those soulless corporations, Dana had never gotten past her middle-class spending habits. That's why Carol had written the letter, making the trip an edict.

Dana didn't realize she was crying until she tasted a tear at the corner of her mouth. With the saltiness of it on her lips and the memory of her friend's laughter, her snarkiness, and her big heart, she realized there was only one way to honor Carol. She needed to enjoy the trip Carol had given her.

Maybe she'd even have an affair with a sexy young Italian.

※

THE GIRLS HAD STAYED AN EXTRA COUPLE OF DAYS AFTER Carol's memorial, and now they were packing their bags to leave tomorrow. Natalie's room was filled with rock star posters while Olivia's still had stuffed animals and the purple carpet she'd wanted when she was thirteen.

Dana had called Natalie into Olivia's room and given them the news.

"Oh my God, Aunt Carol left us each a hundred grand?" Olivia talked from behind her hand.

"That's crazy, Mom," Natalie said.

The girls knew their dad made an extremely good living, but Dana had taught them the value of money. She didn't have to tell them not to blow it on clothes and expensive shoes. Although Natalie would sneak in a pair of Manolo

Blahniks if she could find them on sale, something to remember Carol by every time she wore them. Olivia would be more likely to use a bit of it to buy her first really nice piece of furniture in her first apartment when she graduated and found a job.

"You know you were both like daughters to her."

Olivia sniffed, blinked rapidly, put a finger to the corner of her eye. "I don't know what we're going to do without her."

"I don't either," Dana agreed. "Uncle Thomas said you should have the money in a few weeks." He'd rushed through the bequests. "Carol left something for me, too." She waited a beat before adding. "Some money to spend on a trip."

"You mean like a vacation?" Natalie looked at her with an odd quirk to her mouth. Then she downright gaped. "But you never go anywhere by yourself. You don't even go to a restaurant on your own. In fact, you haven't been out to dinner with anyone except Aunt Carol since Dad left."

Dana pursed her lips. Natalie was absolutely right, and Dana didn't like hearing it. "I agree. To me, going out to dinner is about socializing."

"Then why do you want to go on vacation by yourself? Isn't that for socializing?" Natalie was always the more outspoken, but Dana could see the questions in Olivia's eyes as well.

"Because it's time. In fact, the very morning Carol had the hemorrhage, we were talking about that very thing. Vacation. Something to jumpstart my life again."

Natalie snorted. "Well, no wonder she had a hemorrhage."

Dana gasped, so did Olivia. Natalie put her hand over her mouth. "I didn't mean that the way it sounded. But you know what I mean. It's just so out of character for you."

She wanted to say that getting dumped by her husband of close to thirty years was out of character, too. Though dumping his wife and getting his girlfriend pregnant obviously wasn't out of character for Anthony. "Taking a vacation is exactly what Carol thought I should do. She wrote me a letter while she was in the hospital, before..." Before she died. But even now Dana had trouble saying that.

"What letter?" Natalie wanted to know. "You never told us about a letter."

"I'm telling you now."

"Can we read it?"

Dana had the feeling that Natalie wouldn't believe it until she read it for herself.

"It's a very personal letter. And I'm not ready to share."

Natalie huffed. "It can't be that secret. What have you got to hide?"

Dana wasn't sure why that rankled. "I don't have anything to hide. But the letter was for me." A tear pricked her eye. "It's something I want to hold close to me. If you don't mind." There was an edge of sarcasm to that last bit.

Sitting on the bed, Olivia touched Dana's knee. "It's okay, Mom, to have something for yourself." She shut her sister down with a look, telling her to cool it.

She didn't want her girls to know all the things Carol had said about Anthony. And she certainly didn't want them to read about any sexy young Italian lovers.

"Okay, I get it," Natalie said. Although the crease between her brows said she was still miffed. "But Mom, you've never been away on your own. Do you even know how to make all the bookings online? I mean, Dad always took care of everything."

That's because their father was picky and controlling and afraid Dana would screw it up. Which she wouldn't have. In fact, there were a number of times she sat with him as he made arrangements and had to point out errors in what he was doing. "Excuse me, but you might remember I have a college degree and I put your dad through law school by working as an accountant. So I'm quite capable of making my own travel arrangements, thank you very much."

"Oh, come on, Mom, you know I didn't mean it that way." But of course, Natalie did. "But really, do you want to do this on your own? I mean, going to a bunch of touristy sites all by yourself when you don't have anyone to enjoy it with?" Then Natalie gave her a sly smile. "Are you sure you're not going with someone?" The line between her brows was replaced by a naughty twinkle in her eyes.

"I'm going by myself. I would have gone with Aunt Carol. But her letter was persuasive, saying how much I needed this. And you know what?" Her voice rose with a lilt. "I've always wanted to see Rome. And now is the perfect time. The idea is growing on me. Even the first day Carol talked about it. With this bequest, I don't see any reason why I shouldn't."

She'd felt like Natalie at first. Why on earth would she go on vacation alone? There'd be no one to share that *Wow!* expression over a gorgeous sunset. No one to tell her whether that designer outfit looked good on her before she bought it. No one to gasp with over a delicious meal. No one standing by her in the middle of the Colosseum as she said, "Remember when we watched *I, Claudius* with that amazing speech Livia gave to the gladiators," and knowing that person understood exactly what she meant.

"I'm starting to see this vacation in a different way. It's like breaking free of who I am. Maybe you're too young to understand, but sometimes you just don't want to be the person everybody has always thought you were."

Olivia looked at her with a light filling her eyes, as if she wasn't seeing her mother anymore, but a woman with her own ideas, her own identity beyond being a mother, her own hopes and dreams.

"And maybe it's even something I want to prove to myself that I can do."

"You don't have to prove anything, Mom." Olivia, her baby, always had the sweetest smile.

"I know I don't. But I've realized this is something I need to do. If I wait for someone to go with me, I might never get to Rome."

"You have us, Mom," Natalie offered. Then she made a face. "Although I'm not sure when. I want to go to summer school, get in an extra semester."

Her bright, beautiful daughter wanted the fast track. "I really appreciate the offer. But I need to do this on my own and I need to do it now."

"I'm so proud of you, Mom." Olivia threw her arms around Dana.

Then Natalie joined them in a wonderful group hug. "I get it, Mom. I didn't mean to question you. After everything you've been through in the last year, you deserve a break."

It was exactly what Carol said, that there were so many things she deserved.

Dana wanted to try every single one of them.

5

Two months later on a pretty afternoon at the end of April, Dana started her journey. She'd dyed her hair, the taxes were done, and she'd caught up on all her client work. After three weeks away, she might have to work a few nights and weekends to catch up on the bookkeeping when she returned, but it wouldn't be too bad.

She went first class all the way, ordering a town car to pick her up at the house and booking a first-class overnight flight where the airline attendants treated her like royalty. After a gourmet meal, she watched a movie, then started another, but she could hardly keep her eyes open and fell asleep halfway through. The seat reclined all the way and the footrest came up and it was like being in bed. She didn't know another thing until the attendant woke her for breakfast.

With the time change, she arrived in Rome in midafternoon. There, she'd arranged for a car to pick her up and drive her to the hotel.

"Thank you, Carol," she said to herself as she sat back in comfort. A lady could get used to this kind of luxury, and she heard Carol's voice in her head. *You deserve it.*

The driver gave her a running commentary— most of which he said so quickly she didn't understand. But who cared? She drank in the amazing sites, beautiful buildings, fountains, statues, magnificent churches. There was so much she would have to explore.

When they drew up in the circular drive of the Palazzo Roma, she saw that it was indeed a palace. An ornate fountain with naked Roman gods babbled in the courtyard. Glorious flowers perfumed the entrance. She thanked her driver, tipping him well as a thank you for the mini-tour from the airport.

Everyone spoke English in beautiful Italian accents. The bellboy took her luggage and at the registration desk, the hostess made up her keys.

The sumptuous lobby was tiled in extravagant marble mosaics. Fashionably dressed women lounged in opulent chairs, drinking espresso, fruity cocktails, or champagne. A waiter passed through with drinks and hors d'oeuvres, and a pianist in a white tuxedo played romantic music. Bougainvillea and wisteria hung from the second-floor balcony surrounding the lobby. The grand staircase at the back, carpeted in plush burgundy, led to a mezzanine level.

The bellboy followed her across the lobby with her luggage on a trolley, telling her in sweetly accented English that he would meet her in the fourth-floor lobby while he took a separate freight elevator. She'd chosen the top floor for its view of the Colosseum.

When she stepped out of the elevator, the bellboy was waiting for her. Directing her to her room, he opened the door and unloaded her bags by the closet.

"Can I get you anything else?"

He was handsome and he was Italian. But he was *far* too young, Natalie's age at best. If she followed Carol's instructions and had an affair with an Italian, she wouldn't hit on anyone in the hotel. Or *that* young. She didn't want her chosen victim— she heard Carol's laughter— to know where she was staying. But maybe she wouldn't do anything all. It was her choice.

"No, thank you." She tipped him generously. That's what Carol did, took care of the people who helped her.

"*Grazie*," he said.

Alone, Dana surveyed her luxurious room.

She hadn't reserved the most expensive, but she'd chosen exactly what she wanted.

The room was on two levels with a huge arch and two small steps connecting the bedroom and sitting room. Sheer curtains could be pulled across to give the bedroom privacy. The bed was a queen-size covered by a cream and gray counterpane and a profusion of matching pillows. In the sitting room, a loveseat upholstered in a bright flowery fabric and two matching chairs faced a fireplace that had once provided the only heat. The bar area contained a coffee machine, a small refrigerator, and bottles of water.

The bathroom was off the bedroom, and Dana sighed her satisfaction when she stepped inside. A large, deep tub sat next to the tiled shower stall. The vanity had two sinks, the floor was marble, and the fittings were gold-plated. The towels looked so thick she could lose herself in them. A fluffy robe hung on the back of the door just waiting for her to step out of the bath.

She saved the best for last. French doors in the sitting room opened onto a balcony that ran the length of the suite. She shoved aside the lace curtains, threw open the doors, and stepped out to a glorious view of the Colosseum. The sun slowly moving down the sky cast long fingers of light across its broken but magnificent facade. She closed her eyes and imagined the ruins two thousand years ago when the emperors ruled.

It was everything she'd hoped for.

She'd been on a few European trips with Anthony— to Germany and London and other countries— but they'd left the girls at home because Anthony said they needed a mommy-daddy vacation. She'd missed them the whole time.

This was different. This was *her* choice.

The Colosseum was crumbling, and she didn't care. It was amazing. She gazed below at the cars zipping by on the road and wondered how often Italians stopped and just looked at their heritage. Or maybe they didn't want to claim the brutal history. Because Rome had been brutal.

Yet now, standing on her fourth-floor balcony, she felt a sense of serenity looking over the city's frenetic calmness. The words weren't an oxymoron because there was something about Rome that brought her peace, even as cars rushed and people dashed and bikes hurtled pell-mell through the traffic. It was the collision of past and present. It was the horns honking as if they were a form of self-expression, a language all their own. It was the Italian voices fast and high-pitched rising up from the courtyard below. It was the fountain splashing and the cobblestones that looked three hundred years old. Even her room was like an old palace, the ceilings plastered in intricate designs, nymphs carved into the fireplace mantel, the marble floor that had felt thousands of feet smoothing its surface.

It was no wonder Carol had loved this hotel.

She could have taken a nap, but the jetlag wasn't bad, especially since she'd slept on the plane. The best way to acclimate was to stay up until her normal time in *this* time zone. She unpacked, hanging the dresses, blouses, and cardigans she'd brought, filling the drawers with her lingerie, her tops, her capri pants, a couple of long pants. The Rome weather in late April and early May could be warm during the day and cool in the evenings. She'd packed for both.

By the time she was done, it was close to dinnertime, and she was beginning to feel hungry. She thought about ordering room service and picked up the menu to see what was offered. Then she remembered Natalie's sarcastic comment. *You've never even eaten alone.*

Rome would be a feast of meals eaten by herself. She would enjoy every moment. And rather than succumbing to jet lag and the room service menu, she donned a pretty dress — Carol had said she was supposed to dress for dinner— and made her way down to the hotel's elegant dining room where she sat on the patio, ordered champagne, and dined on fish with a sweet mango salsa, crisp-tender vegetables, and a pilaf that was like ambrosia.

Instead of bemoaning the fact that she was dining alone in a sea of elegantly dressed couples, she relished the sweetness of the evening, the ability to enjoy her fabulous meal without making conversation or arguing about what to see the next day.

Instead, she thought about the wish Carol had assigned her.

Her family had been torn apart, and like Humpty Dumpty, it would never be mended. She didn't want to wish for a new relationship. Or a new man in her life. There were all sorts of wishes she could make for her daughters. Yet this wish was supposed to be for herself. She could wish for the perfect sexy Italian stallion, but she wasn't sure she wanted that either, no matter how much Carol wanted it for her.

The only wish she truly wanted to make was for the only thing she couldn't have, Carol alive and well.

SHE'D GONE TO BED AT NINE, A LITTLE EARLIER THAN normal, and woke early, around four o'clock while it was still dark outside. When she couldn't get back to sleep, she rose to sit on her balcony with a cup of delicious herbal tea she'd prepared.

Below her, the traffic noise swelled with each passing minute as Romans began their daily life. The Colosseum was a massive outline against the starlit sky. It would be her first stop. She could easily walk from the hotel, and she intended to spend the whole day between there and the Roman Forum and Palatine Hill, the site of many ancient Roman palaces.

As the sun rose and suffused the ruins in golden light, she relished the Rome sunrise, her first ever. Colors, oranges and yellows, bathed the Colosseum's crumbling arcades, turning it into the spectacle it had once been, despite its fragmented walls.

Even as she watched, mesmerized, her eyelids began to droop. Maybe if she took a quick nap, she would be on Rome time when she woke.

When she looked at the clock next, it was later than she'd intended. She washed and dressed quickly, throwing on a pair of capris, a short sleeve top, and plenty of sunblock. She slapped on a favorite hat to spare her face from the sun, and stuffed a cardigan in her bag in case it was cool in the shade. With her sunglasses, she looked like any other tourist. No one would suspect she was completely alone.

And if they did, would it matter? No. This holiday was about everything *she* wanted to do. For the next three weeks, it was all about her.

She grabbed a pastry on the way out, eating it as she walked. The distance was longer than she'd thought when she'd estimated it from the hotel balcony, but a couple of weeks ago, she'd bought a fast-track ticket online for an early timeslot rather than later in the day so her line wasn't terribly long. While she waited, she gazed at the Arch of Constantine and the ruins of the Temple of Venus.

Inside, the crowds were already thronging the passageways, but it would get worse later. Armed with her guidebook, she'd chosen not to purchase a ticket for any of the tours offered. She wanted to go at her own pace, wandering the broken walkways, the fallen walls, breathing in the ancient Roman air. She walked the circumference, climbed to the other levels. It would have been so different two thousand years ago, probably nasty with the scent of animals and dung and slops and men's blood down below but up here in the rarefied atmosphere where the emperor sat, it would have been clean and fresh.

Next on her agenda were the catacombs— the *hypogeum*— which were the bowels of the Colosseum where the gladiators prepared and the animals were caged, starved for the spectacle, enraged for the kill. The gladiators would slaughter each other, they would butcher the animals, or the beasts would tear them to shreds.

"What?" she asked again, not understanding the attendant at the entrance to the *hypogeum*.

He pointed to her ticket and said, "Tour. No entry without tour."

She finally got it. The only way down was on a tour. When she returned to the front entrance, she was told there were no more open spaces today on any of the tours of the *hypogeum*. Stupid, stupid. She should have looked more carefully.

Didn't these people realize that was the most important part for her?

"All right," she whispered to herself. "Just do it another day." After all, she had three weeks in Rome.

What she could do now was stand on the ramparts above gazing down into the gaping maw of the crumbling subterranean tunnels. Two thousand years ago, those passageways and chambers would have been dark, dank, and cold. The *hypogeum* would have been covered by wood and an ocean of sand, with trap doors for animals to rise up, prisoners to pour forth, and gladiators to suddenly appear. Brightly dressed people would be cheering or jeering in the stands. Thumbs up, thumbs down. Determining a man's fate. Deciding an animal's life. It was breathtaking. It was awe-inspiring. It was ancient history made almost real below her.

Removing her sunglasses, she closed her eyes and tipped her head back, replaying that marvelous scene in *I, Claudius*, one of her favorite Masterpiece Theatre productions, when Livia had given that amazing speech to the gladiators. She imagined Livia's passion, the frenetic activity around her, the clanking of shields and weapons, the low growl of a lion, the stomping feet, and Livia, wife of the great Emperor Augustus, telling them all that they were scum and she wouldn't put up with the degrading tricks they pulled to try to stay alive.

"You know, you can actually see the Colosseum better if your eyes are open."

The male voice was close, it was deep. And it was sexy.

Dana didn't open her eyes. Instead, she said, "That might be true. But right now, I'm a gladiator and Livia is telling me she wants her money's worth in blood and guts and brutal death and a good show."

His chuckle vibrated by her ear, that's how near he was. "*I, Claudius* was remarkable."

She snapped her eyes open. Looked at him. He was utterly gorgeous. Tall, clean-shaven, silver-haired. But though his eyes were a gorgeous chocolate, he wasn't Italian and he wasn't younger, rather, he was American and probably in his early fifties.

The most amazing thing— the only thing that actually mattered— was that he understood the reference. Good Lord, hadn't she thought about that when she'd considered coming alone? And here, like a miracle, was a man who understood. "You're so right. They just don't make shows like *I, Claudius* anymore."

He nodded agreement. "Now there's just Marvel Comics, live-action Disney movies, witches, vampires, zombies, and remakes."

"Well—" Putting her sunglasses on against the bright sunlight, she raised her eyebrows. "There was *Buffy the Vampire Slayer*. And while not quite up to the caliber of *I, Claudius*, Buffy was fabulous."

He laughed. "I missed that one. Sorry."

"Well, it is twenty years old now. But I'm sure you can catch it on streaming," she said without even a wrinkle of a smile.

"I still prefer *I, Claudius*. Do they have that on streaming? I haven't watched it in ages."

"I've never looked." She let a smile shine out. "But I have the entire series on disk."

He raised one brow, it was curious and yet somehow mischievous. Like a little boy with a secret. And for a moment, a very brief moment, she thought he might ask to watch it with her sometime.

Of course, this was Rome, the city of *Roman Holiday*, *Three Coins in the Fountain*, and romance. And she was letting herself get carried away by a sexy smile, deep brown eyes, and the low, seductive tone of his voice.

But he didn't ask, and the moment was over. She tried to hustle him away, not because she wanted to be alone again or because he was lecherous, but because he could upset her plans for the holiday.

"Your tour is moving along," she pointed out to him. "You better catch up."

He hesitated a beat, then said, "Want to come along?"

She shook her head. "I didn't pay for a tour." Then she admitted the truth. "I didn't even realize you needed a tour to get down in the hypogeum." She held up her guidebook. "I thought I could do the whole self-guided thing."

"I paid for two tickets. She didn't show up."

She felt the infinitesimal sinking of her heart. He was attached. She glanced at his hand, but it was ringless.

"My sister," he said. "I bought tickets online before I left. She was supposed to meet me here in Rome, but something came up."

"You travel with your sister?" She realized how odd and even rude the question sounded as soon as it came out of her mouth.

He didn't seem offended. "She's been through a bad divorce," he said. "It seemed like a good idea to get away."

"I know exactly how that can feel."

He raised one brow in a Spock-like look. But he didn't ask, and Dana figured she'd already said enough.

"It just so happens that we're going down to the *hypogeum* now. So you can get your tour. And if you come along, we can imagine you're Livia and I'm a gladiator you're entreating to provide a glorious death out in the arena." He held out his hand.

The *hypogeum*. She wanted it badly. She could imagine him as a gladiator. He would have been a sight to behold.

Maybe she should have hesitated. Maybe she shouldn't agree at all. But she was in Rome and she could do whatever she wanted.

And she put her hand in his.

6

Marshall— he'd introduced himself as Marshall Garrison— was an interesting and entertaining companion, murmuring amusing anecdotes about the hypogeum while the tour guide talked and answered questions. They remained at the back of the crowd to avoid the dirty glances of the tourists trying to listen.

Dana enjoyed every moment with Marshall, who was more knowledgeable on all things Roman than their guide. And better looking, too. "Why are you even bothering with the tour?" she asked. "You already know everything."

He gave her the Spock eyebrow again. "Are you saying that I'm a know-it-all?"

She laughed. "Knowing it all isn't the same as being a know-it-all."

"I'm not sure I see the difference."

"I could explain it to you, but I'll let you work it out on your own."

"Would I be a know-it-all if I told you that Livia couldn't have given that speech in the Colosseum because it wasn't even built for another seventy years?"

She put the back of her hand to her brow, sniffed dramatically. "Oh no, you've destroyed all my illusions."

He laughed softly. And she liked the way his laughter touched her on the inside.

But Carol had said her lover had to be young and Italian.

And really, she was enjoying Marshall's company too much to want to throw sex into the mix. Because sex changed everything.

They shuffled forward, the tour guide pointing out things Dana had already read in her guidebook. Finally, they stood atop the grand stadium again, Marshall shoulder to shoulder with her, well, not quite, maybe more like biceps to shoulder. She liked a tall man. She didn't compare Marshall to Anthony's five foot ten. Not even for one second.

"Can't you see Russell Crowe out there?" Marshall said. "Wounded but still powerful, hiding his bloodstains and stepping onto that field of battle to meet Commodus."

She sputtered a laugh. "I don't think it's pronounced like commode, the toilet. I think it's more like Commodus." She changed the accent on the syllables.

"But I always thought he was a bit of a commode." His face was straight, not even the crack of a smile.

Dana had to agree. Didn't everyone cheer at the outcome? "*Gladiator, I, Claudius*. What other hidden Roman depths do you have?"

"The miniseries *Rome* was magnificent. Until the second season had its production funding cut off at the knees."

"I do miss Titus and Vorenus," she said mournfully. "But then there was *Game of Thrones*."

He snorted softly. "Sorry, no *Game of Thrones* here."

"Don't tell me you didn't watch that either?" She pointed a finger at his chest.

"I was never much into the fantasy element. I prefer raw history."

"I watched it with the girls." Then she realized he didn't know anything about her. "My daughters. Two of them. They're in college now."

"Ah," he drawled. "Now I get the whole Buffy thing."

"I'm not brushing it off entirely on them. Maybe they got me to watch in the first place." Though she had purchased *Buffy* on DVD because the girls were too young when it first came out. She hadn't let them watch *Game of Thrones* until Olivia was fourteen, and even then, the blood and guts made Dana cringe. "But I loved those shows."

"*Buffy* and *Game of Thrones*. Maybe I'll have to broaden my horizons."

She laughed at him. "Yeah, right."

"What, you don't think I can?" he asked.

She just smiled. Then the tour guide was pressing them on, while Dana would have loved to stay and breathe it all in, the ghosts of history that wandered these ruins. And Marshall's deep voice in her ear.

"Of all the emperors, I admire Marcus Aurelius the most," Marshall mused as the tour guide talked about all the emperors and dignitaries who had presided over the games. "Have you ever read his essays?"

She flashed him a smile. "No, I haven't. While your education is sorely lacking in *Buffy* and *Game of Thrones*, mine is lacking in philosophers and emperors."

"Then I actually have something to add to your repertoire, too."

He went into a dissertation on Marcus Aurelius, and she found herself utterly fascinated. Even when the tour guide stopped them for another must-see site, she wanted to listen to Marshall.

He had a wonderful deep voice that resonated inside her. He was intelligent, handsome, and funny as well. His anecdotes were highly entertaining.

But the day was fading away, well after lunchtime, and all she'd snacked on was a couple of granola bars and some apple slices she'd carried with her on the plane. She'd had nothing substantial since she'd bought the pastry in the morning. Not that a pastry could be considered substantial. Now the lack of food was making her lightheaded.

As the group broke up, she said to Marshall, "Thank you for allowing me to join the tour on your dime." She leaned in close to softly say, "You were much better than the guide."

He winked. She was taken in again by his handsome face, just the hint of a beard on his jawline, the distinguished gray of his hair, the chiseled jaw like something Michelangelo would have sculpted out of stone.

"You're very welcome," he said. "Are you going to the Roman Forum and Palatine Hill?"

She'd planned to, but it was later than she'd thought and she didn't think she could take any more crowds. "Not today. Since the ticket is for two days, I'll do those tomorrow." She creased her lips in a rueful smile. "Right now, I'm starving so I'll just go back to the hotel for something to eat."

"In that case, would you join me for a meal?"

He wasn't what Carol had ordered, not young, not Italian. But he was sexy. Even more, she liked him. He was fun, a good companion, he'd watched *I, Claudius* and knew that exact scene with Livia. What better recommendation could there be?

She gave him her most gracious smile. "I'd love to join you."

༄

MARSHALL TOOK HER TO A LITTLE CAFÉ WITH PATIO seating, but then everywhere in Rome had patio seating. It was nice in the shade of an umbrella, and they sat drinking limoncello and watching the street teeming with tourists and street artists and ladies with baskets of flowers and old men chatting on benches. On the sidewalk, a guitarist serenaded the passersby amid the sounds of traffic and honking horns.

She ordered what was basically a shrimp salad with a fancy name, then settled in to talk. "So you're traveling with your sister," she said. "Except that something came up."

"I'm here on business, but doing a little touring at the same time. My sister was dying to get away, and she wanted to join me for part of the trip." He shrugged. "It'll just be different days than we'd planned. She should be here next week."

"I hope she's not ill," she said politely. She sipped the delicious limoncello, letting it go to her head. It was quenching after a day in the sun of the Colosseum. She could only imagine what the heat would be like in full summer.

"Trouble with one of her boys. A ninth grader," he added. "Divorce is hard on everyone." He sucked on an ice cube a moment. "I'm surprised you didn't wait until summer so your girls could come on this trip with you."

She waited a beat, deciding what to tell him. And she chose the truth. What did she have to lose? "I couldn't wait until summer. I came to make a wish. I just haven't decided what the wish needs to be."

"A wish? You have me intrigued."

She had every intention of telling him the whole story. Suddenly it felt good to talk with someone who had absolutely no stake in anything she did. "I'd hoped to come with a friend of mine. Unfortunately, Carol died a couple of months ago."

"I'm so sorry to hear that."

She felt the same twinge in her belly she always did when she thought of Carol and how much she missed her friend. "It was sudden. An aneurysm burst." She didn't go into all the technical jargon. "I thought I got her to the hospital in time." She looked down at her hands, feeling the ghost of pain and terror. "But she had a relapse a couple of days later."

"I'm so sorry," he said again, his voice soft with sincerity.

"Anyway," she said, waving her hand as if she could possibly wave away the grief. "She left me a letter with strict instructions that I'm supposed to make a wish in the Trevi Fountain."

"The Trevi Fountain." He smiled, gentle and comforting. "That's why everyone comes to Rome."

She laughed, both sad and sweet. "Well, yes. But the only thing I really want to wish for is to have my friend back. And that's never going to happen."

"A wish is supposed to be for the impossible."

"That's more than impossible. It would be miraculous." If she was going to wish for the impossible, shouldn't she be wishing to patch her marriage back together? But losing Carol was so much worse. And that said a hell of a lot about her marriage.

"Tell me about your friend."

Her smile felt glorious. "We knew each other since we were eight years old. She was the new girl in my class and she made me laugh over some silly thing she said in her introduction and we were best friends from then on." She told him how they'd remained steadfast through junior high and high school. They'd never vied for the same boys. They backed each other up in squabbles with other friends. When they were adults, Carol had always believed in her. "She was my rock. I like to think I was her rock, too."

"I'm sure you were." His coffee eyes sparkled with amber. "You went to college together as well?"

"Of course." She told him about meeting their future spouses, the double dating, the shared wedding dress, how they'd weathered everything together from marriage to childbirth to her parents' deaths to her divorce. It was marvelous to talk about Carol when she didn't have to worry about anyone else's feelings but her own. At home there'd been Thomas's desperate grief, her girls' chagrin about the Rome trip, and her inability to ever tell them that losing Carol was so much worse than losing their father. The grief over the divorce and his remarriage and the new baby paled in comparison to her grief over Carol.

She talked so much that by the time Marshall's plate was empty, her salad was only half eaten.

Yet she couldn't stop spilling her guts. "She was a divorce attorney. High-profile. She represented some big names that will blow your mind. But of course, I can never tell." She sighed with a sense of relief over just being able to talk. "She handled my divorce, too."

She felt like the female comedian on *Mrs. Maisel*, who poured out every dirty detail of her life in her comedy sketches. Dana spewed it all on Marshall. "She got me the most amazing settlement in the history of California, I think." She laughed slightly, remembering Carol's glee at sticking it to Anthony with everything she could. "He cheated with his paralegal, now he's married to the woman, and she's pregnant. I never told my girls that he cheated, but one of them understands him and the other hates him. And Carol was my rock."

She ate a shrimp then went on until she didn't have another word left. She wondered what Marshall thought of her. Her spewing was a bit cringe-worthy. "You must think I'm terrible airing all my dirty laundry, as my mother would have said, and never asking about you."

Instead of answering right away, he gazed at her for a long, speculative moment, one that made the hairs on her arms rise. "On the contrary," he said. "Compared to your life, mine is completely boring. I never married, never had kids, been married to my job, climbing the corporate ladder, and even when I go abroad for a trip, it's always combined with business."

"That doesn't sound boring, all the business wheeling and dealing, foreign trips, commanding people. But what exactly do you do?"

"I'm a CEO." Then he laughed. "I can't tell you what the hell I do because it's different every day. There's always a fire to put out."

"CEO. That's a big job. Who do you work for?"

He hesitated, as if he thought it might be violating some nondisclosure agreement. Then he told her a name that literally made her jaw drop so far it could have landed on the table.

To cover her gasp, she shoveled arugula into her mouth, then said as mildly as possible, "I may have heard of the company. Isn't it headquartered in San Francisco?"

"Yes." He smiled because anyone would know *that* company. "That's where I'm from."

She smiled. "Coincidentally, so am I. I live on the Peninsula."

He laughed, such a deep, masculine, goosebump-inducing sound. "An amazing coincidence. A love of *I, Claudius* plus the Bay Area." He leaned close, a sexy smile on his lips. "But since you know my company, please don't call up the newspapers and tell them I'm in Rome working on a business deal."

"I wouldn't dream of it," she said, so straight-faced that her cheeks ached. Finally she added, "Thank you for making me laugh. For making me remember Carol and letting me talk about her endlessly. You know when you're with family and friends, they can't listen to your grief because they have their own grief to deal with. It makes everything worse because you can't seem to talk about it."

"I don't know much about grief." But he nodded as if he

did know. "My parents died when my sister and I were in our twenties, but we'd never been close with them." He sighed and gave a slight shrug. "I'd like to say it felt bad, but honestly I can't remember the feelings at all."

"I'm sorry. I'm not sure whether it's better to feel this grief or not to."

"Feeling grief means you felt love. That's a good thing." He smiled then, his eyes crinkling. "So now I've got all the background, tell me why Carol wanted you to make a wish in the Trevi Fountain."

She was horrified she'd talked and talked and hadn't gotten to the original question. But he encouraged her so nicely. And she told him about that terrible day, because it was all part of the story, the walk in the park, that talk, then Carol on the ground, holding her head.

Marshall put his hand over hers, squeezed. "I'm sure that was terrible."

Dana breathed in, steadied herself. "Yes. It was. Thank you." Then she tried to shake off the emotions and told him the rest. "Anyway, she said I needed to go on a trip, have some fun since the divorce was final and my ex was remarried, and that I was stagnating. We were supposed to go on the trip together." Although all along Carol had said Dana needed to go on her own. "We talked about making a wish in the Trevi Fountain. And—" She finally smiled, though it was a little embarrassed and a lot rueful. "Carol said I needed to come to Rome and have an affair with a sexy, young, gorgeous Italian man." She waited for his reaction, her face burning.

Marshall's eyebrow went up and his mouth curled in a half smile. "Now this sounds intriguing. I need to hear more."

7

Dana ate another shrimp speared with arugula, then blurted it all out.

"Carol said he needs to be at least twenty years younger than me." She laughed. "Speaking of more impossible wishes."

Marshall smiled softly, his eyes tracing her face. "Any young Italian would be lucky to have an affair with you."

She crossed her eyes at him. "You don't have to be kind. Someone that young will make me feel like his mother." Then she shrugged and smiled and winked at him. "But I have to do whatever Carol says since she left me instructions in her last letter to me."

"Ahh." He nodded sagely. "Since he has to be young and Italian, then I'm completely out of the running." There was such a twinkle in his eyes that she knew he wasn't even hurt by the idea.

Her heart skipped a beat, and her first inclination was to grab his hand and say he was definitely in the running. Yet she'd told him far too many intimate things. And *if* she had an affair with him, she'd no longer be able to tell him all her inner longings the way she had today. And she wanted that so badly. She wanted a friendship more than she wanted an affair.

He looked around the tightly packed patio. "Let's pick out a young Italian for you right now. How about our waiter?"

"Our waiter?" She gasped. "He's way too young. How old do you think I am?"

His smile sparkled in his eyes. "I made a deduction that since you're supposed to choose someone twenty years younger and that you probably don't want a teenager, then this young Italian, who appears to be twenty-five, would be a good fit for you."

"How very diplomatic of you." She should have been embarrassed, even mortified that she'd told a complete stranger absolutely *everything*— except that Anthony hadn't had sex with her in the nine months before she found out he was cheating— so why not tell him her age? "Thank you for shaving five years off. But despite what Carol said, he's—" She pointed surreptitiously at the waiter. "—just too, too close to my daughters' ages."

"Fair enough." He pointed a finger at her. "But you need to give yourself some leeway to find the perfect match. So we're looking for a thirty to thirty-five-year-old sexy, gorgeous young Italian male." He smiled widely. "Do you want one night, a week, or the whole vacation?"

She laughed, making the couple at the next table turn their heads. "I'm not sure I can really do this at all. It's just so —" She circled a hand in the air searching for the right word. "Calculated."

"I beg to differ. It's not calculated at all. Men do exactly the same thing. Why should *you* need to be any different?" he stressed. "You can have whatever you want. And you deserve it."

Echoing Carol's words made her think of her friend's letter and all the things Carol claimed she deserved.

She could only look at him for several heartbeats as a round of drinks was dropped off at a nearby table amid a burst of laughter.

How could he understand what Carol said in her letter? "Why are you being so nice to me?"

He sat back in his chair, let out a long sigh, his head tipped to the side. "Don't you think you deserve someone to be nice to you?"

Carol had said the same thing, and long before the letter, too. But as her best friend, Carol was supposed to say things like that. But this man didn't even know her.

"I'm not sure." She was once again completely honest. She didn't know what she deserved, not anymore. There was too much anger and loss and grief, not just over Carol, but her whole life as she'd known it.

"You remind me of my sister Laura. She was the best wife." His mouth creased in a rueful smile. "Of course, I'm biased since I'm her brother."

"Except when siblings hate each other and then you'd think she didn't deserve anything good at all."

"Touché," he said with a quirk of his mouth. "But she's a good person. She was a good wife, and she's an exemplary mother. Her dirty, low-down, rotten cheating husband didn't deserve her. He left her for a trophy wife, but I know he had affairs before that."

"How do you know?" She felt a tremor in her belly. She'd wondered if Anthony had others before Kimberly?

"He was a flirt. He laughed it off, said that it was just his nature. But Laura found odd charges on his credit cards." He leaned in, braced an elbow on the table. "What kind of man charges his affairs on a credit card that his wife pays the bill for?" He pointed a finger. "Only a man who has no respect for her." His voice was stiff, his features even harder. "And he always had an answer. Oh, that was dinner with a client." He waved a hand, imitating the feckless husband. "Oh, that was a hotel room he had to book for a client. No worries. It's reimbursed on his expense report." He narrowed his eyes, gazing into the distance. "And it conveniently explains all the late hours."

She thought of Anthony's late hours. She thought about how he'd had his credit card bill sent to the office so that she never saw it. She thought about the times he went through his suit pockets before he gave them to her for cleaning, the times he'd crumpled papers in his hand and instead of throwing them in the trash, he shoved the wads into his pants pocket. She thought about the two cell phones he had, the personal number she used, and the other one he'd said was for client emergencies. The one he always left the room to answer.

That had been going on long before Kimberly joined his paralegal team.

She'd been so gullible and so stupid. But then she'd also been a victim of her own desire for the status quo, to never rock the boat, to avoid change at all costs. She hadn't wanted to know.

"I understand your sister," she said. "You have kids, and there's so much you decide you can ignore, deluding yourself into thinking nothing has to change."

"Until…" He left it at that.

"Until…" She agreed.

"That's why I say you deserve more." His voice was gentle, commiserating. "Because Laura deserved more. And if husbands can do it with impunity, I certainly don't know why wives can't."

She heard Carol's voice. *You deserve this, you deserve that, you deserve everything.* "Ex-wives certainly can."

He raised his limoncello, and she tapped her glass to his. "Here's to you getting everything you deserve." He saluted her.

She got bold— maybe it was the limoncello— and asked him a burning question. "Is that why you never married? Because you don't trust marriage?"

Sitting back, he folded his arms, and she couldn't read what was going on inside his head. Until she looked deeper, into those deep brown windows into his secrets. "I didn't like my parents' marriage. And quite frankly, over the years I've seen very few marriages that don't have massive cracks." He flourished a hand. "It might be cheating, it might be spending too much money, it might be an unequal partnership and someone gets resentful." A soft smile lifted the corners of his mouth. "I'd rather be married to my job." Then he laughed outright, not loudly but fully. "Not that corporate American isn't just as fickle and cheating as individuals can be. And there's a hell of a lot of underhanded tactics. I enjoy controlling those tactics in a business atmosphere, beating down the people who use them. It's almost a game." He shook his head. "But I don't want to come home to more of the same."

She tried not to gape at him. His attitude was absolutely foreign to her. "You mean you've never fallen in love? Not ever? Not even once?"

He shrugged, with the slightest smile on his lips. "Oh sure, there was a high school thing with a girl named Pamela in my sophomore history class." He waved a hand nonchalantly. "But that was just lust. Or puppy love. Or whatever the hell you call it when you're driven strictly by your hormones and it ends badly."

"Wow," she said.

"Then my parents started fighting, and I figured out the truth about relationships. That's why I'm glad my sister is out of her marriage and why I think she deserves so much more. She's one of the good guys."

Wow again. His parents' divorce had really messed him up. He didn't believe in marriage, and he certainly wasn't good relationship material. But then she'd already decided she needed an Italian romance. With Marshall, she'd end up wanting more, especially since he was from the Bay Area, and he'd never be able to give it. But he was certainly a good listener, and he was super supportive of his sister, which was exactly the kind of man Dana needed right now.

She matched his smile. "I like your sister already." And she liked him despite his views on marriage.

"Perhaps you'll meet her." He looked skyward, not quite an eye roll. "As long as she makes it here the way she's promised."

"That's why you're such a good listener. Because you've listened to your sister and you understand."

"She didn't have anyone else to talk to. She was afraid to tell her friends. Friends always say you've gotta leave that schmuck," he imitated in a harsh accent.

"Brothers can say that, too." Though she didn't know because she was an only child.

"I figured out she just needed somebody to listen."

She gave him a mock gape. "I cannot believe a man actually said that. Men are solution-oriented. You tell them a problem, and they have to solve it." Anthony never let her vent. If she brought up an issue, he'd have the perfect solution. And if she didn't follow his instructions, he got mad and wouldn't listen to another word on the subject. In the end she stopped telling him anything. That was long before he'd stopped having sex with her.

"But I didn't have a solution to her problem," Marshall said, his tone remorseful. "Marriage is messy, and the party you're rooting for doesn't always come out on top. She didn't leave him even though I thought she should." He shrugged. "And in the end, the asshole took it out of my hands by finding a replacement. As far as the money went, it worked out well since he was a cheating ass and she obviously had as good a divorce lawyer as you did.

She sipped her champagne, smiled behind the glass. "I had Carol."

He smiled, nodded. "And she stuck it to him."

Dana beamed. "Oh yeah."

"Which allows you to take fabulous vacations in Rome."

After everything she'd told him, she felt comfortable with the truth. "Carol paid for it. She left me some money and said I had to spend it on this trip." She leaned forward, her elbows on the table. "She outlined everything I'm supposed to do, buy new clothes, new shoes, everything the best. She even told me the hotel I had to stay at."

"Don't forget the wish in the fountain and the sexy young Italian."

She groaned. "Those two are the hardest. Buying new clothes is easy."

"I can help make it easier for you."

She thought he'd offer again to take the place of her young Italian. Instead he said, "I'll keep my eye out. Together we'll find you the perfect candidate." He let out a breath with a smile, and his eyes seemed just a little darker now. "I'll also help you figure out your wish." He held up his finger. "Just don't discount wishing for the impossible."

A part of her drooped with disappointment that he didn't want to be her lover. Yet the day had been so wonderful, having all her feelings validated, as if a man truly listened. If they became lovers, the dynamics would change completely. She'd no longer be able to tell him everything, because he would become a huge part of what she'd need to talk about. He was handsome, and the sex would be phenomenal. Especially since it had been so long since she'd had sex. If Carol had been with her, she'd choose him. But Carol wasn't here. And what Marshall had given her today was the unconditional support she needed so badly from a friend.

She wasn't about to give that up for a fling.

❦

MARSHALL WALKED HER BACK TO HER HOTEL. DANA SHAW was beautiful, her hair curling past her shoulders, a luxurious red that was a beautiful contrast to her pretty green eyes. He'd long since stopped looking at ingenues. He preferred a woman in her prime. If he'd met Dana under any other circumstances, if he hadn't encouraged her to unburden herself, he might have made his move.

But she was too much like Laura. Vulnerable, fragile, hurt, and abandoned. If it was just a divorce, he still might have gone for it, giving her back her sense of self-worth, showing her she was a deeply desirable woman, that she could have him eating out of the palm of her hand.

But the loss of her friend had broken something inside her. He didn't want to cause more damage. After seeing everything Laura had been through, in all good conscience, he couldn't take advantage of Dana. Even though he could make her feel so damn good in every sense of the word.

Though he didn't like the idea of her finding some sexy young Italian, the best thing he could do was play the big brother and check out any man she wanted to date. He could be her watchdog as well as her sounding board. And he'd keep her safe.

He chose the role he would play. And it wasn't holiday lover.

In the hotel's lavish lobby, she asked, "Would you like to

stay for a drink?" She pointed a thumb over her shoulder at the bar behind them.

"I'd love to, but unfortunately I have an early business meeting tomorrow. Perhaps we can meet for dinner in the evening." He winked. "Unless you've found a date."

She had such a sweet, musical laugh. "I can't work that fast."

"You won't have to work. They'll come flocking to you."

She snorted daintily. "Give me a break."

He reached for his wallet, pulled out a card. "Let's say dinner at seven tomorrow night." Then he shook his finger like a big brother watching out for her. "And I don't want you going any off with a stranger unless you call me first."

She gave him that tinkling laugh again, like a piano sonata. "But aren't you a stranger?"

"I feel more like your brother now. It's my duty to look out for you." He wanted to touch her, just a finger down her cheek, a tactile sensation he could recall later. But he didn't. He'd chosen another path with her. "Do I have a promise?"

With laughter in her eyes, she said, "I promise."

He bent chivalrously over her hand and left a lingering kiss on her skin. It was the tactile sensation he craved, but still courtly rather than salacious.

He straightened, pointed at the card. "Call me if you suddenly make plans with a sexy Italian." He waited a beat. "But if I don't hear from you, I'll pick you up here at your hotel at seven o'clock."

Then he left her.

The urge to look back over his shoulder was almost irresistible.

Yet he wanted his last sight of her to be that sweet, bewildered expression after he'd kissed her hand.

8

In a café down the street from the hotel, Dana breakfasted on an assortment of meats, cheeses, and fluffy scrambled eggs that melted on the tongue. She sent the girls a selfie to show that she could easily eat on her own.

She decided to do the Roman Forum and Palatine Hill in the afternoon, even though it would be more crowded. She had very important things to do this morning. Like shopping.

Her dinner with Marshall tonight had nothing to do with the decision.

When she stepped onto the street, she flagged down a taxi, with a driver who understood that she wanted designer shopping. She'd heard the best was near the Spanish Steps, and he dropped her off on a street emblazoned with designer names she'd only read about. She strolled past storefronts, their windows filled with gorgeous clothes, black cocktail dresses, colorful day dresses, swimsuits and handbags, jewelry and shoes. Languages of every nationality swarmed in the air. She could pick out the Australian, British, and of course

American. She loved the hectic pace, so different from her life at home.

Then she found them, the perfect shoes. She stood long minutes gazing in the window, Italian leather in the deepest, darkest, midnight black. The impossibly high heels were studded with gold jewels that looped around, leading like star beams to the tip of the pointed toes. They took her breath away. She wouldn't be able to walk in them, but that didn't matter. These shoes weren't made for walking. They were made for dazzling men like Marshall.

Inside, a row of seats down the middle was surrounded by pedestals displaying women's footwear, from evening shoes to casual flats to sandals. Two older ladies inspected a pair of low-heeled pumps, and a couple, the man much older than the pretty woman, strolled past the display of high heels.

As soon as she entered, a salesman swooped in. He was a magnificent specimen, like the Italian guy in one of her and Carol's favorite romcoms, *Only You*. His hair was dark and curly, his eyes almost black, his teeth sparkling white, and his smile enormously wide. His skin had that lovely Mediterranean glow, his chin clean-shaven with the promise of a beard that would grow out thick. She guessed him to be around thirty-five, the perfect age for an affair.

"Hello, signora." His hand against his impressive chest, he introduced himself. "I am Giancarlo. May I help you today?" Then he added, "I saw you looking at all our beautiful shoes, all designed for a sophisticated New Yorker such as yourself."

He'd pegged her immediately as an American. She laughed, she was no New Yorker and no sophisticate. And he was excessively polite. She opted for saying she was from San Francisco because it was better than admitting she was a suburbanite.

He smiled that dazzling smile again. "San Francisco. I've always wanted to walk across the Golden Gate. You must have done it many times." He spoke quickly, his accent musical and understandable, unlike the cabbie.

She was happy to say, "Yes, I've walked the Golden Gate several times with my daughters. If it isn't foggy, you can see the whole cityscape against the backdrop of the bridge." She had many pictures.

Giancarlo gazed at her feet and her comfortable sneakers. "You have the perfect shoes for that. But may I assume you're here for a pair to go with your many beautiful cocktail dresses?"

He made her smile. She couldn't help enjoying the male attention as his eyes traveled down her body once again to her shoes.

"I found the perfect pair in the window," she told him.

He held up a hand, holding her off as he leaned into the display. "Don't tell me," he commanded. "I know just the pair."

Sure enough, he picked the jeweled high heels. When she nodded, he made a flourish at a comfortable armchair on the plush carpeting. "Let me measure you for your proper size."

She took the seat. "You don't need to measure. I know my size."

Once again Giancarlo held up his hand. "These are very special shoes, signora. Bottega Veneta. They require an exact fitting. I'm sure your American stores are competent, but in my store, it is a point of pride to make sure we fit you precisely."

He pulled up a stool and placed his hand beneath her heel, drawing her foot between his legs on the slanted footrest. She was wearing white Capri pants with a colorful sleeveless top and didn't have to roll up her pant legs. He untied her laces, then delicately slipped her foot from the shoe.

There was something electric about having her foot

between a handsome, sexy, young Italian's legs while he had his wicked way with her feet.

But she thought of Marshall and that delicious kiss on her hand. If the touch of a man's hand on her feet was electric, then the feel of Marshall's lips on her skin had been like a bolt of lightning.

Her salesclerk set her foot onto the measuring scale, pushing her heel back against the curve. There was a lot of touching to get her correct size, her heel, her ankle, her toes. He bent his head, his hair as curly and full on top as it was from the front.

She wished for Carol so badly right then. Carol would wink over the fact that a man was almost between her legs.

Right now, gazing down at the sexy Italian, Dana smiled for the two of them.

Then he straightened, giving her that wide grin. "*Perfezione*. I will retrieve the shoes along with a selection of others that might also appeal. So that you have a choice. A lady always deserves choice."

He brought a stunning array, from two-tone, to red, to plain but elegant black, to ones with ties up the ankles. Sitting once again in the stool in front of her, he asked, "Would you like to try the Bottega Venetas first or save them for last like the cream on top?"

As a child at Halloween, she'd always separated her candy into the really good stuff and the not-so-good stuff and the stuff you wanted to throw away. She'd always saved the best for last while Carol had always eaten the best first, gobbling it down. Then she wanted to share Dana's good stuff.

Did she want to save the good stuff for last? Or did she want to be like Carol and gobble it now? Carol whispered in her head. *Since the gorgeous Giancarlo will be touching your feet the whole time, we should save the best for last.* "I'll try the jeweled black ones at the end."

He looked at her, his dark eyes thickly lashed. "That's a wise choice, signora."

She tried on red and white and rhinestone. There were pointed toes and rounded toes and square toes. There were chunky heels and thin stilettos. When she paraded through the store, there were pairs so high her calves hurt, and pairs so pointed she thought she'd have to lop off her toes just to walk a few steps. Like the emperor in the Colosseum, she gave them each thumbs up or thumbs down, and Giancarlo set them in two piles.

"Now we come to the last, and perhaps the best, everything we've been waiting for," he said like a fashion show commentator.

The box on his lap, he opened the top slowly, ceremoniously. Rather than cardboard and tissue paper, the shoes were cradled in a satin-lined wooden box. The heels glittered with the shine of star beams. He removed one shoe from its satin lining and held it up to the light, the brightness dazzling her.

And she fell totally, ecstatically in love.

Setting aside the box, he carried her bare foot to the slant of the stool and deftly lifted her heel to slip on the shoe. She felt like Cinderella with the perfect fit.

He guided her foot to the carpet and picked up the other, once again ceremoniously sliding on the high heel.

They looked down, their heads only inches apart.

"*Bellissima*," he said reverently.

Dana knew it was true.

"Please, dear lady, walk for us."

Two more salesclerks and five new customers wandered the shop, but she felt as if all eyes were on her in those shoes as she promenaded to the long mirror.

The high heels took her breath away. She'd never coveted a pair of shoes. But she *needed* these shoes.

She wanted to see Marshall's expression as she walked across the lobby.

She glided back to Giancarlo, and her pulse raced at the look in his eyes. She was fifty, she dyed her hair, and she wore loose-fitting tops to hide the baby belly that had never gone flat again. She had decent calves, toned from all her walking, and she was in fairly good shape.

But in these shoes, she felt truly *bellissima*.

Giancarlo was still seated on the stool as if he were worshipping at her feet. "You have definitely saved the best for last."

Dana had to agree one hundred percent. "I'll take them." She didn't ask the price. That would ruin everything. This was what Carol had wanted her to do.

Giancarlo held out his hand, helping her to sit once more. "You have made the perfect choice. These classic shoes will last a lifetime. You could even leave them to your daughters in your will."

Natalie would try to steal them the first chance she got. "My daughters will absolutely love them." And neither would believe their mother had actually purchased them.

He lifted her foot once more, removed the high heels, first one, then the other, replacing them in their satin-lined box. When she would have slipped her sneakers back on, he lifted her feet and put them on himself.

She laughed. "I can barely stand to put these old things on again."

"We have casual walking shoes," he said quickly. "I can show you."

She shook her head. "No, thank you. Just the high heels." While she might be able to pay an exorbitant sum for a pair of high heels she would probably wear only once, she wasn't about to fork over money for designer walking shoes.

She handed her over credit card and still perched on his

stool, Giancarlo removed a handheld machine he wore on his hip in a small holster as if it were a handgun from the old West. He ran her card through and when he turned the machine for her approval, her chest heaved. She could buy a state-of-the-art laptop or a 4K Ultra HD TV for that amount.

She hit the approval button. Carol would have been proud of how quickly she'd signed away that much money.

Giancarlo gazed at her a moment with those gorgeous dark eyes and thick lashes. Then he said, "Perhaps you would do me the honor of wearing the shoes for me tonight for dinner at a fine restaurant."

Oh my God. The man was asking her out. Her skin heated with embarrassment. The first thought that came to her head was why on earth would this handsome man ask her out. He probably thought she was a rich American, and he was hoping to cash in.

Then Carol's voice was in her head.

You're a desirable woman, that's why.

It was so like Dana, always looking for a reason why a man wouldn't be attracted to her. She never simply thought that she might actually be attractive.

"Please, I do not mean to embarrass you."

He was gorgeous. He was fifteen years younger than her. And he was sexy. Here was an extremely attractive, young Italian asking her out, exactly what Carol said she deserved.

"Yes," she blurted before she could stop herself. Before she could overthink it and turn down his offer. "I have a dinner engagement, though. Perhaps we could meet for a drink afterward." She liked the idea of a drink rather than dinner, a shorter duration just in case.

He smiled so wide, she thought the whiteness of his teeth might blind her. "*Perfezione.*" He jumped up. "I will get a bag for your beautiful shoes."

She waited in the chair, all the clerks watching her surreptitiously, and the other customers trying to pretend they hadn't heard. She felt the craziness of what she'd done. They probably thought she was some desperate American housewife.

So what? It was just a drink. And she did look amazing in those shoes. She deserved a drink with the handsome Italian. She deserved an evening of being admired. She wasn't desperate. She wasn't even lonely. She had a good bookkeeping business back home and an excellent divorce settlement. She had half her life left.

When her handsome Italian returned, bringing a carrier bag with her very expensive shoes, she boldly said, "Do you have a card with your phone number? I'll text you later and we can discuss the details."

He dazzle-smiled her again, a card already between his fingers.

"I know a club," he said. "I have written the name and the street on the card. Tell any driver and they will know exactly where it is. Is ten o'clock too soon after your dinner engagement?"

She was meeting Marshall at seven. "That'll be perfect."

She left him calling *ciao* over her shoulder like she was a breezy young Italian.

She liked Giancarlo, but she felt better being in control of her own transportation. She could leave whenever she wanted.

Before she wouldn't have been able to wait to tell Carol.

Now she couldn't wait to parade in front of Marshall wearing her new heels. And to tell him about her date.

9

"I went shopping," Dana said, utterly delighted with herself.

She was utterly gorgeous. And Marshall was utterly smitten.

"I can see that. And it's a lovely outfit."

Her glossy red hair hung in ringlets over her shoulders, and her subtle makeup enhanced the green of her eyes. She wore a sleeveless black jumpsuit with gold trim along the edges. It delved deep into her cleavage and the back straps left a triangle of bare skin that tantalized him as she turned to give him the full view.

Then, putting her hand on his arm, she raised her pantleg and pointed her foot, revealing a high heel covered in sparkling gold jewels against the black leather. "Aren't these the most beautiful pair of high heels you've ever seen?"

"I find myself speechless. You take my breath away." He wanted to drag her back to her room and strip her out of everything but the high heels.

She laughed and hooked her arm through his. He

wondered if she could hear his heart beating and feel his pulse racing.

"I spent an exorbitant amount of money." She touched the leg of her jumpsuit, then held up a small purse on a gold chain slung over her shoulder. "Of course, I didn't have anything to go with the shoes so I had to buy a whole new outfit, too." She gazed up at him, her eyes glittering. "Do you like it?"

"You look amazing." He could have used so many more superlatives. Sexy, enchanting, mouthwatering, seductive. The extravagant hotel lobby was awash in elegant, beautiful women. But Dana eclipsed them all.

She eyed him a moment as if she thought he *had* to say that. "Well, thank goodness I got your vote. I've always needed Carol there to tell me whether something looked good. This time I had to do it all on my own."

"Your taste is impeccable."

She laughed again and led him out of the hotel. "I thought I'd be sick when I saw the prices. But I had to tell myself that Carol ordered me to splurge." She rolled her eyes and lowered her voice, clinging to his arm. "Honestly, though, I'm done with shopping. Except for gifts for the girls."

He liked that she talked to him as if he were her BFF, with the ease of knowing someone for years. "The outfit is worth every euro," he told her. "You deserve beautiful things."

She smiled her thanks as he helped her into the cab. He was glad he'd chosen a restaurant they had to drive to. He couldn't imagine making her walk any distance. Those heels weren't meant for walking. They were meant for sex.

The cabbie turned left out of the driveway while she chattered about her day, the shoes she'd tried on, the clothes, the jewelry she'd drooled over. She cupped her hand beside her mouth and leaned close. "I even bought lingerie. They talk about French lingerie, but I thought the Italian stuff was amazing."

He wanted to see her in every scrap of lace she'd bought. But he liked her ease with him. As if he were her friend and confidant.

"What about the Forum and Palatine Hill?" he asked, redirecting his licentious thoughts.

She batted a hand. "Oh that. I made it before the end of the day. Fabulous sites."

Marshall laughed. "Are you sure you really made it?"

"Of course." Then she smiled. "Okay, I admit I kind of rushed through." Her lips glistened as she smiled. "But the shopping was so fun." Then she turned the conversation back on him. "How was your day?" she asked, her eyes bright with enthusiasm and interest.

"Just meetings, nothing very interesting." They'd been hellish. The negotiations weren't going smoothly, but then they usually didn't. The dialogue always seemed to start out badly, but eventually coming round to an agreement.

"I suppose it's all hush-hush." She zipped her lips. "So word doesn't leak out and the stock price goes the wrong way."

He chuckled. "Are you fishing for stock tips?"

She put her hand to her chest in an I'm-so-innocent gesture which was anything but innocent. His mind rushed to all the ways he could make her feel good.

The driver dropped them off at the end of an alley, and Marshall gave her his arm as he led her through an ivy-covered trellis. The restaurant patio was separated from two others by tall hedges in planter boxes. Marshall asked for an inside table so Dana didn't have to put on a sweater over that gorgeous pantsuit.

It was a cozy, elegant dining room recommended by one of the associates at the firm he was working with. The tables in white linen were spaced far enough apart to allow private conversation, and the noise level was low. Patrons were dressed tastefully, and potted flowers scented the room sweetly. Their waiter was short with an unfortunate comb-over, and he spoke excellent English. Dana ordered a champagne cocktail, which she said was her favorite drink, and he ordered Campari and soda.

"What's that?" she asked once the waiter had left.

"It's an aperitif, very common in countries like Italy." He cocked his head. "Somewhat bitter if you're not used to it."

When the drinks arrived, he offered his glass. "Give it a try."

He liked the idea of her lips on his drink.

She tasted, making a face, and he had to laugh.

"*Ewwe*," she muttered, covering her mouth and almost shoving the glass back at him. "Thank you but no thank you."

"I told you it was bitter if you're not used to it."

Her face still screwed up, she said, "I'm not sure how it could ever grow on me."

But she was definitely growing on him. She was divorced, her daughters had left home, her friend had just died, yet she had a certain *joie de vivre*, as the French would call it.

"You should stick with your champagne cocktail then."

She sipped hers. "I most certainly will, thank you very much." Then she held out the flute. "Would you like to try?"

He smiled and shook his head. "It'll clash with the Campari. I'm glad you had a good day out."

"I'm not normally a big shopper." The flickering candle on the table bathed her pretty features in flattering light. "But this was fun."

Their waiter arrived once more.

"What would you recommend?" she asked. "I'd like to try something different from what I'd get back home in the U.S."

Trying new things was definitely on her menu. New shoes, new clothes, new lingerie, and maybe a new lover.

He wasn't enamored of that last part. Unless he was the lover.

"To start, may I suggest the aged ham paired with our aged cheese?" The waiter beamed with the description. "An outstanding combination of flavors. Our ham had been cured and aged thirty-six months, and the cheese stands at twenty years."

"I didn't know you could age ham and cheese that long." There was a teasing twinkle in her lovely eyes, an even deeper green in the restaurant's low lighting.

"Aged to perfection, signora. To bring out the robust flavors. And together they are *delizioso*." He kissed the tips of his fingers to show exactly how delicious it would be.

As delicious as she was.

"Does that sound good to you?" she asked, her gaze warm on Marshall.

"Absolutely," he agreed.

"And now for your dinners." Their waiter smiled widely. "May I suggest our carbonara with pancetta in a creamy white cheese sauce topped with parmesan for the lady?"

"It sounds marvelous." She clasped her hands, elbows on the table, looking up as if mesmerized by the description.

Marshall chose the Bolognese. When you were in Rome, you had to try the fresh pasta.

When the aged ham and cheese arrived, their waiter giving the Italian name for everything on the plate, Marshall was glad they'd ordered it. The sounds Dana made as she nibbled the morsels were something close to orgasmic. He added inhibition to the list of things he liked about her. He wondered if she would be so open, so free, so unselfconscious if she thought this was an actual date. He wondered if there would come a tipping point where wanting her in his bed would become greater than the pleasure he found in her friendship. Maybe that was a matter of when rather than if.

She waved her hand over the champagne and cheese and ham. "I'm going to have some marvelous stories when I get home. Some I can tell them and some I can keep to myself."

Something about the sparkle in her gaze made him ask, "Dare I venture that you've found your sexy young Italian?"

She bit her lip. She smiled. She nodded lightly. And finally, she shrugged. "I did meet a man. But I have no idea if it'll go anywhere."

He raised one brow, egging her on, though he knew she was dying to give him the dirty details, just the way she would have told her best friend Carol. A part of the him was dying to hear, while another part, maybe the bigger part, was envious, even jealous. Yet he enjoyed the feeling. It made his blood pump with elements of the high he got during a business negotiation. But this had a sexy man-woman edge to it that made his skin heat.

She needed no further prodding. "Believe it or not, he was my shoe salesman."

If he hadn't seen the curve of her lips, he would have tried harder to stifle his laugh. "Your shoe clerk hit on you?"

With a piece of ham spiked on her fork, she waved him down. "That's what's so crazy about it. I mean, he was sitting on that stool in front of me with his legs spread wide, and I put my foot on that little slanty part of the stool—" She leaned close. "—right between his legs," she whispered, her voice so soft he had to read her lips. "His hands were all over my feet, touching, measuring, testing. I think he brought out ten extra pairs of shoes just so he could keep touching me. I'm pretty sure he had a foot fetish."

Marshall almost snorted out his Campari. Did she know how utterly delightful she was? How sexy? How badly he wanted to be her shoe salesman with his hands all over her feet? "Maybe he just had a fetish for *your* feet." A slow burn was rising inside him.

She shrugged, wrinkled her nose. "His hands were all over my feet, and he was making all sorts of eye contact. Then he made a comment about... well, it could have been something about how sexy my calves are."

"Your calves?" He could think of so many sexy things about her. But her calves were what the guy talked about? Maybe he did have a fetish.

"It was probably because he was still sitting on that stool. All he could see were the shoes and my calves."

The waiter chose that moment to bring their pasta, fragrant with cheese and garlic and bacon and tomatoes.

After he'd topped their meals with fresh parmesan and retreated, Dana leaned over her carbonara, breathing in deeply, eyes closed. "This smells divine." She speared a small forkful, twirling it in the sauce and bringing it to her lips, tasting. Then she groaned.

Marshall almost did as well.

"God, it's so amazing." She gave him a satisfied sigh followed by a dreamy smile. "The bacon is so crispy. Not just bacon bits from a jar but the real stuff. How's yours?" She pointed with her fork.

Watching her, he hadn't tried his yet. "Extremely good," he said after he'd twirled the pasta and sauce onto his fork. The real pleasure was listening to her, her sighs and tantalizing moans as she ate.

"You were telling me about your shoe salesman." He wasn't letting this one go.

"Oh my God, yes." She closed her eyes to savor another bite of bacon and bucatini smothered in the creamy, cheesy sauce.

"Okay, so, in front of the whole shop— there were two other clerks and some customers— he asked me out for dinner tonight." She gave him an incredulous wide-eyed look, which only emphasized the gold flecks in her green eyes.

"Yet here you are with me." He liked that she'd turned down the shoe clerk with a foot fetish in favor of him.

"I told him I already had a dinner date, but that I'd make it for a drink afterward." Her smile was wholly seductive. It seduced him, and had probably seduced the shoe salesman. Maybe she'd even seduced herself.

It was evident that Dana had a distinct lack of admiration in her life. Her husband was a jerk. He'd banged his employee. He was a complete and utter ass. And he was an idiot because he didn't recognize what he had right in front of him. Marshall could almost guarantee that if Dana checked in with the new trophy wife a year or two from now, she'd be just as neglected.

"Where are you meeting your shoe salesman?" he asked.

"He gave me the name of a nightclub. I'll meet him there. He doesn't have my number or know where I'm staying, and I'll take a cab so I'm never actually alone with him."

But she'd bought shoes from him, and he had her name and credit card information. Maybe that was enough to do some real damage. Marshall found himself worrying about her like he would worry about Laura. "And you're actually thinking of meeting him?"

He hoped she'd change her mind. It was one thing to talk about a theoretical affair with a sexy young Italian, quite another to actually do it.

"I've thought about that all day." She turned serious. "I mean, I'm in an unfamiliar city, taking a taxi to an unfamiliar place and meeting an unfamiliar man. And yet—" She dropped her voice. "It's so nice to be admired."

"I admire you," he told her. "You're a beautiful, sexy, funny, desirable woman."

"But you're my friend. You've heard all my tales of woe. You have to say that."

By choosing to be her friend, as the proverbial saying went, he'd been hoisted with his own petard. "I'm your friend. But I can still say you're attractive, sexy, beautiful, and desirable."

Maybe he should have taken her to bed immediately, giving her physical proof that she was desirable. But then he would have missed this, the trading of secrets, the openness, her complete lack of inhibition in telling him her inner thoughts. And she'd come to Rome with two missions, a hot sexy affair and a wish. She needed a complete stranger to go wild for her, turned on by just her looks. And he no longer qualified for that.

"Well, then I'm going to sound like a big brother, if you really want to do this."

Her smile was soft and dreamy with possibilities. "And, pray tell, dear brother, what advice do you have for me?"

"Have you got your phone with you?"

She fished in the tiny purse that by some magic actually fit her phone.

"You've got my card. I want you to call me so that my number is already programmed into your phone."

"Then you'll have my phone number," she said without inflection.

"Yes, I will. And that means I can send you texts. And you can text to tell me what you're doing."

Her lips parted, her eyes widened. "You want me to tell you what I'm doing?"

He let a smile crease his lips. "*Everything*," he underlined with emphasis. "I want to know you're safe. And if you're not, I can run to your rescue."

"Yes, dear brother." She pulled his card from her bag, an

exceptionally good sign that she'd carried it with her, as if he were part of her landscape now.

She punched in his number, and his phone vibrated. He swiped to answer the call, keeping his eyes on her, then shut it down. "There, my number's in your phone and your number's in mine. If I don't hear from you, I promise I will call you."

The tilt of her head, the sparkle of her eyes, the curve of her lips all testified to how much she enjoyed this. "Should I text you every half hour?"

He gazed at her a long moment, letting his eyes trace the line of her lips, the pretty cheekbones, the lovely eyes. "Every fifteen minutes is better.

She growled. He felt a fire in his belly. "You've got to be joking. What if..." She let the question hang.

"If..." He let it hang, too. "If I don't hear from you every fifteen minutes, I'll give you an extra ten, then I'll text you anyway. And if you don't answer, then I'll have to call you. Over and over until you answer."

"He's only supposed to take half an hour for..." She deliberately paused. "*That?*"

Marshall would take all night for *that*. He didn't believe the shoe salesman would get that far. He certainly didn't believe she'd invite the man to her hotel. But he wanted to play the game with her. "I have a suspicion he's going to be so enamored and so hot." Her cheeks flushed at his words. "And he's going to lose complete control after ten minutes with you in his arms."

Her cheeks tinged a color that almost matched her hair. Her breath quickened, the rise and fall of her breasts visible. He was doing things to her, even if he was only talking.

He was playing with fire, too, because beneath the table, his body showed the evidence of how much he wanted to be the man losing his cool and making her scream.

10

The nightclub Giancarlo had chosen was a combination restaurant and cabaret like something out of the forties, a big band, old-time music, singers and dancers.

"It has been open only a few months, but already you can see what a hit it is." Giancarlo had dressed in a stylish suit and slicked back his hair.

"I wouldn't have thought this music was your style."

"Very retro," he said in American slang, then gave a very Italian shrug. "Who knows how long it will last. We Italians like our dalliances, then we get tired and want something new."

Was that what she was, a dalliance, something he would get tired of? Not that it mattered, of course. She only wanted a dalliance. And she'd be gone in three weeks.

He'd chosen a table close to the front and ordered a bottle of champagne.

"I like it. It's not what I expected at all." She could actually hear the music instead of having it blasted against her eardrums.

"I wanted to show you something different that Rome has to offer." He took her hand in his, stroked a thumb across her skin.

The gesture was too familiar. She didn't know him.

And this was nothing like Marshall's kiss on the back of her hand.

Marshall. Her mind kept going back to him. The rules he'd set down were a delight. She'd enjoyed their dinner immensely. Of course, she did all the talking, once again telling him too many secrets. But she'd liked that, too, the freedom to say anything she wanted. And his rules made her feel safe, protected. She felt feel sexy, too, with the way he looked at her in her beautiful new jumpsuit.

It was a good thing he was her friend and off limits. Because she could fall for that look in his eye.

She realized Giancarlo was saying something and put a hand behind her ear. "I'm sorry, the music," she said, excusing her distraction.

He squeezed her fingers politely. "I was simply asking about your life back in America."

"I have two daughters in college." She had no intention of hiding her age. In fact, she wanted him to accept her exactly the way she was.

"I'm sure they are as beautiful as their mother."

Flattery would get him everywhere, she thought. And she told him all about Natalie and Olivia, how amazing they were.

Until a woman practically threw herself on him as she passed their table. They chattered in fast Italian, his arm hooked around the woman's waist. She was young, probably only a couple of years older than Natalie, and slender in a tight, thigh-length dress, her hair hanging down her back in glossy black waves. Her lips were plump, her gaze saucy, her eyes darkly lined.

She looked from Dana to Giancarlo, firing off another

volley of Italian, a smile on her lips, Giancarlo replied, and they laughed. All the while, even as his arm was around the girl, he was holding Dana's hand, squeezing her fingers. Finally the girl toddled away on her high heels.

"I am so sorry," he said, his face dramatically apologetic. "The younger sister of my good friend. She's a very sweet girl."

She'd looked barely legal, and Dana suspected the good friend wouldn't like the proprietary arm Giancarlo laid around the younger sister.

"It's all right." Her phone lit up with a text. She felt no qualms about saying, "I need to check in with my friend," and angled herself slightly so that Giancarlo couldn't see the text.

He better not have his hand on your thigh.

She laughed softly.

"What does your friend say?"

"Just asking if I'm having a good time." She let go of Giancarlo's hand to type.

We haven't gotten to my thigh yet. He's just holding my hand.

She smiled sweetly. "I said I'm having a wonderful time."

Giancarlo's smile was wide enough to dazzle the entire nightclub.

Another number started, and people flocked to the dance floor. His hand out, Giancarlo seemed about to ask her to dance. But another woman threw herself at him, her arms around his neck, her breasts stuffed in his face. She was older than the last one, though not by much.

Her hair was long and blonde with dark roots, and her dress barely covered the essentials. Dana feared she was giving the dance floor behind her a show as she leaned over to hug Giancarlo. Her Italian was rapid-fire, her lips pouty, her smile sexy, her eyes smoky. She giggled and simpered. Maybe she liked older men. She glanced at Dana, her expression turning haughty. More rapid Italian, giggles, a few laughs from

Giancarlo. Then he smacked the girl on the rear, and she sauntered away with an extra wiggle to her hips.

Hmm. Was smacking a woman's bottom acceptable in Rome?

"Again, I am so sorry."

"Another friend's sister?" she asked, the words sarcastic even as she affected a light flirty tone to take the sting out.

He waved his arm expansively. "No. A friend of my sister's."

He had a lot of friends, extra touchy friends. Would his sister like the way he'd slapped her friend's bottom?

Dana wondered if this was jealousy. Well, not so much jealousy as resentment of the looks the girls gave her. As if they were laughing at her. Maybe she was overly sensitive.

"Would you like to dance?"

A few minutes ago, she would have, but now she didn't want to leave her phone or her purse or even her drink unsupervised on the table. "In a little bit," she said. "I'd rather talk about you. Where did you learn such excellent English?"

He waved his hand. "Here and there. But my life is very boring. I would rather know everything about you." He picked up her hand again, stroked his fingers across her knuckles.

She thought of Marshall's lips against her skin.

"Married?" he asked. Not that he'd seemed to care when he asked her out.

"Divorced."

He beamed as if that was exactly what he wanted to hear. "Tell me how you spend your days. Having coffee with friends, going to the salon, spa, perhaps tennis in the morning, golf in the afternoon?"

Her life to him was a cliché.

She was just about to tell him no, that she was a bookkeeper who worked from home, dispelling the "rich American" myth. But another pretty young thing grabbed his arm, trying to pull him onto the dance floor. He did his best to extricate himself between bouts of laughter, pointing to Dana, a flurry of Italian, the girl pouting and finally sauntering away.

"Another friend's sister. Or friend of *your* sister?"

He pursed his lips. "I apologize again. She's my brother's girlfriend. He's working tonight and she just wants to dance. He will not allow her to dance with anyone but family. He's the jealous type."

She didn't want to degrade herself by pointing out the difference between her age and that of the parade of pseudo female relatives. But there was a fourth girl, then a fifth. As much as she'd like to give Giancarlo the benefit of the doubt, the feeling she had was turning unpleasant. She began to imagine he was telling them all to leave him alone while he worked his magic on the rich American divorcée. She wasn't being unfair to herself. But there were the girls' smiles, the sly glances at her, the laughter, the flurry of words.

The man was working, and she was his mark.

At just the right moment, her phone lit up with another text, and she grabbed the device like it was a lifeline, reading quickly.

He better not have his hand up your skirt.
I'm not wearing a skirt, remember.

Then she turned her screen blank and looked at Giancarlo, affecting a woebegone look. "I'm so sorry. I have to go. My friend needs me right away." She stood, phone in hand. "Thank you so much for the champagne."

Before he could stand, before he could even reach for her, she darted across the club. She hoped that one of his many admirers would latch onto him before he could follow. Luck was with her, and as she stepped outside, a taxi was just letting off its passengers. She jumped right in.

Settled in the back, she texted Marshall.

I'm in a cab on the way back to my hotel.

It was barely two seconds before he shot back.

I want to make sure no one is hijacking your phone. Tell me what you had for dinner tonight when you were with me.

Carbonara with the most delicious crispy bacon all over it.

All right, it's you. Call me when you get back to the hotel. I want to hear everything.

The thought of rushing back to call Marshall was so much more thrilling than her evening with Giancarlo.

Then Marshall texted again.

Better yet, call me after you pour a glass of champagne and get into bed.

She liked that idea immensely.

❀

THE CELL PHONE RANG, AND HE STARTED WITHOUT preamble. "Are you in bed?"

"Yes."

"Do you have your champagne?"

"Yes." Then she laughed. "Aren't you supposed to ask me what I'm wearing?"

"What are you wearing?"

"A nightgown."

"A sexy nightgown?" That was how he imagined her, sexy, see-through lingerie.

"Is this phone sex or something?"

He thought about pushing it, telling her that he was naked. "Do you want it to be?"

"Isn't phone sex all raunchy and nasty?"

"Not necessarily." He could explain to her how hot it could be.

"I'm probably too old for phone sex."

He could show her that she wasn't, that she'd like it. But then tonight, he'd acted like her big brother. Phone sex right now might be over the top. Even if his body was ready for it.

"Tell me about your date."

"Are you dying to know?" she teased.

"You know I am." He was dying for so many things from her.

"He took me to this fabulous new club. Please don't ask me where it was because I have no idea. I just gave the taxi driver the address and he dropped me off."

"Tell me about the club."

"Actually, it was really kind of cool, like something out of the forties with the dance floor right in front of the big band and a stage and singers and dancers. The dance floor was ringed by small café tables. And the champagne was really good."

She did love her champagne. "Did you dance?"

"No. He wanted to, but I said no."

Marshall was glad. He didn't want her dancing in another man's arms. "Why say no?"

"I didn't want to leave my purse and my phone unattended."

That didn't sound good. "Was he skanky?"

"Isn't the word skanky for a woman?"

"I have no idea. So did he try to put his hand up your skirt?" He teased himself with the image, but it was his hand on her thigh, not some skanky Italian.

"You know I wasn't wearing a skirt. Anyway, I wouldn't call him skanky."

"Then what was he like?"

"He was actually attentive and sweet. And he did hold my hand." A long pause. "That was all."

He was inordinately glad that was all. He was starting to think being her big brother watchdog might be the death of him if she wanted to sleep with one of these sexy young Italians. "You're still not telling me why you were afraid to leave your purse unattended."

"Well, it was actually the parade of young women that kept stopping by the table."

"How young?"

"Between twenty and twenty-five. All dressed in tight clothing with all their assets hanging out, really pretty, very stacked.

He chuckled. It was amusing that the Italian gigolo was trying to seduce her while all his other girlfriends wouldn't leave him alone.

"They were all friends' sisters or his sister's friends or his brother's girlfriend or... I lost track."

He laughed out loud. "Now *that* sounds suspicious."

"He's older, like maybe thirty-five. It felt weird that all these pretty young things were hanging on him. None of them seemed like someone's sister or the girlfriend of somebody else."

"If they really are the sisters of all his friends, I suspect he gets beaten up regularly."

She laughed. "He didn't have any bruises that I saw."

"But you said he was attentive."

"Oh, he shooed them all away, and he apologized profusely. But there was always this flurry of Italian between them, and of course I didn't understand a word, but I didn't like the way the girls looked at me."

"Like what?"

"Honestly, like I was the rich American divorcée he was trying to bamboozle."

He listened for a hint of sadness or dismay or even anger, but her tone hadn't changed. Yet he was affronted for her. "I'm sure it wasn't like that. They were all jealous because you're so gorgeous."

She snorted as if she didn't believe him when he meant every word. She was amazing and beautiful and sexy.

"Yeah right," she said. "It was also the oddest place for all these girls to be, too. I mean the music was big band and I half expected a Judy Garland impersonator to step out on the stage at any moment. The dancing was ballroom stuff. So why were all those young women there?"

"Maybe it's the 'in' place to be right now."

"That's what Giancarlo said."

"Oh, Jean Carlo," he said with exaggerated smarminess.

"Not like that. It's Giancarlo, like Giancarlo Giannini, the actor. A very sexy name."

He chuckled, but was that jealousy giving him heart burn? "I didn't know you were a big fan."

"Did you ever see him in *Seven Beauties*? He was amazing and hilarious and sad and pathetic all at the same time."

"I missed that one, too. I'll have to add it to the list along with *Buffy the Vampire Slayer*." He'd have to ask to borrow her complete set. To watch the whole thing with her. Laying on his couch. His arms wrapped around her.

Damn, he was getting carried away.

Her voice was soft and seductive. "I'll have to test you about all the movies and TV shows you've missed and set them up in your Netflix queue for you."

"I'll give you full access to my account." She could have full access to anything of his that she wanted.

"Anyway, after the fourth or fifth girl, or it might have been the sixth, I knew it wasn't gonna work. In fact, I'm not sure I can go through with Carol's plan for me and have a holiday fling with a complete stranger."

How about a non-holiday fling with someone who'd stopped being a complete stranger sometime yesterday when she'd told him all her secrets?

He still didn't detect any sadness or hurt. "You were

married a long time. And I don't believe you even looked at another man during that whole time."

"I didn't. I was pretty boring, I guess."

She was far from boring. He found her fascinating. "My point is that it won't be easy to jump in bed with just anyone. You need to know a man. You need the dance of flirtation."

He could provide it.

"I don't know what I need. Maybe I just need to enjoy this vacation for what it is. Without scheming to find a man. If it's going to happen, it'll happen. And if it doesn't, I'm enjoying myself anyway."

He wanted to tell her she didn't have to look any further. But he knew in his gut she'd shut down the minute they got intimate, that they wouldn't be *friends* anymore.

He was tired of talking about other men. "What are you going to wish for?"

"I'm just going to wish for the most memorable vacation I've ever had in my life. Like in the movie *Roman Holiday* with just one sweet kiss at the very end before I have to return to my life as the princess of bookkeeping."

He could definitely give her that, one beautiful, memorable kiss. Except that he'd want a lot more. "You're truly a romantic."

"Yes, and that's what I'm going to wish for."

"We need to start you off on the right track then. I have tomorrow free and two tour tickets for Pompeii. My sister obviously isn't going to make it. Would you consider being my guest?"

She gave a sharp intake of breath, either excitement or shock. "I'd love it. But I want to pay for the ticket."

"Oh no you won't. They're already paid for. Since they'll be going to waste if you don't come, it'll be my treat."

"Then yes, thank you, I'd love it."

Praise the Lord. "It's a bus tour, so there'll be a bunch of old folks. The tour also includes a hike to the top of Mount Vesuvius."

"A hike up Vesuvius sounds exciting. I've got my sturdy walking shoes."

"I'll pick you up at quarter to seven. The tour bus leaves at seven, and it's quite a drive to Pompeii since they take us down there on a more scenic route than the highway. They'll provide lunch and drinks. Just bring your hat and your sunscreen."

"My hat, my sunscreen, my sturdy walking shoes, and a bunch of old folks. It sounds terribly romantic."

He laughed. "You have no idea." Anywhere with her would be romantic.

Her voice softened then. "Thank you for listening to me."

She didn't need to thank him. He'd wanted to hear her voice. "Thank you for texting me. Now I know you're safe, I can sleep." Except that his dreams would be filled with images of her.

"You don't need to look out for me, you know."

"I want to."

"Then I'll see you tomorrow at quarter to seven in the hotel lobby."

"I can hardly wait."

He lay in bed a long time listening to the street traffic.

Giancarlo was an idiot. But the thought of Dana in bed with a sexy Italian made Marshall's instincts for warfare rise, like Paris battling for Helen of Troy.

He'd never wanted to battle over a woman's affections. But he would for Dana.

He didn't even feel bad that he'd lied about the Pompeii tickets. He'd looked at the website before, but he hadn't purchased a tour until the moment she said yes.

He liked looking at her. He liked listening to her. He wanted to touch her.

Tomorrow, maybe he would.

※

She lay in bed watching the play of Rome night lights outside the French doors. The conversation had been so sweetly intimate. The lights out, the champagne on her bedside, and his voice intimately in her ear. So much better than the evening with Giancarlo.

She couldn't let Marshall keep paying for her. And what was he going to do when his sister arrived? Take the same tours all over again?

But she liked the idea of spending a whole day with him, touring the ruins, hiking up a volcano. There was an air of romance about going to all these fabulous sites with a handsome man she barely knew.

Even if she felt like she'd known him forever and could tell him anything.

11

There were definitely a lot of old people on the bus, all nationalities, all languages. Their guide said everything in Italian, then repeated it all in English. So hopefully the Dutch couple and the German group and the Scandinavians understood.

The elderly crowd were quite lovely, very polite, and quick to laugh.

"Did you eat breakfast?" Marshall asked Dana. "I should have picked you up earlier and taken you for a nice breakfast first."

Marshall was always looking out for her. "No, I'm fine. I ordered room service and ate it while I was getting ready."

He was casual in a T-shirt and cargo shorts. She'd worn Capri pants again and lots of sunscreen. She'd have hat hair by the end of the day, but that was better than burning.

"The scenery as we're driving along is magnificent." She gazed raptly out the window.

The road was narrow and sometimes steep. They passed hills crammed with houses climbing up the sides like mountain goats, almost perched on top of one another. Marshall let her have the window seat, leaning over to look at whatever she pointed out to him.

"You smell good," she told him. "What's that aftershave?"

"Are you sniffing me?"

He seemed to love teasing her, enjoying every moment, especially if she blushed. "I was not sniffing you. I wanted to know because it would make a good Christmas present for Thomas, Carol's husband." She hadn't been thinking about Thomas at all.

Marshall laughed. "Well, that puts me in my place, doesn't it? But I have to admit it's just the shampoo from the hotel."

His scent was enticing, tantalizing. And it wasn't just his shampoo. He had a unique male scent all his own.

The guide picked up her microphone again and chattered about the town they were passing through.

It might only be spring, but it was warm when they reached Pompeii. Some of the women carried parasols. Dana was glad she had her sun hat. As part of the tour, they were able to skip the main entrance lines.

The ancient city was amazing, and their guide was full of interesting tidbits. The people had died almost where they stood, sometimes in families, most of them killed by the gases or the heat before they were covered by volcanic ash. Plaster casts had been made in the hollows where bodies had simply turned to dust. The casts been placed where they were found, some huddled in terror, lovers dying in each other's arms, families lined up in rows as if they thought they could shelter in their homes, a lone man caught even as he was praying.

The place had an almost mystical feeling to it, as if the souls of so many dying all at once somehow still permeated the atmosphere. It made you walk softly, talk reverently.

"It must have been terrifying." She leaned close to

Marshall. "Nowhere to run. Nowhere to hide. It happened so fast."

"And they were so close. There was another town about ten miles away called Herculaneum. Many of them made it onto boats."

"I guess that's why you don't build a town at the base of an active volcano."

He bumped her shoulder for stating the obvious.

There were many exhibits about what life had been like in Pompeii. And there'd certainly been no taboo about sex. Some of the houses served as bordellos, with penises displayed on their signs. Archeologists had unearthed erotic statues, penis-shaped charms, frescoes and mosaics of men and women coupling in astonishing positions. She blushed and tried not to look at Marshall.

Of course he couldn't help teasing her. "All these artifacts are shocking the panties off the little ladies here."

"The American and British couples for sure. But the Scandinavians seem to take it in stride."

After the guided tour, they were given free time to explore the site, after which a late lunch would be served. Together they wandered the town, drinking in the sense of antiquity mixed with desperation and terror.

But the fascination wasn't just with the destruction, it was also about life in ancient Roman times. The streets were paved in stone, some of them with parallel ruts in the road used by chariots and wagons. "Sort of like trolley tracks," Dana mused. There were communal privies with holes in long stone slabs— "Not for me," she had to say— and even hot food and drink bars much like a soup and salad bar of modern times. There were the remains of elaborate homes, their courtyards filled with beautiful fountains and intricate mosaics, stunning murals depicting mythological tales.

At the gift shop, Marshall bought an illustrated book of

Pompeii as well as a pack of erotic playing cards, handing the cards to Dana. "A souvenir so you'll always remember what Pompeii had to offer."

"You're so thoughtful," she said, humor running through her voice. "I can use these to play solitaire on the flight home."

"Just don't show them to your daughters or they'll wonder what hell you were doing on this trip."

He held her hand as they walked, and it was so pleasant, not as if he were expecting anything, just a sweet, caring gesture.

For lunch they had homemade pizza. The cheese came off in strings, the dough fluffy and light, the sausage mouthwatering in the fresh tomato sauce.

"This isn't anything like pizza at home." She licked sauce off her finger. "It's to die for.

"Maybe I need to take an Italian cooking class when I get back home."

"Oh my God, don't tell me you cook," she said around a mouthful of pizza, holding her hand up so he couldn't see.

He laughed. "If I don't want to eat out all the time, I have to cook."

"That's amazing."

"I take it your husband didn't spend time in the kitchen."

She snorted. "Not likely." She'd worked, putting Anthony through law school, cooked all his meals, and done his laundry, too. Nothing changed once the girls came along. Okay, that sounded bitter. She cut off the negative thoughts.

They talked with the rest of the group, all of whom spoke English, asking questions about where they were from, whether they had kids, all the usual polite conversation. Then Marshall held up the playing cards, and said, "Dana insisted I buy them for her. But I told her only if she promised not to use them for solitaire on the flight home."

They all laughed. If Anthony had done that, she would have felt like the butt of his joke. But Marshall was funny, and she loved the raised eyebrows, the cheeky smiles.

With lunch over, they all slathered on extra sunscreen and headed up Mount Vesuvius. The trail was crowded and they were once again glad of the tour bus which allowed them special parking. The sides of the trail were dotted with wildflowers, and while the day had started out warm, the higher they climbed, the cooler it grew. The view stretched for miles over the Bay of Naples and the magnificent city.

It was two miles up a switchback path until they reached the steeper climb to the crater's edge. She'd wondered how this relatively elderly group would make it, but it turned out many were experienced hikers, walking even faster than she did and with less breathlessness. Thank God she was used to walking the steep hills in the park with Carol.

At the top, they strolled along the rim of the massive crater, looking down at the destruction of Pompeii, and she slipped her hand into Marshall's. "Thank you for bringing me. On my own, I would have taken the train, done the tour of Pompeii then gotten right back on the train and missed all of this." She would have missed him.

He rubbed up against her shoulder. "You're welcome."

She had the urge to kiss him, just a sweet thank-you kiss, nothing sexual.

"What are you going to do with your sister when she gets here since you've already done Pompeii and the Colosseum without her?"

He winked. "I'll just get her another tour, put her on the train, and send her down to Pompeii." Right. He'd do no such thing. If his sister wanted to, he would do Pompeii all over again. But it would be worth a second trip.

"She loves to shop," he added with a shrug. "I'm sure she'll want to make the rounds of all the exclusive designer stores."

He squeezed her hand. "Maybe you can help me out by taking her so I don't have to." He rolled his eyes and whispered, "Shopping."

"I'd love to. Even if I've spent my quota, there's always time to shop. Especially when someone else is doing the buying."

"It's a date then. Thank you for saving me. I'll even take you both out to dinner afterward."

It was the least she could do to pay him back for all he'd done for her, considering that he was on a business trip.

She fell asleep on the bus ride back, leaning against Marshall's shoulder. He woke her up as they rolled into town, and she stretched. "Oh my God, I missed all the amazing views."

He smiled. "They were the same on the way back."

Out on the sidewalk beside the bus, they thanked their guide and waved goodbye to their companions.

But she wasn't ready to leave Marshall. "I'm hungry again. Can I take you to dinner?"

"You don't have to take me out." He gave a slight shake of his head.

"I want to. A small way to pay you back for today. And for the Colosseum and last night's dinner and on and on for everything you've done. And especially for listening to me."

"I like listening to you," he said simply.

"It's my treat anyway. Deal?"

"Yes." He had such nice eyes, always with a hint of sparkle, as if he laughed a lot. "Where are you going to take me?"

"I heard about this great takeout spaghetti place."

"Takeout spaghetti?" He made a face. "You're kidding."

She slapped his arm playfully. "Yes, I'm kidding. Although," she said with a singsong voice, "the takeout spaghetti place I read about online is right near the Spanish

Steps. We could eat it right on the steps, then have gelato afterward."

"I hate to burst your bubble, but you're not allowed to eat on the steps, not even gelato. Not even if you promise not to drop it." He was laughing at her now, with that sparkle in his eyes and a deep chuckle in his throat. "I don't think you're even allowed to sit down anymore. All those pesky tourists are worse than a flock of pigeons pooping on the famous steps."

"Oh no," she cried, her hands to her cheeks. "And another dream died."

"But we can still walk up them from the Piazza di Spagna to the Santissima Trinità dei Monti Church."

She smiled. "All right, deal."

THE WOMAN CERTAINLY KNEW HOW TO ENJOY HER FOOD. The dinner had been fabulous and expensive, even if he'd tried to talk her out of the exclusive restaurant near the Spanish Steps.

He'd seen pictures of the steps, but they didn't show the scope of the magnificent view. They walked up, surveyed the church from the outside, then gazed at the piazza below. And walked back down hand in hand.

The day had been good. They shared a gelato, fingers entwined like new lovers. It was on the tip of his tongue to say that she didn't need a young Italian lover. He could be better for her.

Yet as soon as he said the words, everything between them would change. The ease she felt with him would disappear. A woman like Dana, married for close to thirty years, would want more that a holiday fling. He couldn't offer her that, and he didn't want to see her get hurt in the end.

So he took her back to her hotel, leaned in close to kiss her cheek and breathe in her scent.

Still holding her hand, he asked, "What's on your agenda for tomorrow?"

"The Vatican."

"You'll enjoy it. I've got back-to-back meetings tomorrow, along with a dinner I have to attend. Can I call to see if you've got time to get together in a couple of days?"

"Absolutely."

He wanted to cancel all the meetings, beg off the business dinner, spend all his time with her. But he was a businessman first and always. And he didn't want to smother her.

He kissed her cheek once more, this time lingering a little longer. Then he watched her enter the hotel, her hips swaying.

Did he imagine there was a difference to her walk, more bounce to her step? As if getting away from home for a holiday in Rome, the eternal city, had given her a new confidence.

He watched until she disappeared, his lips still tingling with the taste of her skin.

12

The Vatican museums were amazing, but the highlight, of course, was the Sistine Chapel.

Despite being early for the tourist season, the crowd was still thick, almost moving her along like a wave, the sound of voices rising until the monks told everyone to quiet down and show respect. The noise would subside for a few minutes, but inevitably the voices would swell once more.

She felt the majesty, gazing up into the vault filled with Michelangelo's masterwork until her neck ached. His rendering of *The Last Judgment* over the altar gave her chills for its intricacy and beauty. That's what everyone marveled at, Michelangelo's work. But there was so much more, including Botticelli and Rosselli, and she could have studied the Raphael tapestries all day, especially since she'd read they weren't usually exhibited in the chapel.

But there was so much to see in the museums, miles and miles of paintings and sculptures and statues. And sometimes her mind wandered to other things. Like being with Marshall and their fabulous day in Pompeii, the invigorating hike, the delicious dinner, the shared gelato at the base of the Spanish

Steps, Marshall holding it, each of them taking bites, standing so close, so intimate. She wasn't sure she could wait a couple of days to see him again.

She thought about what she'd told Marshall, that she'd wish for the best holiday of her life.

This trip was already the best holiday ever, mostly because of Marshall. And of course, because of Carol. She would never have done this without Carol.

In many ways, her daughters were right. She'd always done things with someone else, never on her own. She never even went to a movie theater by herself. If she couldn't find someone to go with her, she waited until it came out on DVD or streaming. True, she'd gone to the Colosseum and Pompeii with Marshall, but the fact was that she hadn't needed to. She could have done it all happily on her own. Even if it wouldn't have been as fun or interesting.

After her day in the Vatican, she had dinner in a café all by herself, almost defiantly. She asked the waiter what he recommended and chose what amounted to a panini filled with delicious meat and cheese.

She no longer needed to wish for the best vacation ever, since she already had it. Maybe she should wish for her bookkeeping business to really take off. She sipped her espresso, which she was beginning to get a taste for.

If she wished for the business to grow, then it would take more time. She'd rather have time for yoga and coffee with friends. Coffee dates would never be the same without Carol, but she had friends, and coffee chats could still be good. She didn't want to be tied to her home office. She wanted the freedom to pick up and go whenever she liked. With the current state of her business, that's exactly how it worked. And she didn't need the extra money.

But she was still left with deciding what to wish for.

That evening Marshall texted her goodnight, saying he

was still busy. She felt a slight pang, but he was here on business, and she couldn't monopolize him. So the next day she took off on her own. Honestly, after the Vatican yesterday, she didn't feel like fighting the crowds at St. Peter's Basilica or any of the major tourist sites. She decided on a walking day to get the feel of Rome away from the tourist crowds.

Strolling along narrow cobbled streets decorated with flower pots, she gazed up at geraniums and tomato plants hanging from balconies and clothes lines suspended from windows, the scent of fresh laundry almost like perfume in the air. She passed great walled-in homes with huge Italian pines or cypress or palm trees standing tall above the stonework, birds suddenly shooting up into the air as if something inside those walls had startled them. She wandered through vegetable markets and window shopped, breathing in the scents of a bakery or eyeing the meats in a butcher's shop. Old men sat in outdoor cafés sipping espresso and talking in loud voices. Mopeds were parked everywhere, lined up along the streets like dominoes. Young people dashed along on electric scooters, accompanied by the ever-present sound of traffic and car horns and church bells.

The cacophony of Rome was almost musical.

She enjoyed a respite on a café patio with some amazing concoction of coffee, cream, and chocolate that sat in a parfait glass in layers, a chocolate truffle on the side. She slipped through the beaded curtains of a little grocery packed with elderly ladies, string bags on their arms as they picked out their daily goods. Outside the fruits and vegetables looked freshly picked as women haggled over them in high Italian voices. She drank orange soda as she walked and treated herself to lunch at an Indian restaurant. She passed fountains in almost every square and churches on almost every block, one of them perched on a hill, tourists sitting on the steps below, enjoying gelato.

So it was only the Spanish Steps you couldn't sit or eat on.

Then she found it, a hair salon, its open door crooning to her. She felt as if she were Audrey Hepburn looking at her reflection in the glass and comparing it to the picture of a more modern look.

Dana flipped her hair in the reflection. She didn't dislike her hair, but she'd been wearing it this way for so long. She didn't know if she could go as far as cutting it in a bob, that just didn't feel right.

She examined herself and said softly, "You can do whatever you want. You deserve it." It wasn't Carol's voice, it wasn't even Marshall's, it was her own. And she marched through the shop door.

The salon throbbed with activity, women under dryer bonnets or with foil in their hair, women in all the available seats, their high-pitched Italian voices trying to overpower the roar of hairdryers. If not for the Italian language, it was exactly like her hair salon at home, smelling of perm solution and hair dye overlaid by something floral, perhaps the shampoo they used.

The receptionist bustled over to her, speaking English immediately as if Dana had a scarlet "American" written on her chest.

"May I help you, signora?" She reached out to fluff one of Dana's waves. "Perhaps a little straightening. Or a cut, something layered, that will turn these waves into curls." The woman snapped her fingers and a man rushed over. Dana realized then that she wasn't a receptionist but probably the owner. In her fifties, she had gorgeous skin, and Dana was dying to ask her what her nightly regimen was.

"Lorenzo," she said with a long drawl on the name. "We have a lady all the way from America." She paused, looked at Dana. "You are American, correct?"

Dana nodded. She hadn't said a word so far, but the woman had guessed nonetheless.

She smiled with beautiful teeth. Everything about her was immaculate. "La signora is here because only our amazing Italian stylists can give her what she needs," she called out to the entire shop. "She cannot get this at home. We will give you an amazing cut," she said once more to Dana, "and your hair cutters back home will be able to copy what we do."

It was a delightful act, building up that only *Italian* stylists, *her* stylists could know what Dana needed. "That would be wonderful. I'd like a change, but nothing too drastic. No shorter than my shoulders." She wasn't about to give them carte blanche.

"Signora, we will bring out the *dazzling* color of your hair, the *stunning* curls that are just waiting on the cusp. You will be *amazed*." Then she turned to the man. "Lorenzo, wash the lady's hair. Then—" She put a finger to her high cheekbone and tapped. "She will do best with—" Her voice was slow, considering, her gaze roaming the busy salon. "Give her to Nario. He will know exactly what to do."

Dana wondered which one— the stylists were all men— was Nario.

"Nario speaks very good English, and he will be able to tell you exactly what you need."

She didn't argue as Lorenzo whisked her away to a room filled with sinks and rows of hair products on shelves where he snapped a cape in place to protect her clothing. He was young, perhaps twenty, maybe in training to be a stylist. Good-looking with an aristocratic nose, his fingers were miraculous. The water was warm, soothing, and he washed her hair with a scalp massage that was so good it almost put her to sleep.

Then he brought her back to the main salon. Another young man, this one perhaps thirty, kissed the fingertips of a woman with a beautiful bouffant of white hair. They exchanged cheek kisses, then the man turned.

He was quite beautiful. She imagined a statue of the mythical god Apollo. His bone structure was flawless, the slope of his nose stately, his lips full, his eyelashes long, his eyes a deep dark brown. He wore his hair in short ringlets slightly glazed with some sort of oil that seemed to shine in the salon's lights.

He held out his hand, and she let him lead her to the only empty chair in the salon.

He played with her hair a moment, then whispered, "Absolute perfection. I am Nario. Let us find the perfect style for your face." He spoke excellent English.

He stood behind her, watching in the mirror, fluffing as the locks air-dried, the waves and colors emerging. "Your hair is an amazing shade, not orange, not fire engine red, as they say, but a bit of mahogany and cherrywood and rosewood, and just the taste of some other color." He picked up the strands, lifting them, letting them fall, testing them in the light. "I feel you need a touch more gold. But first we cut. I suggest curls, more on top." He drew his hands down her cheeks. "They will accentuate your beautiful cheekbones and your glorious face." He gestured with his hands, as if he expected her to see what he imagined.

All she saw was a middle-aged woman. The moment the thought hit her, she hated it. So would Carol. *You're always picking. You're beautiful. All this other crap is Anthony's fault.*

Was it really Anthony who had made her feel so undesirable? Perhaps she'd been desirable all along, but his lack of attraction had sapped all her belief in herself.

But she liked Nario's words, liked his description of her hair, and she wanted it. Closing her eyes, she said, "Yes, let's try what you suggested."

He picked up the scissors and started cutting. The shorter

the hair became on the top of her head, the more the curls grew. He sniffed and shuddered, sighed and shivered, as if the feel of her hair and the new cut he was giving her were sensual delights.

While he cut, he talked. "You are American, signora. Where are you from?"

"San Francisco," she told him because there was no reason not to.

"I would love to see Frisco. What do you do there?" He snipped and shaped.

"I'm a bookkeeper."

He nodded sagely. "And do you have beautiful children?"

She smiled. "Yes, two very beautiful girls."

He talked the whole time, asking her questions about herself, her life, nothing terribly personal that she didn't feel like answering. She told him about her daughters, how amazing and smart they were.

He didn't cut much off the length, taking it just below her shoulders to get rid of the split ends. Under his ministrations, her face began to look fuller rather than gaunt, lighter rather than haggard.

"We will add a little gold now," he pronounced. "And then we will finish off the cut. But what do you think so far, signora?"

"You're amazing, Nario." She might have looked like a middle-aged woman when she walked in, but now she felt a bit like Angelina Jolie.

"I can only work with what you bring," he said effusively. "Your beauty is all there beneath the hair. I only bring it out."

He snapped his fingers, and Lorenzo ran over with pots and brushes and bits of foil, and Nario began highlighting. The owner drifted over to gaze and coo. "Nario is a master. I rue the day he will open his own shop."

Then finally her hair was laden with foil and Nario

whisked her away to sit under a dryer as the signora ushered another woman to his chair. Leaning down before he turned on the dryer, he murmured, "Have no fear, I will be back to check on you often. The lady here doesn't require much, coming in once a week for a set. You have my full focus."

He handed her a magazine in Italian, and she flipped through the pictures, the hairstyles, the makeup, the beautiful women, while Nario popped over every few minutes to check that her hair wasn't turning orange. He worked on his elderly client, then checked Dana one last time, lifting the bonnet to test her curls.

He snapped his fingers and Lorenzo came running. "Five minutes with a clarifying treatment, then wash with hair cleansing cream and let it sit for five minutes, then another five with extreme conditioner." He leaned down to Dana. "Your hair will be like silk."

It was complete luxury, Lorenzo's fingers constantly in her hair, rubbing her scalp, massaging in the products, washing them out. And finally she was done, Lorenzo leading her back to Nario's chair as he escorted the elderly woman to the dryer Dana had vacated, setting the bonnet over her head.

Nario began to blow-dry Dana's hair, fluffing, making a few more snips, punctuating them with a moan or a groan as if he were having sex with her hair.

"Your American friends will be envious, will they not, that you had the courage to allow me, Nario, to take command of your hair."

She laughed. "Yes. They'll be shocked." Carol would have cheered.

"I can tell you must have many friends, very popular."

"A few," she said, still smiling.

"Rarely do I have the honor and pleasure of working on such beauty." He probably said that to all the ladies.

It was her usual attitude, that compliments didn't mean

anything, that they weren't really for her but for ulterior motives. She'd done the same thing days ago, believing Giancarlo thought she was just a rich American woman, an easy mark.

"*Bellissima*," he said on a reverent breath when at last he was done, standing behind her, gazing at her reflection in the mirror. "Do you feel how beautiful you are, signora?"

"Yes, I do," she said with all honesty in that moment. Her red hair was now rich with gold tones, curling on top, waving down the sides, curls brushing her shoulders.

She wondered if Marshall would find her beautiful. He complimented her, but he hadn't tried terribly hard to take the place of her sexy young Italians. But did she really want him to? She adored him as her friend. Would the day trip to Pompeii have been so good if he were trying to woo her or she wanted to woo him? The teasing would probably have made her nervous.

With an Italian fling, she could walk away. With Marshall, she didn't think she could do that so easily. But then Marshall wasn't a relationship man anyway.

Nario gestured, calling over Lorenzo, the signora, another stylist who'd just finished his client. They chattered effusively in Italian, gesticulating, smiling, congratulating Nario on his work. And he had done far more than she expected.

Once they'd drifted away, Nario did some last-minute primping on her hair. "Would you do me the honor of having dinner with me tonight at my uncle's *ristorante*. I know he would like to meet the American woman who allowed me to bring out the beauty of her hair."

She looked at him in the mirror for a stunned moment. He was certainly handsome, and fairly young, she suspected around thirty. He was sexy, too, extremely masculine and in excellent shape, his biceps bulging in his short-sleeved shirt. She wasn't buying thousand-dollar shoes, she hadn't even given him her credit card. She didn't feel that he saw her as a mark.

And she was free tonight since Marshall was with his customers. Maybe the food would be extra special at a local restaurant. It could be a lovely dinner. And why shouldn't she? She deserved an evening with a handsome younger man at his uncle's restaurant.

She met his gaze in the mirror and smiled. "I'd love to."

She didn't feel the need to text Marshall since she would be at a family restaurant surrounded by Nario's family.

His uncle's *ristorante* turned out to be four blocks away from the square, and off the beaten tourist track. Nario was sweet, reading the menu for her, which was all in Italian. It wasn't the fanciest restaurant and only half the tables were full. The red tablecloths were plastic, easily wiped clean, and the napkins were paper. The chairs were plain wood, a little hard beneath the bottom, and candles and flowers in jelly jars decorated the tabletops. Nario's uncle was sweet and attentive, and she could hear Mama yelling in the kitchen.

"My nephew is named for me, I am Nario, too," the uncle announced proudly.

They got down to the business of ordering. When Nario thought she should order this, Nario's uncle decided she should order that. When Nario suggested that wine, Nario's uncle suggested this one. He spoke surprisingly good English, but as she tried to order, the two argued in Italian, smiling good-naturedly.

When Uncle Nario brought their meals, he stood over Dana waiting for her approval.

She gladly gave it. "This is absolutely the best pasta I've ever had."

He clapped his hands. "Mama makes it special for the most beautiful lady. And my nephew, he is amazing with the hair, no? You are gorgeous. He is a genius, no? I tell him he should be in America doing the hair for all the starlets. But he's such a good boy, not wanting to leave his family."

Nario the younger blushed as his uncle lauded his talents.

"I tell him that in five years, he will have the biggest salon in Rome. He will have twenty stylists. Celebrities will come from all over the world to his shop. He will be on TV like those celebrity cooking shows in America, but his will be for hair. No?"

"I believe it," Dana agreed.

"Uncle, can you not see I'm trying to woo a beautiful woman?" Nario made a shooing motion, and Uncle Nario groused at him in Italian. Then he smiled and blew Dana a kiss before returning to Mama in the kitchen.

"Your uncle is obviously proud of you."

Nario gave her his pearly whites. "He is more like my papa. And Mama, she is—" He gave a very Italian shrug. "She is the only mama I have ever known. He and Mama raised me." He didn't offer an explanation for what happened to his parents.

"He would like me to go into the family business here. But when I decided not to, he never said a bad word. All he and Mama wish is for my success in whatever I choose to do."

The pasta was excellent but the plate was huge, and she kept Nario talking as she waded through it. "He obviously has faith in you."

Nario chuckled. "Yes, he sees me as the next Sergio Valente. But I have only just made my start. It is good to— what do you Americans say?— cut my teeth?" When she nodded, he went on, "But the salon is just a backstreet."

"The shop was completely full."

He snorted softly. "All we get are Italians. If we want the big time, we need to cater to all nationalities. You're the first American who has stepped through our doors in six months."

"But your business seemed incredibly good. Doesn't that count?"

He gave another snort, twirling his spaghetti onto his fork with a spoon. Before he put it in his mouth, he said, "You walked in and we were able to seat you almost immediately. That is not good. People should be waiting, appointment only." He shoveled the spaghetti into his mouth, chewed, swallowed, then added, "Did you not wonder why Lorenzo washed your hair first?"

She shrugged, her mouth full of the delicious pasta in simple tomato sauce.

"La signora knew I only needed ten more minutes and I could take you. She didn't even care that it made finding your perfect style much more difficult. She cares only about the money." He rubbed his fingers together. "Not about the client."

She made a sympathetic noise.

"In my shop, women will need to make appointments two months in advance. But when they are in my chair, they will get all my attention. Of course, I shall leave little holes in the schedule for the more prestigious clients who cannot plan that far ahead. Or," he shook his finger, his eyes bright with planning, "I will hire two or three stylists who are only for walk-ins." He shrugged eloquently, so Italian. "Of course, this is how they will get their experience. In my shop. Stylists will be clamoring to get into my shop." His gaze had an almost manic fervor. "People will talk about me in magazines, saying yes, Nario did my hair. I won't even need a last name. Just Nario."

"That sounds marvelous." She felt this young man could make it happen.

They had only just finished their pasta when Uncle Nario descended upon them. "Mama has made her special cannoli. It is—" He didn't add a description, simply kissed his fingers.

She wanted to say she was absolutely stuffed. She should have asked Nario if it was impolite to leave anything on her plate, but she'd already surmised the answer would be a hysterical Mama in the kitchen asking what was wrong with the pasta.

She looked at Nario. "Perhaps we could share."

"Oh, no, no, no," Uncle Nario argued. "I will not allow my nephew to take one single bite of your cannoli."

Her stomach sank. "You're so kind." She hoped he didn't hear the horror in her voice.

"Has my nephew told you all about his plans for his salon?"

Nario shot him the evil eye.

"He is so modest, that boy. He will be famous. His name will be spoken around the world."

Nario was now shooting daggers at his uncle.

But Uncle Nario went on. "All he needs is investors, people who believe in him the way his family does. If I had the money, I would give him every penny, but—" He waved a hand around the half-full restaurant. "As you can see," he left it at that.

"The cannoli, Uncle." Nario's teeth clenched.

"Yes, yes, the lovely lady must have her cannoli." Uncle Nario bustled away.

And Dana knew exactly why she was here. She was the potential patron. "I will find many investors," Nario said. "My uncle is jumping the gun, as you Americans say."

But Dana knew he wasn't. This had been Nario's plan all along, hence the dinner at his family restaurant and his uncle's overzealous sales pitch for Nario's salon.

She actually felt relieved. She wouldn't have to negotiate the after-dinner fumbles, deciding whether she wanted a sexy young Italian lover tonight.

Carol's voice popped into her head. *Right, so you wouldn't have to make a decision.*

It was true. Maybe she didn't need an affair. Maybe she only needed to go out on dates. She hadn't had any practice in thirty years. This could be considered good practice.

Right now, though, she needed to be completely honest with Nario. "You may be under the impression that I'm a rich American. I'm sure your salon will be a huge hit, that you'll find multiple investors, and your name will be all over the magazines. But unfortunately, I'm not rich. A friend left me the money to go on this trip." It wasn't a lie, because though she had an excellent settlement from Anthony, she didn't have unlimited funds. And that meant she couldn't invest in sexy young Italians.

He waved his hands extravagantly. "That is not why I invited you. I only wanted dinner with an attractive woman. I have no expectations about an investment."

She smiled. "Good. And just to be clear, I'm not having sex with you either." It felt good to be blunt and bold. To take charge, to say what she did and didn't want.

Nario laughed good-naturedly. "I feel that I am being told off. You are an extremely attractive woman, and if I could coax you home with me, I would." For a moment she thought she detected a tiny flame in his eyes. "But truly, I did not ask you here for sex or for money." Then he grinned. "I asked you here so that my uncle could see how attractive you are, and the fabulous cut that I gave you today." He leaned close. "I'm not sure my uncle always believes that I can achieve my dreams."

Dana fluffed her curls. "You definitely have talent. You make me feel young and sexy with this hair. Not like a fifty-year-old mother of two college-age girls."

He wiped his hands together. "Then I have done my job."

She pointed a finger at him, giving him a sideways look. "And if you need a referral, I'm your girl."

He rose and leaned over the table, taking her hand, kissing it lavishly. "Thank you, my dear lady, thank you."

And she wondered what Marshall would think of her sexy new hairstyle.

13

She texted Marshall when she got back to the hotel. *What's your schedule like tomorrow?*

She had to admit she'd missed him. Even though it was only days, it seemed like ages since they'd gone to Pompeii, since she'd walked with him, dined with him, laughed with him.

He was back quickly, as if he'd been waiting to hear from her. *Busy. But let's squeeze in a break after I have lunch with some people if you haven't got any tours planned.*

He didn't really have time, she could tell, but it was nice to know he still wanted to see her. She felt warm inside, that tingle a teenage girl gets when the boy she likes gives her some attention. And it felt good. She wanted him as a friend, a confidant, not a lover, but that didn't mean she couldn't enjoy the feelings he brought out in her.

How about meeting me at this little church I found? We can actually eat gelato on the steps. Dessert after your business lunch. My treat.

He sent her a winking emoji. *You can definitely be my dessert.*

When she answered with a red-faced emoji, he sent one with tears streaming down its cheeks. Then he typed, *It's a date*. She sent him the cross streets of the church, and he told her when he thought he'd be available.

Then he asked, *What did you do today?*

It was sexy to lie in the dark texting with a man. Even if they weren't saying anything the least bit sexual.

She wrote back, *Just put on my walking shoes and took off, no destination in mind.*

His answer was, *Sounds great. Tell me all about it when I see you tomorrow.*

She'd tell him about her date with Nario, too, about Uncle Nario and Mama. It would be a good story. She'd make him laugh. She'd had fun, they had a good talk, his uncle and aunt were sweet, and so was Nario himself. He hadn't tried to bilk her out of any money, and he'd given her the most beautiful hair. It seemed like a win-win to her. Even Carol would see it that way.

Before going to sleep, she video-chatted with the girls, telling them what a fabulous time she was having, eating by herself, visiting the Vatican all alone, shopping. She modeled her Bottega Veneta shoes for them. Natalie almost cried, and Olivia almost fainted. It was wonderful fun holding up her purchases for them to ooh and aah over. She didn't mention Marshall and Pompeii.

For right now, Marshall was her delicious secret.

🌸

SHE MADE IT TO THE CHURCH A FEW MINUTES EARLY. SINCE Marshall was on borrowed time from work, she didn't want to be late.

Waiting in line for a gelato, she saw him approach, handsome and sexy in a business suit, white shirt, and striped tie. His jacket slung over his shoulder, the sleeves of his white shirt were rolled up his forearms, tanned and taut with muscles, as if he actually had time for yard work.

He leaned down to kiss her on both cheeks, Italian style.

Then he gaped a moment. She'd taken off her hat, shoved it in her bag, and fluffed up her curls.

"Wow," was all he said.

But the words sent a shimmy of heat spiraling down inside her. She touched her hair, basking in his approving gaze. "Do you like it?"

Once more, he was close enough for her to smell his unique male scent that wasn't aftershave and could have been shampoo, but was really just him. "I adore it. You're beautiful, always have been. Since the moment I saw you at the Colosseum. But the new cut is like the whipped cream and chocolate sauce on my banana split."

She laughed, turning heads. "Was that a subtle reference to your...?" She didn't say the words, but let her eyes do the talking, her gaze sliding down him for a brief moment.

His laugh sent delicious tingles through her.

Just have your affair with him. What could be more perfect?

It wasn't Carol's voice urging her on. It was her own.

"I don't think that quickly when it comes to double entendres, but if you want to take it that way, be my guest." The smile lingering on his lips was enticing.

But she could never have asked that question if he'd been a real date. She could never have raked his body with that saucy look. It was only because he was her friend, because she felt comfortable with him. She absolutely could not lose the ease she felt with him. It was more important than sex. He might not have long-term relationships with women. But she could be his friend.

Then she asked him, "What flavor do you want?"

"Pistachio." He fished in his back pocket for his wallet.

She touched his arm, his skin warm beneath her fingers.

"This is my treat. You go find us the perfect spot to sit." She waved him away, and when she had the gelato, she found him under a row of trees that run up the steps to the church. He'd even laid his coat on the step.

She handed him the pistachio cup. "Your jacket will get dirty."

He eyed her white capris, then patted the jacket beside him. "Just sit."

She plopped down gratefully, only now realizing how her feet ached.

He nudged her with his elbow. "What on earth is that?" He pointed at her gelato.

It was blue with speckles of hard candy crushed inside it. "It tastes like peppermint bubble gum."

She held it out to him, liking the way his eyes went wide while she fed him.

"I prefer the pistachio." Then he pointed at her. "And your tongue is blue."

She stuck her tongue out at him.

"Tell me what you've been doing this morning, besides your hair."

She laughed. He was so easy to laugh with. "Actually, I did the hair yesterday. And today I walked for miles and miles touring the most amazing churches. And just looking at everything."

"I know what you mean. The first time someone visits Rome, they rush around to see all the big tourist attractions. But you have to get into the back alleys to appreciate how beautiful Rome is."

She liked sitting here with him. There were other people on the steps, laughter and talking. As beautiful as they were, the Spanish Steps were mobbed, and this was pleasant, the gelato was good, and they wouldn't get arrested for sitting.

"How many times have you been to Rome?" she wanted to know.

"This is my third trip. It's always business, though, so I don't get as much sightseeing done as I want. But when I get a break, I enjoy walking around. I even carry walking shoes in my briefcase." He warmed her with a smile.

It was only then she saw he'd swapped out his dress shoes for a pair of running shoes.

"And yet you still planned your holiday with your sister while you're working."

He smiled. "That was so I didn't have to do all the shopping with her."

"I forgot about that." She swooped in to take a spoon of his pistachio just for the fun of it.

He swatted at her and missed. Then he asked, "So, did you meet any sexy young Italians?"

"Actually, I did. Yesterday." She fluffed her curls. "Nario did my hair. And he asked me out." She said it proudly, as if she'd accomplished something huge.

Marshall raised a brow.

"I had dinner with him at his family restaurant."

He gave her a sideways glance. "You know you're supposed to check in with me so I can make sure you're safe."

She pursed her lips, letting her eyes do the smiling. "I thought a dinner date at his family's restaurant was pretty harmless."

"And was it?"

She couldn't read anything in his expression. He didn't smile or laugh or glower.

"His Uncle Nario was a sweetheart. And Mama—" She rolled her eyes. "—yelled every time Uncle Nario went back in the kitchen. Although sometimes Italian sounds like yelling even when they're not mad."

"And?" he urged her on.

"It was the best pasta I've ever tasted. I'm not joking. I told Uncle Nario that it truly was amazing. I'm surprised the restaurant wasn't packed but maybe in Italy, everyone makes amazing pasta so it's no big deal."

"Tell me about your *date*." Underlined with a little bit of sarcasm, she wondered?

"Honestly, it wasn't so much a date as an interview. I figured out Nario needs an investor for the hair salon he wants to open."

Something eased in his expression, or maybe it was just his eyes. As if his normal humor crept back in. Maybe he'd really been worried about her.

"Are you sure he wasn't after more than your money?"

She shook her head, smiling at the same time. "No, he was definitely after my money. But in an amiable way. Once I told him the truth, that I owned a small bookkeeping service, and I'm not a rich American, we had a lovely time."

"And did you...?" He raised a lecherous eyebrow instead of finishing the question.

"No, I did not." She didn't even feel demoralized by the fact that the two sexy young Italians she'd been out with were only after her money. "I truly enjoyed myself. I didn't want anything else."

"Well," he said with a shrug, "I'm still available to help you out. Even if I'm not young."

But he was sexy and gorgeous.

She batted his arm. "You're not Italian. The whole point is Italian." She wasn't sure he meant it or if it was a throwaway line.

He was from the Bay Area, too. Maybe they could continue their friendship when they returned home. The thought sent a thrill through her. Someone to attend the symphony with, or go to a show in the city, or even to meet for a nice hike.

It was a pipedream. He'd think it was too much like a relationship.

Their gelato finished, he stood and held out his hand. "I have time for a walk if you do."

"Of course." She took his hand, enjoying the feel of his warm skin and his slightly callused palm against hers.

❀

"You have to promise me one thing," Marshall said as they reached the top of the steps outside the church. From this vantage point he realized just how far they'd climbed.

Her hand was still in his. "What?" she asked.

"If you make any more dates, you absolutely have to tell me ahead of time and text me while you're there, just like we did the first night."

He wasn't truly able to express, even to himself, how glad he was that she'd made it through last night's date with Uncle Nario's nephew. It wasn't just her safety, although there was a huge dose of that. There was also a stab of jealousy, like the little boy who didn't get picked for the baseball team. Or the wimpy kid who was looked over by the head cheerleader when she rushed straight to the football captain. In high school, he'd been captain of the football team, but now he felt what it was like to be totally discounted.

He'd made his offer; she'd seen it as a joke. He hadn't pushed. In addition to the jealousy and in total opposition to it, he liked what they had, the friendship, how she made him laugh, the way she told him everything. The friendship was more important.

Even though he was dying to get his hands on her.

"All right, big brother." She gave him a smirk. "*If*, a very big if." She gave him a smile. "I will text you if any other hot young sexy Italians ask me out. And you can keep tabs on me every single moment."

He raised her hand to his lips, kissed her fingers. "Good girl."

He actually looked forward to her sexy, funny texts.

But he didn't know what he'd do if she actually went home with one of those men.

14

The interlude on the church steps with Marshall had been, how to describe it, absolutely marvelous. Maybe for the fact that it had been so short yet so lovely. Just seeing him and being with him was wonderful. She watched him jog down the steps, turning at the bottom, waving. Then he disappeared around the corner.

She felt... bereft. As if she'd lost something vital. That's how much her friendship with Marshall had come to mean to her.

When they were back home, she absolutely wanted to see him, even if she had to be the one to suggest it. She'd make him see that it wasn't a *relationship*. It was friendship. She valued him too much to let him go.

She'd just have to make sure she didn't get attached. And certainly that she didn't fall in love with him.

She wandered the streets after Marshall left, no real destination in mind, and somehow found herself at the Trevi Fountain.

"It's everything we thought it would be," she told Carol under her breath.

The water was a brilliant turquoise, and while the statues were worn from the minerals in the water, it was a remarkable sight. This was Rome. This was the center of all the pictures she'd seen. This was *Three Coins in the Fountain*. Although when the actresses had stood around the fountain, there hadn't been a gazillion tourists like there was today.

Dana didn't care. She was here in this beautiful place, the stuff of wishes.

She pushed her way to the front. If she was polite, she'd never get there. The bottom was awash in coins, silver, copper, some glinting with gold. What was her wish?

She thought of all the ones that had come to her over the past few days. To have the best vacation ever. To meet the man of her dreams. To find a sexy handsome young Italian for a holiday fling. To grow her business. To find the most fulfilling pathway for her life.

To have her friend back.

That was still the only wish that had true meaning for her.

And it was the only one she could never have.

Even if Marshall said you were supposed to wish for the impossible.

Just wish for whatever comes to your lips first, and don't overthink it.

She dug in her purse for the special coin she'd been saving for this moment.

She held it so tightly, her fingers ached. It was just a wish. It wasn't as if it could actually come true. This was just fun, just something people did, why was she making such a big deal?

Because Carol had wanted her to do it.

What were the three wishes in the old movie? One coin in the fountain means you'll come back to Rome. Two coins means you'll fall in love. Three coins and you'll get married in Rome.

Did she really want any of those things?

She had two more weeks to make up her mind. She could even make her wish on the very last day. Maybe if she stopped thinking about the wish and let it percolate, it would rise to the surface.

She slipped the coin back in its special pocket, turned, ready to give someone else their chance at the fountain.

A man stood in front of her. A tall man. A handsome man. A sexy man. He was younger, maybe thirty-five, his aquiline nose, olive skin, dark eyes, and black hair all classic Italian.

He was like a movie star or a prince from a fairytale, and he stole her breath gazing at such beauty.

"Don't tell me you are not going to wish. Everyone makes a wish. Every wish made in that fountain must come true."

His silky, deep voice was like a caress down her spine. And very Italian.

She'd thought about wishing for the perfect young Italian lover, and without even throwing the coin, here he was.

"I wasn't sure what to wish for," she told him honestly. The crowd flowed around them, pushing them closer together. His aftershave was some mesmerizing spicy scent.

"A beautiful lady can always find a wish to make." He reached in the pocket of his tight jeans that outlined all his proportions and held up an Italian coin. "You're allowed three wishes. Just because you make one now doesn't mean you cannot come back to make another."

"Doesn't it have to be my coin?"

"No. It just has to be your wish made at the moment the coin hits the water. It's all about timing." He pushed through the tourists, taking her with him, right up to the railing. "I'll throw it and you make the wish." He lowered his voice to a note that actually made her shiver. "Watch the coin. And make your wish a good one." Then he threw it.

She didn't have time to think. The wish simply popped

into her head, and it seemed as if everything, the people, the fountain, the tourists, the car horns, the mopeds, everything went silent. She could actually hear the splash of *that* coin above all others. And now it was out there.

Her wish for the perfect holiday lover.

He looked at her, his lashes a mile long. "Don't tell me what your wish is or it won't come true. In fact, do not tell anyone. In that way, you'll know when it comes true that it was all about *this* wish made right here."

She was seduced by his words, almost believing that if she kept her wish to herself, it absolutely would come true.

She didn't tell herself it was silly even though she knew it was.

The man grabbed her hand and pulled her out of the throng of people as if he were afraid they'd be crushed. "May I buy you coffee or a pastry or even gelato?"

She heard Carol in her head. *You wished for it, now go for it.*

"That would be wonderful."

He took her to a patio café around the corner where half the fountain was visible but the tourist cacophony was muted. They sat beneath the shade of an umbrella on padded wrought iron chairs, pigeons walking among the tables.

His name was Aureliano, which sounded like music, and he was an art restorer in the Vatican's back rooms.

"That's fascinating." How did *she* get lucky enough to meet a Vatican art restorer? "To be up close with all those masterpieces, it must be like touching treasure every day."

He shrugged. "It is often tedious, a long, slow process." He held up his hand. "We must use such a delicate touch." He drew his fingers through the air, and she felt it like a caress across her skin.

"Tiny, delicate strokes," he said softly as if he were talking about his hands on a woman's body. "That's what you have to use. You must get close, so close, so that you see every brushstroke and feel it come to life beneath your fingertips."

She flushed, as if he were talking about sex instead of art. When she said, "It sounds amazing," her voice actually cracked.

He was as beautiful as a Botticelli painting or a Michelangelo statue.

Yet even as she gazed into his dark eyes, she thought of Marshall, comparing their faces, the lines on Marshall's that attested to his laughter, his age, his sadness, his joy, his work.

Aureliano was like a restored painting, his beauty glistening, gleaming, his features perfection yet almost unreal.

Yet he was everything Carol said she needed. He'd met her by a fountain, and she was like any other tourist. The tote she carried wasn't designer. He couldn't have a clue about her wealth. He couldn't have a clue about *her*. Yet he'd approached her.

It felt good to be under the admiring scrutiny of his gaze.

He told her about his university degree— she had no idea you could actually get a degree in art restoration— and he talked about his school as if it were prestigious, how hard it was to be accepted, how proud his parents had been. "I was allowed to take them down into the bowels of the Vatican and show them my work. It's not permitted for most. But I'm conscientious, and my touch is highly desirable. So I was granted permission. They want to keep me happy there." His eyes twinkled.

"Your parents must be so proud of what you've accomplished."

He waved a hand. "I'm the youngest. They had no hopes for me. But I've surpassed all my brothers and sisters. That is only because being the youngest I didn't have to go into the family business."

"And what is the family business?"

"We are winemakers. We have a huge vineyard in Tuscany. But I have six older brothers and there's no more work for me there. Thus I'm allowed to pursue the career I choose."

It sounded like something out of a Tuscan romance movie, the brooding hero who breaks free of the strictures of his family and follows his own path.

He asked very little about her, and she liked that. He didn't glance at her finger to see if she had the telltale sign of a removed wedding band. He didn't pump her for information about what she did for a living or how long she'd been divorced or if she had children. His eyes didn't flash with dollar signs. It was refreshing.

When their espressos were drained and the pastry they'd shared was gone, not even a crumb left, he asked her, "I have plans to go to a fabulous club tonight. I wondered if you would accompany me."

Her heart lurched. A fabulous club. "It's not the one where they play big band music?"

He laughed, shook his head. "No. This place has our kind of music." She felt as if he were including her, as if she weren't fifteen years older than him.

She didn't give herself time to think, just as she hadn't thought while making her wish. "I'd love to."

"Shall I pick you up at your hotel?"

"I'll meet you there. What time?"

"Ten o'clock." He grabbed a napkin, and a pen from his pocket, writing down the address. "Any taxi driver will get you there. I look forward to it." He glanced at his watch. "I'm afraid I must get back to the Vatican." He stood, bent over her hand, placed a kiss there.

Then he wended his way through the tables, turned at the outer edge, waved at her, and disappeared around the corner.

She thought of Marshall's kiss on her hand, the way her skin had tingled for long moments.

Had there been a tingle in Aureliano's kiss?

She couldn't be sure.

It didn't matter. She'd meet him at the nightclub and have a good time. Then she'd see what happened later.

That evening she chose a black cocktail dress, having no idea what most Italian nightclubs were like, and the Bottega Veneta high heels. She had a feeling she'd be the oldest person there, not that it mattered. She had a date with a gorgeous Italian man, exactly what all middle-aged women wanted, right?

She was in her prime.

She texted Marshall while she was getting ready, smiling as she typed. *Just like you told me, big brother, I'm checking in. I met a nice young Italian man at the Trevi Fountain.*

It was only a moment before he typed back. *You went to the Trevi Fountain without me to make your wish?*

I didn't know you were supposed to actually make the wish with me.

Of course. I want to be there for the historic moment.

She laughed at herself in the mirror. He was so amusing. *I didn't make my real wish. This was just a throwaway wish.*

She enjoyed bantering with him, and he came back in a moment with, *Very lucky. Because without me you don't have a wish guarantee.* Before she had time to answer, he added, *What was your throwaway wish?*

She typed back equally as fast. *I can't tell you or it won't come true.*

But if it's a throwaway, do you really care?

She laughed even though she was alone. *You should never jinx a wish.*

All right. Did it come true?

I have no idea. But that nice young Italian man asked me out to a nightclub. And I'm going. She was almost out of breath typing so fast.

He took longer to get back to her this time. She was already done with her makeup.

Then her phone pinged. *Remember your promise.*

She was smiling as she typed back. *I remember my promise, big brother. I'm supposed to check in every 15 minutes.*

Where's the nightclub?

She grabbed the napkin Aureliano had given her and typed the information into a text.

Any sign of trouble, you're out of there, right?

Yes, big brother.

In fact, when you're ready to leave, call me, and I'll come get you in a taxi.

She couldn't resist replying with, *No, big brother.*

He sent her a red-faced, snorting emoji, then typed, *If he hurts you*, and followed that with a boxer emoji.

She sent a dancing girl. They traded emojis from praying hands to the handset of an old rotary phone. Then finally she texted him that she was leaving. And he texted that she needed to let him know when she arrived at the nightclub.

He sent a GIF of a bull snorting steam out its nostrils.

She surveyed herself one last time in the mirror, checked that she didn't have lipstick on her teeth and every hair was in place. Her phone pinged once more and he wrote, *You're beautiful*, as if he'd known she was making her last check in the mirror.

She finished off with a heart emoji.

WAS IT RIDICULOUS TO TAKE A TAXI TO THE NIGHTCLUB and wait outside just in case she needed him?

Marshall knew it was. But half an hour later found him doing it anyway.

He simply couldn't leave her alone.

The club was brightly lit, its neon lights flashing across the cars passing by. The music streamed out into the street, loud and pumping. There was a line outside, a bouncer checking everyone at the door.

She'd texted him when she arrived, then answered two more texts, saying she was fine. But there was none of the sexy banter the night she'd gone out with Giancarlo.

He didn't know if that was good or bad.

He paid the driver extra to park down the street so Marshall could watch the entrance.

It was crazy. Because being here was for damn for sure a jealous act. But she was utterly entrancing. Men asked her out every day.

She needed to spend more days with him so there weren't so many opportunities for others to approach her.

Her sex appeal was off the charts. He'd known that the moment he laid eyes on her at the Colosseum. She was hit on at stores, in hair salons, by crowded fountains. Yet she had no idea how attractive she was. And she certainly didn't have any clue how badly he wanted to be her fountain wish.

If she decided she wanted to go home with this guy, Marshall might actually have to beat him off.

He didn't care about being her friend and confidant anymore. Sure, he didn't want that part of their relationship to change, but he was willing to sacrifice. If she wanted her holiday fling or romance or whatever the hell she called it, then he was the only man it was going to be with.

Sitting in the taxi, his heart was pounding, his blood was racing, and he wanted to play the Neanderthal, storming the club to drag her out.

15

Dana decided she really was a middle-aged woman.

Half an hour ago, Aureliano had met her at the front door of the nightclub. Which was a good thing, because she never would have found him in that crowd. The place apparently didn't start hopping until late. How much more hopping could it get?

The patrons who weren't dancing stood at tall café tables littered with drinks, and there were no chairs in sight. There weren't many empty spots, but he found one close to the wall. The music pounded inside her head, blistering her ears. The strobe lights gave her a headache, flashing constantly over the crowd on the floor as they undulated like a massive ball of worms. When she wanted to say something to him, she had to lean close and practically scream. So did he. Her throat was starting to ache, and his breath against her ear was too hot. He stood so close he had to drape his arm around her shoulder.

The scene creeped her out, and she screamed in his ear, "I'm too old for this."

He didn't understand this wasn't her scene. It was her daughters' scene.

He pointed at something on the dance floor, she had no idea what, and when she turned back to ask him what it was, she could have sworn his hand was hovering over her drink.

That couldn't be possible, right? Her nerves were jumpy. She didn't like this place, couldn't stand the noise or the lights. But she looked at him and decided to ask, leaning in close. "Did you just put something in my drink?"

He cupped his ear, and she shouted the question, loud and succinct. "What did you put in my drink?"

He raised his hands, as if proclaiming his innocence. Then he splayed his fingers on his chest in a who-me gesture. She pointed, mouthed the same words.

He drank from his glass, switched it with hers, and gave her a singularly innocent look.

But she could have sworn he'd pocketed something right after his hand had been near her drink. Her mind ran rampant with crazy notions, and she pushed the glass away.

He was standing so close again, and she didn't like his scent tonight. She couldn't pinpoint why. Maybe simply because it wasn't Marshall's scent. Or maybe because there was something off about Aureliano this evening, something she hadn't sensed over coffee by the fountain. Or it was the loud music and the gyrating bodies making her paranoid.

She could just make out his words in the sudden switch of one song to another that had a less pounding beat.

"I would never do that. You can trust me, dear lady. I will buy us new drinks, if you wish, and you can keep an eagle eye on yours all night long."

He signaled, and the waiter miraculously appeared. He ordered another champagne for her as he palmed a bill and passed it to the man, who scooped up the two glasses and whisked them away. "There, we will get fresh drinks, so you have no worries. Would you like to dance?"

Her phone chirped with a text from Marshall.

"No, thank you." She found the words snapping out of her.

Why was she so nervous? Why didn't she just leave? "I need to text my friend back and say everything's okay." It was a comfort knowing Marshall was only a text away.

She typed back that she was fine, but she wondered if she was. She wasn't cut out for the dating scene, at least not in nightclubs with strangers. She didn't get why you'd want to be somewhere that you couldn't even talk.

The waiter returned with their drinks, leaned in, saying something to Aureliano, who palmed him another bill that the waiter shoved in his pocket.

Why would he give the waiter more money? And why would the man put it in his pocket rather than in the small folder of cash he carried on his tray? In fact, most people paid with cards, utilizing the card reader also nestled on the man's tray.

She looked at her glass, the champagne still sizzling, a thick head of foam on the top. Should it still be sizzling this much? Champagne sizzles longer when you added something to it, like a sugar cube.

She stared at the drink, then looked at Aureliano. He raised his glass, toasted her, his smile wide, mouthing the word *saluti* or something like it.

The music had risen again, and she couldn't hear him. It didn't matter.

Because she wasn't going to pick up that glass. She wouldn't drink with him or dance with him, let alone kiss him or go home with him. So why was she even here?

She grabbed her phone once more, typed, *I'm leaving now. Getting a taxi.*

Then she leaned into Aureliano and shouted, "I'm going home." She tapped her ear. "The music is too loud for me."

She held her phone in her hand as she left. Then Aureliano grabbed her elbow. "I'm so sorry," he said when she read his lips. He leaned far too close, his breath hot in her ear as he shouted, "We can go somewhere quieter. Somewhere you would like more."

"No, thanks." She pulled her arm away and kept going.

She powered through the outside door and onto the sidewalk. The effect of fresh air was immediate. God, she could breathe, she could think, she could actually hear, even with the music pounding out onto the street.

Aureliano had followed her. "I'm so sorry, I'm so sorry," he repeated. "I never thought how loud it was. I'm sure your sensitive ears had so much trouble." He reached out to touch her, and she jerked back instinctively.

But she also wondered if she'd imagine the exchange between him and the waiter. Now, she even doubted that he'd been trying to put anything in her drink. Her emotions had been high, close to frantic.

Still, a woman needed to obey her instincts, and hers were shouting to get away.

She waved down a cab, saying to Aureliano, "It's not your fault." But outside, with people all around them on the street and a bouncer at the door to whom she could call for help, she gave Aureliano the benefit of the doubt. "It's just not my kind of place." She smiled with a hint of self-deprecation. "I'm just too old for that scene."

He reached out again. And again she stepped back as he said, "You're not old. You're *bellissima*."

She actually hated that word. First Giancarlo, then Nario and his uncle, and now Aureliano. Their names and faces seemed to slide into one another, as if they'd become one man. Indistinguishable. She wondered if he even was an art restorer for the Vatican. Or if that was a lie, too.

The cab pulled over, disgorging a load of nightclubbers. She could grab it once it was empty yet she was afraid to get too close, that Aureliano might push her inside, climb in, and she'd be at his mercy.

She'd read a book once on the art of self-defense. It hadn't been about learning to beat your assailant to a pulp; it was all about avoiding the situation in the first place. The most important point was to trust your instincts.

"It's not your fault," she said again. If she was conciliatory, maybe he'd back off. As long as she stayed on the street, safe and surrounded by other people.

Another cab pulled up behind the first, which was still spewing passengers, but Aureliano stood between her and the second taxi.

"I'll just go back to my hotel now."

"I will take you. I have a car," he said, his voice pleading.

"No." She shook her head. "I can take my own cab. I appreciate the evening and the drinks. But now the night is over." She stared him down, thinking the look was forceful. He actually stepped aside, leaving a clear path to the cab's door.

Which opened at that moment. And Marshall stepped out.

She didn't give herself a chance to think. She flew at him, wrapped her arms around him, went up on her tiptoes and whispered in his ear, "Thank God you're here." She didn't care about the fear her words conveyed.

Or what his interpretation would be.

"Was that guy bothering you?" He jutted a chin at Aureliano, who took two steps back as if he might actually run away.

Yet instead he smiled wide, waved, and politely said,

"Thank you for a most wonderful evening." Then he melted back into the lights and cacophony of the nightclub behind him.

"Are you okay?" Marshall stroked her back.

She'd been stiff but now she relaxed against him. "I'm fine. It was just so loud in there. And those strobe lights made me want to vomit." She tipped her head back to look at him, finally allowing herself a smile. "I didn't mean you had to drive all the way here to get me. I was going to get a cab back to the hotel."

"I didn't drive all the way here." His arm still around her, he traced his finger along her jaw. "I've been waiting just in case you needed me."

"That feels a bit stalkerish." But she let her appreciation shine in her eyes.

He grinned back at her. "I suppose it is stalkerish." His gaze turned serious, roaming over her face. "But I get the feeling you needed a knight in shining armor. I didn't particularly like the exchange you were having with him. You looked a little nervous."

She closed her eyes, relishing the feel of his arms around her, his deep voice soft and low by her ear, his delicious scent. "I was a bit nervous."

"Let's get you back to the hotel." He bustled her into the cab.

When she would have slid to the opposite side, he tightened his arm around her, gluing her to him. She liked that, too.

His manly scent topped Aureliano's sickly aftershave any day. And while Aureliano had creeped her out in the club, Marshall made her tingle in the cab.

He signaled the driver, giving him the name of her hotel. She looked at her watch. The whole thing had taken less than an hour. She couldn't imagine how that was possible.

"Tell me what happened."

She gave in to the command in his voice. "I was thrown off immediately by the music and the strobe lights and all those bodies flashing in and out as they danced. I'm pretty sure that's what started it all."

"Started what?" he urged gently.

"I started imagining that he put something in my drink with those strobe lights going on and off, on and off. It just seemed to highlight his hand over my drink. I called him on it."

He tipped her chin, smiled down at her, then kissed the tip of her nose. She wanted more than that little kiss. "I'm proud of you for saying something," he murmured. "A lot of women would just write it off as their imagination."

She'd done that, but only after she was safely outside and surrounded by people.

"He bought me a new drink. But I thought I saw him pass something to the waiter. It looked like another bill, and it was just strange the way he slipped it to him. He did the same thing when the guy came back, and the waiter put it in his pocket. Which was all too weird. That's when I texted you."

"You're smart. The signs didn't look good. It's always better to listen to your gut."

She leaned back slightly, letting her eyes trace the handsome lines of his face. "Why are you really here?"

He waited a long moment, as if he were debating what to tell her. "The nightclub scene worried me. I was thinking that if I saw you leave the club groggy or spaced out, I'd intervene. I wish to God now that I'd gone inside and dragged you out."

"Thank you," she whispered. "I like that you're so protective. You've got this thing about being a big brother, don't you?" she asked, humor lacing her voice.

The taxi took a right turn, and she felt herself sway into him, all her nerve endings tingling at the contact.

"I never actually beat one of my sister's boyfriends to a pulp." Then he arched a brow. "However, I would have gladly taken on her husband after the shit he put her through."

Another turn and this time Marshall swayed into her. When they settled again, he breathed in deeply, his exhale warm and sweet across her cheek.

She snuggled closer to him. "I've come to a conclusion."

He made a noise, "Hmmm," encouraging her.

"I'm looking at my three dates like the three coins in the fountain. I tossed the coins, I didn't get anything, and now I'm done."

He sighed. "Thank God. Because your dates have shaved years off my life."

She slapped playfully at him. "You didn't have to keep checking up on me."

"If anything happened to you on my watch, I would never forgive myself."

The cabbie pulled into her hotel's roundabout, stopped at the door.

"Thank you for bringing me home." She sat up straight, pulled away from Marshall.

His gaze turned intense. "I'm inviting myself in for a night cap."

She thought of the defense book again. *Listen to your instincts.* And her instincts were screaming at her to grab Marshall and hold on for dear life.

"Lovely." She reached into her clutch purse for some cash.

"What are you doing?"

"Paying for the cab."

He waved her away. "I've taken care of it, especially since the cab driver agreed to sit on the street for as long as it took for you to come out."

She laughed softly. "I can't believe you did that."

"I couldn't have done anything else."

The cabbie waved and pulled away to find his next fare.

Marshall slipped her hand through the crook of his arm as they entered the hotel. "Would you like the restaurant or the bar?" he asked.

"I have an even better idea. Let's get a bottle of champagne and sit on my balcony. The view of the Colosseum at night is amazing."

16

Her room was luxurious, a mini suite with a bar and sofa and chairs on one side and the bedroom a couple of steps up through an arch. Outside the French doors, the Colosseum lights were magnificent. The balcony was wide enough to fit two comfortable chairs and a small café table.

"There's another set of doors in the bedroom, and I get to fall asleep to this view every night," she said softly, almost in wonder.

Marshall watched as she stood at the bar and popped the cork. "You're an expert."

The cork came out in her hand with a whoosh. "I do love my champagne." She tilted the flute, pouring slowly to keep the foam to a minimum, handed over a glass, then clinked with him. "To the end of my *Three Coins in the Fountain* sojourn." Then she stepped out onto the balcony and settled in the chair, her sexy black cocktail dress riding up to reveal a shapely thigh.

For a moment, he couldn't take his eyes off her skin, his

heart rate several beats faster than when he'd entered the room.

He sat beside her. "You're right. It's beautiful out here." The lights of the Colosseum were romantic, but the night was cool.

She shivered.

"Here." He removed his jacket and draped it over her shoulders.

"Thank you, that's better. But if you get cold, I've got a sweater."

"I'm not cold." Around her, he was hot. They were silent a long moment that led to minutes as they enjoyed the remarkable sight.

"Tell me what your wish was." He'd been dying to know. "Since it was a throwaway wish anyway."

"I guess it doesn't matter now. Since it didn't come true."

"How do you know it still won't?"

"Because I wished for a holiday lover." She shrugged. "And three disasters are three too many."

"You mean a fling with a sexy young Italian lover?"

She put her fingers to her lips. "I forgot to add that part. I just asked for the perfect holiday lover. Anyway, it seemed like enough. But it didn't happen and now I'm done with this dating thing."

But he wasn't done. Far from it. He was old enough to know exactly what he wanted.

And he wanted her.

"You've still got another chance sitting right next to you."

She wasn't surprised, she was tantalized.

He'd offered before but she hadn't taken him seriously.

She hadn't wanted change. She wasn't sure she did now. "You don't have to put yourself out just because I didn't get my fling. It was more about what Carol wanted for me anyway." Then she quickly added, "Not that you're *not* sexy. Because you are. Totally."

"I'm not offering myself up like a consolation prize. In case you haven't noticed, I'm extremely attracted to you. And giving you a holiday fling would be my ultimate pleasure."

Her heart was thumping loudly, but so was her head. If she slept with him, everything would change. She would be a fling. Which means it would end. And she didn't want anything with Marshall to end.

Carol's voice was sharp in her head. *Take a chance, you idiot*.

"I happen to be very good in bed," he added, an enticing sparkle in his eyes.

She laughed. "And modest, too."

"Well, it's obvious I have to sell myself. And that's my biggest selling point."

"Besides being distinguished and sexy and funny and very, very handsome."

"There's that as well," he agreed, his eyes crinkling with his smile.

"Marshall—"

He leaned over, tucked her hair behind her ear, his touch heating everything inside her and effectively cutting off her words. "I know exactly what you're thinking, because I thought the same thing."

"You really can't know what I'm thinking."

He proceeded to tell her. "You're thinking that I'm your friend. But if we're lovers, then you can't tell me everything you feel the way you have been. You'll get all inhibited, and this easy thing between us will fade away."

She could only stare at him. "How can you possibly understand that?"

"Because I love the way you tell me everything. I like our candid conversations. And I don't want any of that to change either." He ran his thumb across her lips. "But we can be exactly the way we are." He leaned in to whisper, "And still have really hot sex."

She couldn't help it, he made her laugh. "I think you're a little crazy," she said with a smile she couldn't hide.

"It's like the romance trope, best friends to lovers."

"How on earth do you know about romance tropes?" she asked, giving him the eye. He left her flustered and amazed.

"My sister loves her romance novels."

"So do I." *He* was a romance novel come true.

He put a hand to his chest. "God, I'm learning something new about you." He gave her a lopsided grin. "You see, you can tell me anything. And I won't hold it against you."

She told him the truth. "The hardest thing about doing what Carol wanted me to, having an affair with a sexy Italian, is that I can't just jump into bed with someone I don't know. I went on these dates, but it never would have gone as far as an affair."

"I didn't think so either."

"I don't believe Carol thought I would. I think she just wanted me to put myself out there. To have a little fun. To find out that men could actually find me attractive."

His finger beneath her chin, he made her look at him. "You don't have any idea how gorgeous you are, how sexy. When you laugh, I feel it here." He tapped his chest.

He made her heart beat faster with every word. She wanted to keep him as her friend, and the only way to make sure things didn't change was to keep on telling him everything. "Maybe," she started, then plunged on. "Maybe there was a reason why my wish didn't include a sexy young Italian."

"Freudian slip," he murmured. "Because you'd already decided you wanted me."

She looked up and found him grinning. "You really are cocksure of yourself."

"I think of myself as hopeful rather than sure. Because you are anything but a sure thing."

She allowed herself the luxury of looking at his handsome face, his welcoming gaze. "I honestly don't know why I'm fighting this. I've made up all sorts of excuses why it can't work. Because it would change everything between us, because we wouldn't still be friends." She bit her lip. Because she could fall for him completely and never want it to end.

He whispered, "Maybe it can work. If we let it." With the tips of his fingers against her cheek, he turned her to him and slowly lowered his mouth to hers.

The kiss was gentle and sweet, tasting of champagne and desire. A spark lit deep inside her. She opened her mouth, let him take her with his lips and tongue. Until a soft moan rose up her throat.

He backed off slowly, looking at her. "Things will change. But maybe you'll find they're actually better."

He smelled so good, she breathed him in, his unique scent, a bit of the outdoors, something that was indefinably him. When he was this close, she could get drunk on his scent.

Yet her mind was clear enough to admit, "I don't like change."

It was the reason the divorce was so hard. It was why she still lived in the same house that she and Anthony bought after the kids were born. She told herself it was because she wanted the girls to come home to something they were used to, but she was rooted to it. Even this vacation wasn't really a change. Because she had the comfort of the house and her daughters and her bookkeeping business to return to.

What she didn't have was Carol.

"I know you don't like change," he said, his voice soothing yet still sexy and deep and drawing her in.

"How do you know that?" But she knew without him saying a word, just by the look in his eyes, that knowing, searching, understanding look.

"Even the things you don't say out loud are written all over your face and in the way you hold your body, the way you laugh, the way you turn sad at the drop of a hat. That's when I know you're thinking about Carol."

"But I don't know anything about you."

He played with her hair, his gaze searching her face. "You know plenty. I told you about my parents. They had a very bad breakup, and if you look at the psychology of a fifteen-year-old kid watching his parents' marriage literally implode, then you know why I never got married, never had kids, why I looked out for my sister when her marriage got trashed. And you know why I'm a workaholic. Because there's not a whole lot else in my life."

She knew he didn't believe in marriage. "But what about women and relationships?" She knew the answer to that, too.

"I like my women fast and my relationships faster."

Yeah, that was scary. "I'm not fast." Sex to her meant involvement, caring, knowing, something that would at least lead to a relationship. "Which is why I couldn't sleep with the Italians." She hadn't been on a date since her husband dumped her because she didn't want to risk anything.

She was struck by the fact that she was censoring what she said to him. It had begun the moment he'd offered himself as her lover. And when it was done, if she actually could make love with him, there would be no friend to go back to when she got home. She would have burned that bridge. She was not the type of woman who could go from lover to friend.

"Did you ever think that the sex can be even hotter

because we know each other so much better than you and your Italian dates?"

"You're right," she admitted. "But I have a hard time with endings."

She waited for him to say it didn't have to end. But all he said was, "I know."

He wanted her and she wanted him, and that changed the entire dynamic. When it hadn't been said aloud, she could pretend it wasn't there. Now she couldn't pretend.

He could have pressed the point, kissed her again, and she would fall into his offer because God, yes, she wanted it badly. But he sat back in his chair. "You don't have to give me an answer now. You don't have to do anything at all. Just think about it.

She would think about nothing else. She would replay every word, every look, every touch. And that kiss.

"I'm just happy you're safe. I'm even happier that you decided no more Italian dates whether or not you choose me as a substitute. We're friends whether you sleep with me or not."

The problem was how they were talking about it, having sex. Not making love. Love required emotion. It didn't have to be a long-lasting thing, but there had to be something.

God, she was deluding herself. If she slept with Marshall, odds were she'd end up wanting something long-lasting. And he didn't believe in long-lasting relationships.

She didn't know if she could live with that.

Thank God he didn't press. "I have the day off tomorrow. Is there anything you'd like to do together?" He fell silent, letting her think of all the things they could still do. Even the sex.

But she took the out he'd given her. "I'd really like to see St. Peter's Basilica."

"It will be my pleasure to escort you."

Tomorrow, maybe she would feel normal again. Maybe the fear rumbling in her belly was Aureliano and what happened in the bar. Tomorrow would be better.

He finished the last of his champagne, then he stood. "It's late. I'll pick you up in the morning, say about seven, then we can have breakfast together and still get to the Basilica before the lines are terrible."

She stared at the Colosseum lights and its magnificent silhouette against the sky. Then he leaned down and kissed her forehead like they were friends again. Like he'd never asked her to have sex with him, never acknowledged that he was attracted to her. Like he'd never kissed her.

"I'll see you in the morning."

She handed him his jacket, feeling a chill run through her. His footsteps echoed on the marble tile as he walked away from her. She felt a scream rising up. Her heart and body craved him, shouted at her to run to him, throw her arms around him.

But all she called out was, "Goodnight. Thank you. See you in the morning."

※

HE'D NEVER GIVEN UP ON ANYTHING IN HIS LIFE. EXCEPT marriage. But that wasn't so much giving up as having the fear of it imprinted on his DNA. Marshall brooded all the way back to his hotel. He wasn't angry or jealous or hurt. She wasn't turning him down because of who he was. It didn't really have anything to do with him. And that was the problem. If her fears had nothing to do with him, then he had no way to fix it.

She'd gone on those dates, but she never intended to sleep with them. She was simply doing what her friend Carol wanted her to. The other men had built up her ego, but then they'd let it crash, wanting something from her that had nothing to do with who she was as a woman.

He wanted her for exactly the person she was, sweet, loyal, loving. She was smart and funny and sexy and seductive. He even appreciated her for her fears, the fear of change, of being unattractive and undesirable, of getting hurt again. Except for his sister, he'd never known a woman as well as he knew Dana.

But where most women were concerned, he never let things progress. He compartmentalized. He stayed separate. Emotionally unattached. He never pursued.

Yet something had changed the day he saw her in the Colosseum. The moment she quoted from *I, Claudius* and tried to talk him into watching *Buffy the Vampire Slayer*.

And now he couldn't give up until he'd shown her how desirable she was.

17

In the morning, she rose early, choosing just the right outfit for both Marshall and St. Peter's Basilica, black capris that covered her knees and a silky, black-and-white, short-sleeved blouse. She fluffed her hair to perfection, the way Nario had. The way Marshall had said he liked it. She applied eyeshadow and eyeliner and mascara and blusher to her cheeks, then lipliner and lipstick.

She wanted to say she hadn't primped for Marshall before, that this was a change. That their conversation last night had transformed everything.

But she'd been primping for him all along.

She made the bed, picked up her clothes, straightened the chairs, and put the glasses and champagne bottle on the bar to be cleaned away.

Then she left a tip on the bathroom counter for the maid and went out the door to meet Marshall.

He was sexy in long pants— part of the dress code for the Basilica— and a polo shirt. It wasn't what you normally thought of as sexy, like a nice business suit or tight jeans, but then there were a lot of sexy things about Marshall. She'd been noticing all along.

They stopped at a café on a side street not far from her hotel and had what they'd been told was a typical Rome breakfast, café lattes and a plate of *cornetti* to share. The morning treats were the equivalent of croissants but a little sweeter, filled with jam or custard. Marshall had purchased a selection for them to try.

"They're delicious," she told him.

He didn't mention last night, didn't talk about his offer or ask if she'd decided. But she couldn't stop thinking about it as his big strong hand carried his latte to his mouth, as his lips pursed to sip as if he were puckering for a kiss. She couldn't stop imagining the stroke of his fingers across her skin as he talked, or feeling the timbre of his voice deep inside her as if it were an actual touch.

He wasn't a relationship kind of man. But she couldn't stop wondering how much she'd regret it if she never tasted what he offered.

"These are the best croissants I've ever tasted," she said, licking a dot of custard from her fingers. She wondered how his skin would taste if she licked him.

He smiled, and even his smile was a caress. "They say the Mediterranean diet is good for you, but I'm not sure a *cornetti* exactly fits the bill."

She could live on a diet of him alone.

With the breakfast done and their coffee cups empty, they headed for the metro to Vatican City. Marshall slipped his fingers around hers.

She wanted so badly to turn and lead them back to her hotel. To spend the rest of the day in bed with him. Wasn't that why she'd made the bed and cleaned up this morning instead of waiting for the maid to do it? Of course it was.

He'd opened her mind to the possibility, and now she couldn't get it out.

He was a fast walker, but she kept up, her mind in a flurry. Hands linked, he slipped through breaks in the people on the sidewalk, the old ladies with their shopping bags, the young men in suits, leisurely tourists, two nuns with a gaggle of school children following them like ducks.

If she didn't do something, would she regret it for the rest of her life?

To get rejected and hurt? Or never to have taken the chance at all? That was the question.

The line at St. Peter's Basilica wasn't too bad since they'd breakfasted early and the tourist season wasn't in full swing yet. They hadn't purchased tickets for a tour, so no line-skipping, but she didn't mind, holding Marshall's hand as they chatted about anything and everything. She talked about her daughters, her bookkeeping. He talked about his sister, his nephews, what books he liked, where he'd gone to school, about his work.

Despite the chitchat, she kept wondering what it would be like to let herself go with Marshall, to take a chance.

Then they were inside, gazing at the Michelangelo sculpture of Mary holding Christ. They wandered through, keeping their voices low and reverent. "Wow," she whispered at they looked up into the magnificent dome, the sun streaming down through the windows along the rim. "I mean, the Sistine Chapel is stunning for the paintings and tapestries, but this..." She didn't have words for the majesty.

"It's the largest church in the world," he told her. "And it took over a hundred years to complete."

She smiled. "You know something about everything."

He laughed. "I read about it last night so I could sound knowledgeable." Then he pointed up. "Do you want to climb into the dome? It's something like five hundred fifty steps, but we can take an elevator partway."

"Oh my God, yes, let's do it." She bit her lip and sighed her pleasure, and somehow it was about the pleasure of being with him, too, not just the church or the dome or being in Rome. "But no elevator. We have to climb all the way."

There was a separate entrance, and they waited in another line, but it was worth it. Partway up, Dana turned to Marshall behind her. "Thank God I climbed all those hills with Carol."

Marshall wasn't even breathing hard. She had the irreverent thought of what it would take to make him lose his breath.

The climb was definitely worth it. They stepped onto the roof with the sculptures of Christ and the Apostles they'd seen from the square below. Up here, they found a maze of smaller domes and the light towers that spread sun through the basilica below. Amazingly, there was also a gift shop and coffee bar.

Up more stairs inside the dome, they stepped out onto the gallery overlooking the basilica's interior, the mosaics on the walls intricate and awe-inspiring.

"But look down here," Marshall called softly.

The sound of quiet voices rose up to them as they walked around the dome. Marshall took her hand while they gazed down upon the splendor of the scene below, Bernini's bronze canopy over the papal altar, the intricate flooring, the decorated columns, the paintings on the walls of the dome itself.

"We look so much higher up than it seems from down there," she whispered, as if speaking in a normal voice were a sacrilege.

But the feel of Marshall's hand engulfing hers could only be called miraculous.

Then they started to the top. Since it was late morning, the narrow stairwell was crowded and they had to stop along the way, waiting for the line to move on. The slant of the dome almost made Dana feel like the walls were closing in, and it was hot in the close confines.

The stairs widened just before they reached the spiral staircase, and then they were out in the sunshine overlooking Vatican City and all of Rome.

"It's spectacular," she said, pulling her hair away where the breeze had blown it across her lips. "I could stay here forever." With her hand in Marshall's.

God, she wanted what he offered. She knew it couldn't be forever. But it could be the amazing holiday affair Carol had said she needed.

All she had to do was risk the pain of parting.

The thoughts consumed her even as they climbed down again. Could she ask for it?

"You hungry?" he asked when they left St. Peter's.

She nodded, still questioning herself.

They stopped for lunch at an outdoor café with one empty table remaining and ordered a meal of meat and cheese and fresh bread. The sun was gloriously warm. She enjoyed the noise of voices and laughter and car horns on the street, hoping it would stop the rush of thoughts in her head.

And finally he said, "You're awfully quiet."

"I'm just thinking."

"About what?" His voice was neutral, as if he had no clue what could possibly have been consuming her the entire morning.

"About what you said last night," she admitted.

He laughed softly from deep in his chest. "I said a lot, as I recall."

She was going to have to say it out loud. "That the sex would be hotter because we know each other."

His voice dropped to an even deeper note. "So much hotter. Especially if you tell me exactly how you like it."

Her cheeks heated in a rush. So did the rest of her. Suddenly she was wet between the legs, and it was the most delicious feeling. Had Anthony ever asked what she wanted?

Would she actually have the courage to tell Marshall that she liked this or she didn't like that or that he was doing it too hard and too fast and she needed it slow?

But Marshall was asking. She had to be bold enough to tell him. "I haven't been with anyone else but my husband—" She started again. "I haven't been with anyone except my *ex*-husband in thirty years." She felt the heat burrow deeper into her cheeks. "That must sound so unsophisticated to you."

"On the contrary, it means you're loyal and faithful, all qualities I respect."

It meant she'd never cheated. She certainly couldn't say the same about Anthony. She wondered again exactly when the cheating had started. Was it only with his new wife? Or was she just the last in a long line?

But thinking about Anthony would ruin everything.

"What it means is that I don't know what I want. I'm not even sure I know how I like it."

He reached across the small table to take her hand in his. "Then we move slow. And you tell me what you like and what you don't like. And I'll do more of everything you enjoy."

"That's sexy," she whispered.

He squeezed her hand and his eyes ate her up. "Do you like to kiss for a long time?"

"I've forgotten what it's like."

"I'll remind you. And I'll make it better. Are your breasts sensitive?"

The café tables were small but fairly close, and the patrons chattered in different languages, including English. She and Marshall spoke in low tones while the conversations around them were boisterous, and she felt sequestered in intimacy with him.

"Not really." Except now, when he'd started talking about sex.

"Maybe they will be with my mouth and my lips and my tongue on your skin."

Dana looked down at her chest and knew he could see how his words affected her.

"I can spend hours on them," he murmured, his voice so deep and so close, sending thrills through her.

"I don't know what it's like to spend hours in bed."

"I'll show you. I'll show you what it's like to have my mouth all over you and my tongue inside you."

She was melting right next to him. "Would you like it if I put my mouth on you, too?"

The muscles of his face tensed slightly. "Hell yes. But only if you like it. Do you?" The question came out as eager as a child's.

She laughed. "I think I'll like it with you."

"Only do what you want to. Because what we do together is all about you."

"What about you?"

"My pleasure is in making you feel good. Believe me, that's all I need to make me come harder than I've ever come before."

She blushed at his frankness, and yet she loved his seductive words. She understood now what sexting was all about. It was foreplay. That's what they were doing right now in this café. Foreplay.

If she didn't ask for it, she'd never know what it was like. Could she handle never knowing what he could do for her? No, she didn't think she could.

But could she handle it when their holiday was over and they went back to their separate lives?

She knew what Carol would tell her to do. She wanted to

know, *needed* to know what it would be like with Marshall. And the heartache later be damned.

Right now, the regret for what she'd miss was bigger than the fear of getting hurt.

The boldness inside her was dying to burst out. "I've had enough sightseeing for today. What about you?"

Heat flared in his eyes. "I can think of some things to do that might be more fun than touring a Gothic cathedral."

She held his gaze a long moment. "Maybe you should take me back to my hotel and show me."

❦

The maid was making up Dana's room.

That gave him time to ask. "Are you sure this is what you want?" He stroked her face with just his gaze.

They stood alone in the hallway, his heart pounding. Christ, what she'd done to him with that brief, sexy, seductive conversation in the café. Talk about zero to sixty in under a minute. His heart was racing at way over a hundred.

If she said she'd changed her mind, he might actually go mad.

But he needed her to be sure. This moment would change everything between them. He couldn't afford to let her have regrets.

"The only thing I'm sure of is that I want you. And if I don't let you in my room, I'll never know what I missed." She cupped his cheek. "And I need to know."

It was the answer he'd wanted, echoing his feelings. He was wild to kiss her, and he gave in to the impulse despite the maid running the vacuum in her room and the ding of an elevator stopping on their floor.

She tasted of the sweetened lemonade she'd had with

lunch. She tasted like sex and desire and wishes yet to be fulfilled.

He pulled back when childish laughter filled the hall as a couple raced their two children to the room next to Dana's.

"I hope they're not staying," she whispered.

"Why?"

"I don't want to disturb them when you scream with pleasure." A flirty smile lurked on her lips, not quite blossoming.

He wanted to wrap her in his arms, pull her tight against him, let her feel what she did to him. "I'm going to make sure you're the one who screams."

"I never scream." Her voice was so solemn, yet that teasing smile was a hint on her lips.

"I do believe you've just challenged me. I have to warn you that I always win a challenge."

"We'll see," she said flippantly.

Christ, that made him hotter, her new attitude, sexy, flirty, and fun. As if she'd let her fears and inhibitions go when she asked him to take her back to her room.

The maid opened the door, apologized profusely in Italian, put all her things away, and pushed the cart down the hall. Then the door of the next room burst open, and the two kids raced out in swimsuits. Mom and Dad followed, carrying bags and sunhats and pool toys.

Dana dragged him inside her room and threw the Do Not Disturb sign on the door.

"All right," she said, a saucy lilt to her voice. "Let's see if you can make me scream."

HE HAD HER UP AGAINST THE DOOR IN ONE SECOND, HIS mouth hot and hungry, consuming her. She lost herself in the taste of him, sweet and spicy and sizzling. He surrounded her with his arms, his big body, his heat.

He'd asked if she was sure. Yet even as she'd flirted and teased and tried to make things light, she wasn't sure.

Until now, this moment, when there was nothing but him, no thought, no fear, nothing but sensation. Her toes tingled, her heart raced, her fingers tangled in his hair. Pulling him closer, tighter, sealing their mouths together. Her skin was hot, her body on fire. She wanted him to rip off her capris and take her right up against the door. Just when her lungs were oxygen-starved, he backed off, his eyes blazing. When he put his fingers to the buttons of her blouse, she felt them tremble against her skin.

"Slow down," he whispered. "Gotta slow down."

He was talking to himself. She'd never brought a man to his knees. Not ever. But she felt the tremors of his desire for her, and it was the most powerful thing she'd ever known.

"I don't want you to slow down."

Finally, he looked at her, his gaze hot. "I want to make it the best it's ever been."

"It's already the best. You want me. That's all I need."

He dropped his hands to her hips, pressed tight against her, letting her feel the hard ridge of him. "God, you have no idea how badly I want you."

"I want your skin against mine." She opened her own buttons while he tore his shirt over his head.

"Christ, you're gorgeous. Is this the Italian lingerie you bought?" The sexy bra and panties she'd bought with him in mind even though she'd told herself it was for some mythical Italian lover.

"Do you like it?"

"Oh yeah." He trailed a finger along the edge of her bra, the lace almost see-through.

But no Italian lover could compare to him. His chest was

a wall of muscle covered in a dusting of silvery hair. She put her hand to his beating heart, his skin burning beneath her fingertips.

He toed off his shoes and socks, and she did the same. Then he hauled her up against the door again and wrapped her legs around his waist. He was right *there*, so *right* there. Then he feasted on her mouth.

She'd told him she'd forgotten what long, slow kisses were like. And he gave her glorious minutes of it. Until she couldn't think anymore. Until there was only the feel of him. The taste of him. The heat of him.

She had never been wanted like this.

Then he put an arm around her back and a hand on her butt and carried her to the bed. She clung to his neck, and with every step, he rubbed deliciously between her thighs. Then, slowly, slowly, he let her feet slide to the floor until he stood inches above her.

"You are the best I've ever had," she said in answer to something he'd said hours ago. Or minutes. Or even seconds.

His eyes locked on hers, he reached for the snap of her capris. "I've wanted this. From the moment I saw you." The snap popped. "But I kept telling myself you needed a friend more than a lover." Her heart beat fast and hard, loving the way he talked to her. "But you have no idea how jealous I was every time you went out with one of those guys." His fingers hooked in her waistband. "I wanted to beat my chest like Tarzan, storm in, and drag you away."

She had only a moment to think about how he knew exactly the right words she needed to hear, showing her how desperately he wanted her. God, how she wanted him to be desperate for her.

Then he yanked her capris down, and she stepped out of them.

Her bloodstream suddenly filled with panic, her heart

pumping so loud she almost couldn't hear. She could only feel his eyes on her body as he rose to his full height again, seeing every inch of her imperfect fifty-year-old body, the stretch marks of two children, the weight of her breasts, the softness of her belly and thighs. She felt as if all the heat had drained out of her body, and she stood shivering before his perfection.

"Jesus," came out on a mere breath. "You are so damn beautiful."

The look in his eyes and the harshness of his voice made her melt inside, turning her heat to high again. It said he was on the edge, just the way she was. It screamed how badly he wanted her, as if her imperfections meant nothing.

"Take off your clothes." It sounded like a command when really it was a need. She *had* to see him.

When he stripped off his pants, she lost her breath for so long she turned lightheaded just looking at him. He was magnificent. Like one of the statues she'd seen all over Rome, in the Vatican, in the museums. He was solid, his muscles hard, and his boxer briefs framed the thickness of him.

"You are so perfect." She trailed a fingertip down the center of his chest through the arrow of hair that disappeared into his briefs. She felt him tremble and twitch at her touch. And she felt the power in that.

It made her forget that she wanted to hide her body from him.

He reached around her and tugged on the comforter, rumpling the pillows, launching some of them to the floor. "I want to see you splayed out on this bed." Then he smiled, wicked, seductive, sensual. "And then I'm going to tear those sexy panties off with my teeth."

She laughed, and it broke all the tension inside her. Her body couldn't be completely undesirable if a man wanted to rip off her panties.

She shimmied to the center of the bed, then flopped back

on her elbows, her legs slightly spread, and demanded, "Take off your briefs."

She gasped with the unveiling.

He was big, he was thick. And he was very hard. Her mouth actually watered. She wanted to taste Marshall and bring him to his knees with the pleasure of it.

When a tiny voice came— *Do you even know how to do it right?*— she squashed it.

He crawled over her on the bed, took her hand, wrapped her fingers around him. "Touch me," he begged.

She loved the plea in his voice.

"Christ," he muttered through clenched teeth, his eyes closed. She reveled in the fact that she could do this to him, drive him out of control.

"Too much." He pried her fingers off. "Wait." He breathed deeply as if he had to calm himself. Then he looked down at her. "You make me feel like a teenager ready to get off with one pump of your hand."

She savored the harshness of his voice, the need in his words.

No matter what happened between them after this, Marshall was the right choice. No hot sexy young Italian would have done this for her.

Only Marshall.

18

He leaned over her, the hardness of him against her belly as he deftly flicked open the clasp of her bra. Then he licked the skin between her breasts in one long swipe. She shivered and a moan fell from her lips. Arching her neck, she pushed her head back against the mattress. He'd barely started and she was already trembling.

He slipped the lacy cup aside. "Beautiful," he whispered.

Easing down beside her, he draped one leg over hers, his knee between her thighs, and braced himself on an elbow as he traced a finger around her nipple. She shuddered as her flesh peaked. He did the same with her other breast, then finally lowered his head and took a hard bead into his mouth.

Sensations zipped through her like shooting stars, straight to her center. She tangled her fingers in his hair and held him down. He licked and sucked, moving from one breast to the other until she could barely breathe. Until her body arched and writhed. Until she wanted to beg for his touch between her legs. But this was too soon. She wanted the rising tension, the build toward climax, then an explosion that rocked her world.

Just when she thought she might actually come with only his lips on her breast, he pulled away. Rising over her, he took her mouth, kissing her deep, seducing her, devouring her, mesmerizing her. When he was done, her bra was gone, tossed across the room, and she didn't even remember him having pulled it off. All that was left was the lacy bikini, and Marshall began to kiss and lick his way down.

"You taste so good." Lick, caress. "Your skin's so soft, your body so smooth and sweet and hot." Sigh, moan. "I want to make you feel good." Touch, stroke, lick. "Your skin trembles when I touch you." He teased her belly button. "I can smell how wet you are."

When he reached the line of her panties and slipped a finger beneath the elastic, she shivered with anticipation. All his pretty words and soft caresses heightened her arousal.

Then he touched her, right there, and her hips arched and a moan sighed out. She wanted to cry and scream and make him do things she'd never asked for aloud. He dragged her panties down and slid between her legs, and she didn't have to beg at all.

"Christ, I dreamed about doing this to you," he whispered.

God, she dreamed about it, too. "Yes, please, do it."

"Do what?"

She'd known he'd make her ask. He loved words. He would want to hear. Maybe he'd want to make her beg, too.

"Lick me. Quickly." She'd say anything he wanted.

He put his finger on her, circled, making her a little crazy, then dipped his head down until he touched his tongue to her and made her a lot crazy. It was so sweet and hot and perfect that she almost shot off the bed, her hands twisted in the sheets the only things anchoring her to the bed. He played her expertly, setting every nerve on fire until she was trembling beneath him. "More," she chanted. It wasn't like her, she didn't talk, she didn't make a lot of noise, she didn't moan and beg.

But with Marshall, she wanted to do it all.

Her skin was warm and flushed pink. Her breath was fast and hot in her throat.

He gave her more. Licking and sucking her flesh the way he teased her breasts. Then he filled her with a finger, two fingers, and she cried out. It was so so good, too too much. She let go of the sheets to fist hands in his hair, holding him down, rocking against him.

"I've never, I've never," she cried, not even able to finish.

She'd never felt like this. Not the way he did it, as if he loved it, as if it wasn't a chore. Nothing had ever been this good. She wasn't herself anymore. She was a sexual being, living only for the sensation, crying out, as if she had no inhibitions at all.

He found a spot inside, a perfect, wild, and sensitive bead, riding it as if he knew her body, as if he knew she was on the very edge and with one more swipe of his tongue she'd shoot into the stars.

Then she was soaring. Someone was screaming out in pleasure. And Marshall held her down, made her ride that edge of ecstasy forever. She began to laugh before she came all the way down. Spontaneous and unstoppable. Maybe she was crying, because her eyes were wet.

Then she was wrapped in Marshall's arms, their bodies tight together without even feeling him move.

"Oh my God," she was finally able to whisper. "I can't believe I screamed."

"It was more like a wail."

She batted his shoulder. "That's not any better."

"I loved it." He kissed a tear away from the corner of her eye. "I want you completely uninhibited. If you're thinking, then you won't come as hard."

"I think it was actually better because I made noise, like it freed me. I usually like to be quiet." She was suddenly embarrassed. She was talking about her sex life with her husband.

"I never want you to be quiet. I want you to do whatever you need to make it feel the best it can."

"If I get to do whatever I want, I want this." She pushed her fingers through his hair and pulled his head down, kissing him openmouthed. She tasted herself on his lips and tongue. It was new and unique and perfect. "I want everything to be new with you."

"It is, all of it." He pulled her leg up over his, stroking her bottom, between her legs, then down her thigh and back up again, trailing her own moisture over her skin. It was decadent and erotic and sexy.

Suddenly she needed more. She needed to take charge. She slid her hand down between them, wrapping her fingers around his hard length. He moaned into her mouth and slid his fingers a little deeper along her cleft. "Christ, I love how wet you are."

"I love how hard you are."

He thrust into her hand, and she swore he got harder, bigger. "This is what you do to me," he murmured.

She felt a warm, wet drop on her fingers and swirled it around his crown. Then she did something totally alien to her, raising her hand to her mouth, licking his essence off her thumb. "I like it," she whispered, then kissed him with the taste of it. As if they were sharing absolutely everything. "You're amazing."

He was fifty-five and yet he was rock hard and ready to go like a twenty-year-old.

He caressed her behind. "You're gorgeous and beautiful and you dazzle me."

"I want to taste you now."

"I'm all yours." He lay back, opening himself up, putting everything on display for her.

She stroked him lightly, breathing in his musky male scent, relishing all his beauty.

Then she licked him tentatively, just the tip, tasting another salty drop. And it was good, so good.

He stroked her hair. "Oh, yeah." He didn't push her, letting her take it slowly.

She wanted it slow, she wanted to savor.

"Are you sure about this?" Marshall caressed her hair, her cheek, ran his thumb across her lips.

She felt as if she were a fragile bud he was afraid of crushing. But she was a fifty-year-old woman who'd been married for decades and raised two girls. She didn't want to be fragile. She wanted to demand the things she wanted. Like Carol always did.

"I need you in my mouth," she said softly but surely. Then she pushed him back and slid down his body.

She tested him, tasted him, stroked him. And finally she could want nothing more than all of him in her mouth.

She felt the power of what she was doing in his groans and the quiver of his body. He spread his legs and guided her free hand to the sac beneath his hard length, showing her what he wanted, the light pressure, the rhythmic movement. Then he flopped back on the bed and his voice became a low growl, without words, just sensation. She slid him deeper into her mouth, taking as much of the big, thick length as she could. His taste was salty yet somehow sweet, too. Then she slipped all the way back up to his crown, circling the taut flesh with her tongue, and down again until her lips touched the curl of her fist around him.

"Slow, just like that, Christ," he ended on another low groan. "I'll tell you when I need it faster."

She liked his instructions, as if they were working him

together, and she wanted to learn exactly the way he liked it. She sucked hard on the way up, circled him slowly with her tongue, and slid back down again, over and over. Until his legs writhed beneath her on the bed. Until he shoved his hands into her hair and guided her rhythm, increasing it. She did exactly what he wanted and loved every moment. She could feel what it did to him, how much he loved it.

The act was beauty and power and connection. It was as if she had complete control of him, that he was hers all the way down to his marrow.

Dirty words slipped from his lips, and she loved every one of them because they meant he no longer controlled his body or his mind. She did.

He started to shake, and he chanted, "Jesus, that's good, Jesus, so good, so good." He held her down, and she felt the pulse start at his base where she'd wrapped her hand around him. Then he filled her, and she drank every drop, loving the taste because it was *his* taste. She savored his essence, the beauty of taking it from him. She rubbed his sac, squeezed her fist around him, and drew out every ounce of his climax.

Until finally he pulled her off, "Too much. Too good." And he hauled her into his arms.

She wiped her mouth, but she didn't want to lose the taste of him, not yet.

"I didn't mean to do that. I wanted to wait until I was inside you." His arm wrapped around her, he rolled with her until she lay next to him, her cheek against his wildly beating heart.

"That's exactly how I wanted it. What I did to you. What you did to me." It wasn't that she couldn't say it to him. It was simply that they'd done something so momentous she couldn't find the right words to make him see how important it had been.

He hugged her tight against him. "Your husband didn't like to go down on you?"

She liked the way he bluntly said exactly what it was, and she answered honestly. "When you're married, you just get right to the main event without wasting time."

"Holy hell. I'd never call that a waste of time."

They lay there as their hearts slowed and their bodies cooled. They hadn't completed the act, but they'd still made love.

And she wanted it again.

❀

HE FELL ASLEEP WITH THE FEEL OF HER ALONG THE LENGTH of his body. She'd exhausted him, mostly because he'd never known such an amazing release. He'd held out as long as he could, until it was like spontaneous combustion and there was no stopping it.

When he woke to the feel of her in his arms, he admitted he'd never known such perfection.

He'd wanted to make love to her, but in the midst of the cataclysm she'd started in his body, he had enough brainpower left to know she needed to take control of his climax, to be the one who wrenched it from him.

There would be time enough for all the rest.

❀

"MY GOD, I FELL ASLEEP."

She was wrapped safely in his arms, the room humid with their sex, the perspiration dried on her body but somehow deliciously sticky.

It was midafternoon and she was in bed with a man. In bed with Marshall. His breath wasn't the slow, even rhythm of sleep, and she tipped her head to meet his gaze. "Wow." She wanted him to know the magnitude of what they'd done.

He smiled crookedly. "*Wow* isn't big enough. Something more like awesome or out of this world or mind-blowing." He stroked the hair back from her face.

She needed him to know what she'd done was special, all for him. "I like the sounds you made. The way your body trembled. It told me how to do everything right for you."

"It wasn't just right. You made me forget who I was. There was just your mouth on me, your hand around me, and wild, crazy sensation. That's exactly how it's supposed to be."

"Thank you," she whispered.

"I'm the one who needs to thank you."

"I mean thank you for teaching me what you like, putting my hand where you wanted it, taking my head in your hands and guiding me."

"I didn't teach you anything. It was all naturally you."

Oh, how she wanted to be a natural at lovemaking. When you'd been with only one man for almost three decades, it became routine, always the same, whatever way was the quickest because you had to get up early in the morning and get the kids dressed, make their lunches, get them off to school.

It wasn't that everything with Anthony was bad. She'd just been too busy to really let go. And that's what she'd done with Marshall. She let go. She stopped thinking about how she looked, how she sounded, if someone would hear. And she let herself feel every skyrocketing sensation.

"We're not done. I want to be inside you. I want to feel you around me, the way your body clenches on me," he whispered into her hair.

She felt herself heating all over again. She'd never known how important words were, how they got you going before you even touched.

"So that means we need some fuel. Let's go out, take a walk, find some dinner." He kissed her ear. "Build up your strength."

"I like the sound of that."

They showered together and he soaped her up, sending her into orbit all over again with his fingers inside her and his mouth taking her lips. But when she tried to do the same to him, he said, "I'm saving that for later." She slipped a hand over his hard length until he imprisoned both her hands in his. "I can probably do twice in one day. But I'm not so sure about three," he said with a reminder of his age.

"You know you're amazing. I thought men your age had to take a little blue pill."

"When I'm around you, I don't need any extras."

"You certainly didn't this afternoon."

He hugged her tight. "I can never get enough of you."

She didn't ask if she was different from the other women he'd been with, if he'd needed help from a pill with them, or if he was just highly sexed. She didn't want to talk about other women. This was her holiday fling, and she didn't want to think about her failed marriage or make him remember another woman.

As they dried each other off, he went down on his knees, taking her with his tongue. She leaned against the wall, and when the tumult was over and she could breathe again, she asked him, "Aren't I supposed to wait till later, too?"

He stood, laughing. "You get to come as many times as I can make you." He kissed her long and sweet, making her breathless again and leaving her wanting more.

As they headed out of the hotel, she felt energized, completely alive in a way she hadn't in years. This was what good sex could do for you. And she wanted it every day.

"I have an idea, if you're willing."

She gave him her most seductive chuckle. "I love all your ideas, and I'm very willing."

He bent down for a quick, hard, mind-altering kiss. "We need to go to some of the major fountains so you can throw your coin in and make your wish. It's the right time."

Her heart stilled. Because now there was a wish she was terrified to make, a wish that this didn't have to be just a holiday fling, a wish she knew couldn't come true.

"I want you to wish to have your friend back. I want you to wish for the impossible. Because it's time to make the impossible possible."

To make the impossible possible. To make a man who didn't believe in relationships want a relationship with her.

It might actually be more possible to wish Carol alive again.

19

"Let's grab a cab," Marshall said, and a valet waved one in for them. Helping Dana inside, he added, "We'll walk back and have dinner along the way." It seemed as if he'd been planning this.

"Why do you really want me to make this wish?"

As the cab pulled out onto the wide esplanade, Marshall picked up her hand. "Because I believe you need it. Because once you put your wish out there, how badly you want her back, somehow she'll know and you'll have told her how very important she was. And that will help you put her to rest."

"I put her to rest two months ago."

He squeezed her fingers, then reached out to tip her chin toward him. "No, you didn't. You went out on three dates with Italian men you didn't know because that's what she wanted for you. But is it what you wanted for yourself?"

What she wanted was to feel attractive, to see desire for her in a man's eyes, to feel like she wasn't a washed-up, middle-aged woman heading into menopause. But things had changed between them. Because yesterday she would have said that to Marshall, and today she couldn't. Yesterday, she would have revealed her innermost fears. But now he'd become one of those fears, fear that he would get tired of her, that everything would end when this trip was over.

So instead, she agreed with him. "It's time. I like your wish."

"It's your wish, not mine. Just believe in it."

If she divorced herself from all her fears and mixed feelings, she knew he was right. She'd been fighting this wish, and yet it had been the only one she wanted to make.

At least until today. Yesterday she'd made a wish for the perfect holiday lover.

Today she had exactly what she'd wished for.

Maybe impossible wishes could come true. Maybe it came in a form you never expected. And maybe, too, he was right, that she needed to lay Carol to rest. This trip was homage to her friend, and the biggest homage she could pay was to make a wish the way Carol had wanted.

Then her friend could rest. Maybe Dana could, too.

The driver took them along a wide avenue, then turned right and left and right again, the streets getting narrower with every turn. He finally let them off, pointing down a small side street with a sign pointing to the Piazza Navona, the first stop, home of three famous fountains.

The alleyway was short, filled with women hanging out windows, shouting at each other to be heard above the roar of the crowds in the square.

The sun was still high, long before the Italian dinner hour, and the piazza was teeming with people, clusters around each of the fountains. Stalls of fruits, vegetables, and trinket sellers ringed the square. There were scarves and T-shirts and baseball hats and postcards of the fountains. The restaurant tables all faced the square, their patrons sitting in the shade under awnings, sipping coffee, eating treats, and watching people.

They entered the piazza at the far end by the Fontana del

Nettuno, the Fountain of Neptune. The statues were magnificently sculptured, their features careworn by centuries of Italian weather. "It's beautiful." She leaned in close, her hand cupped over Marshall's ear. "But isn't his penis kind of small? I mean, he's Neptune, after all. He should be as big as you."

He laughed, loudly, his mouth wide, his eyes sparkling. Wrapping his arm around her, he hauled her in for a fast, hot kiss. "You do amuse me."

She grinned with him. Yes, there were some things she could still say to Marshall. And she could laugh with him.

Taking her hand, he pulled a coin from his pocket, ready to hand it to her. "No," she said. "It needs to be my coin." She had plenty of them just for wishing, plus the special one for Trevi. This had to be her coin and her wish. Even if Marshall had prompted her to make it.

Hand in hand, they pushed through the crowd surrounding the fountain, the picture takers, the wish makers, the tourist mothers.

"Maybe they don't throw coins into this fountain," she said.

"People throw coins in every fountain. So throw yours and make your wish." Standing next to her at the railing, he stroked a finger across her cheek, tucking her hair behind her ear, then bending down for a sweet kiss. "I told you what I thought your wish should be, but it has to be all your own."

She turned around, her back to the fountain, threw the coin over her shoulder, and made her wish silently in her head. *I wish to have my friend back in my life.*

When she opened her eyes, he kissed her again, a little longer, a little sweeter, until someone nearby said, "I think I know what she wished for." A man, an American accent. Dana blushed.

But Marshall merrily said, "And may all your wishes come true as well."

They headed to the piazza's center and the huge obelisk rising out of its fountain, Fontana dei Quattro Fiumi, Fountain of Four Rivers.

She brought Marshall's clasped hand down by her side and leaned against his shoulder. "I love the Golden Gate and the view across the bay to the city is amazing. But there's such history here, statues that have stood for hundreds of years and monuments thousands of years old. It's just different, maybe not better, but stunning just the same."

"I know what you mean. The history makes it even more special. To think these wonders were built by kings and emperors and popes that have been dead for hundreds and even thousands of years."

Once again, he elbowed his way through the swarm, bringing her to the edge of the railing a few feet from the water. After long minutes of taking in the glory of the fountain's river-god statues and the ancient obelisk, she threw her coin and made her wish. To have her friend back, to feel the closeness that allowed you to say anything, everything, to cheer on each other's hopes and dreams and joys and commiserate with the fears and anguish and sorrow.

Once again, Marshall sealed the wish with a kiss, then smiled down at her. "It helps, don't you think?"

"Yes. It really helps." Between the fountains, there were less people, with the crowds congregated around each spectacular monument. "I wonder what it's like late at night when all the tourists have gone to bed."

"I don't think Rome ever sleeps."

He pulled her to a stall blooming with colorful scarves and picked out one for her, a brightly colored peacock he wrapped around her neck. "It's perfect with your hair and eyes."

"Thank you. I love peacocks. I have needlepoints of them all over the house."

He swooped in for a kiss, chuckling. "I can imagine you doing needlepoint."

She laughed with him. "You mean like an old granny in a rocking chair?"

"You're no old granny." He hugged her tight, flush with his body. "No old granny could do to me what you did today."

She wrinkled her nose at him. "And love it."

They smiled at their secret.

Then they pushed through to the railing surrounding the piazza's last fountain, Fontana del Moro, the Fountain of the Moor.

She made her wish at the foot of the Moor. All the wishes were slightly different, yet all the same. Somehow, in some magical way, she almost felt as if they could come true.

At the far end of the piazza, she took a picture straight across, the huge obelisk the centerpiece of the square. Then Marshall, with his long arms, took a selfie of them, the fountains in the background, the obelisk rising right out of the throng.

She thought about sending it to her daughters, saying she'd met someone, but she could imagine the variety of emojis flying back at her, the crying face, the terrified face, the shock face, even the poop emoji. Then all the explanations she'd have to make.

She'd keep the picture just for her.

"Do you want a coffee?" he asked. "Or push on to the Pantheon?"

The Fontana del Pantheon was in the Piazza della Rotonda in front of the iconic Pantheon itself.

"Let's find the Pantheon," she said and Marshall checked his GPS, pointing them in the right direction. The lanes were narrow and crowded with people, vendors, cafés, and shopkeepers. There was noise and laughter and car horns. Rome was never quiet.

When they stepped into the piazza, the magnificent Pantheon was straight ahead. It had stood for two thousand years. As magnificent as the Colosseum was, the Pantheon was amazing because it was intact. Tourists poured in and out of its doors.

"Let's go in," she tugged on his hand. "I read somewhere that it's free."

When she stood in the center, gazing up into the dome, sunlight falling through the oculus— the hole in the top through which it could rain or even snow once in a while— all the tourists seemed to fade away. She'd felt the same the day she'd stood in the Colosseum, her eyes closed. Now she could almost hear the great Emperor Augustus's voice, his wife Livia right beside him.

Marshall's fingers slipped around hers. "I can feel them all, can't you? Julius and Augustus and Livia, Tiberius and Caligula and Claudius." His voice was soft with reference.

She hadn't researched the Pantheon and didn't know exactly when it was built. She didn't know if Caesar had ever stood here. Whether or not he had, the place was still powerful, magnificent, the house of a thousand ghosts.

"It's beautiful." They stood hand in hand basking in the glory for long moments, until voices and people and the cacophony began to intrude once again, and Marshall led her back out into the late afternoon sun.

"Need more coins?" he asked.

"I've got plenty, thank you."

Here in the square, it wasn't as crowded around the fountain as Piazza Navona since most of the tourists were trying to get into the Pantheon. She held the coin in her hand a moment, contemplating the wish. In her mind, it became more of a plea. *Please give me my friend back.* She tossed the coin and made the wish just as Marshall took a picture. Then he stood beside her, throwing his arm around her shoulder.

Touching came so easily now, the handholding, the kisses, some short and sweet, others lingering.

"This spot should really give your wish some weight." He pointed at the Pantheon. "A two-thousand-year-old structure right before us." He turned to her. "What do you think?"

"All I have to do is believe, right?" If she believed, could she make this fling with Marshall last longer? "And I believe," she said, because she had to.

She jutted her chin at a café on the opposite side of the square, its cloth-covered tables facing the Pantheon and the fountain. "Can I buy you coffee and a pastry? You're always treating me."

He hugged her to him, kissed the top of her head. "I would love for you to treat me."

A waiter seated them, and they ordered coffee and two pastries. As they waited, she snapped pictures of the fountain, the Pantheon, the people, then she turned, leaning back to take a picture of Marshall's smiling profile. She didn't have enough pictures of him that she could moon over when she got home.

The waiter returned with their lattes and treats, and she asked him to take a picture of the two of them. More memories to store away.

Marshall pulled her close for a kiss. "Thank you for this afternoon."

His breath warm across her cheek, she felt the same tingles she had in her bed. The moment was perfect to ask for what she wanted. "Will you spend the night with me?"

"If you didn't ask, I was going to beg." He sealed the words with a sweet, hot kiss. Then he picked up his pastry and fed her a bite.

As he licked powdered sugar off his fingers, she had a powerful urge to be the one to lick him clean.

They sat close together, taking tiny bites to make their

pastries last, sipping their lattes instead of gulping, and drinking in the sights in the square.

The waiter eventually brought the bill, and Dana counted out the change. Then she stood and held out her hand. "I'm ready for the Trevi Fountain and my last wish."

"Isn't it all the same wish?"

"I said it different ways every time." She let a smile take over her face. "We'll see which one works."

The Trevi Fountain was even more crowded than the day she'd met Aureliano and made that throwaway wish. In a way she had to thank him. It was through him that she and Marshall had come together.

Her hand in his, Marshall said, "Are you ready to brave the ravening hordes?"

She laughed out loud. She'd laughed more with Marshall in the last few days that she had with Anthony in the last five years of their marriage.

She stopped in the middle of the piazza, before Marshall pulled her down the steps to the fountain itself. When he realized she wasn't coming with him, he turned, raising his eyebrow in a what's-up gesture.

"Thank you," she said.

"For what?"

"For reminding me how to laugh. I haven't laughed so much since Carol died."

He reeled her in until he could wrap his arm around her waist and hold her tight against him. She leaned back to look up into his beautiful face.

"She'd want you to laugh again." He nuzzled her nose. "Life isn't worth much if you're not laughing at it, at yourself, and at everything around you. A good belly laugh can cure anything." His smile was so sweet and endearing that everything inside her melted.

She wanted to ask him why, if he believed in the power of

laughter, he didn't believe in marriage and relationships. Even after her spectacular marital failure, she still believed.

Maybe she could believe enough for both of them.

Then she let him lead her down the steps to the fountain, holding tight to his hand as he parted the wave of tourists. She found a tiny spot by the railing between a lady with three children and two teenagers taking a million selfies.

She wedged herself in, her back to the fountain, while Marshall stood in front of her, his camera in his hand. "Throw the coin high and wide," he told her. "If you actually hit the statue, the wish works even better."

"I've never heard that one." She laughed.

"If it isn't part of the tradition, it should be."

She reached in her bag, found the coin in its special pocket. She was glad she hadn't wasted it that day at the fountain with Aureliano.

Marshall reached out before she threw it. "What's that?"

She held the coin flat on her palm. "A Sacagawea dollar. I figured that a special wish calls for a special coin."

"It'll work. Absolutely." And he rolled her fingers around the coin. "Now close your eyes, make your wish, and throw it hard over your shoulder."

Despite all the people around them, the shoving, the pushing, the laughter, the shouts, she felt as if she were in a bubble with Marshall. As if the rest of the world had vanished. She closed her eyes, his silhouette still burning against her eyelids as she prepared her wish in her mind. She raised her arm, let the Sacagawea dollar fly as she made her last wish. *I want my friend.*

Maybe it was her imagination, maybe it was wishful thinking, but she was sure she heard the loud plink of the coin against the statue of Oceanus, then a plop as it hit the water. A great cheer went up, and she wanted to believe it was for her coin and her wish.

She wanted to believe that the impossible could truly be possible.

She opened her eyes and Marshall was in front of her, big and strong and beautiful, his eyes trailing over the contours of her face. He held out his hand as if they were still inside the bubble she imagined, all the people like a fadeout in a movie.

Then he kissed her, so tender, so sweet, so right.

And she felt as if her all her wishes could come true.

"SHALL WE GET SOME DINNER?" HE ASKED.

The sun was setting as they left the Trevi Fountain, winding through narrow streets, dodging people, their hands tight together as if afraid they might lose each other.

There'd been a moment at the fountain when Marshall felt as if they were completely connected, as though a tether between them would ensure they'd always find their way back to each other.

It was a fanciful thought, because feelings like that never lasted. But he relished it for its novelty.

"I'm not hungry for dinner right now." His hand still in hers, Dana turned, stopped in front of him, pulling him close, close enough that their clasped hands were nestled between her lush breasts. "I'm hungry for *you*. You're the only thing that can satisfy me right now."

He wanted her. Badly. So badly that he feared no one but Dana would ever be able to satisfy him again in his life.

20

He was kissing the nape of her neck, making her crazy, and her fingers fumbled with the key card in the slot. Until finally the door opened and she almost stumbled inside. Marshall caught her against him as he slammed the door. It was so sexy and elemental. His desire. Her chaos.

He had her stripped out of her clothes in two seconds flat, and with one more second, he was out of his. He hauled her naked body up against his, and she felt him hard between her legs.

"I want to take you right here up against the door, pounding so everyone can hear." He braced her there, taking her lips in a mad, wild kiss that flung her up in the air like a roller coaster and down again, her stomach pitching.

"But then I want you long and lingering on the bed, making you come for hours, then sliding deep inside you and just sitting there for long minutes as your body milks me."

It was the words she loved, an essential accessory to the sensations, to his hands and lips on her, his body against her.

Yes, this was what sexting and phone sex were all about, the all-important words.

"On the bed," she said, as if he were giving her a choice. They'd left the covers rumpled from their afternoon tumble, and the delicious scent of sex in the air heightened all her senses.

He carried her to the bed and came down on top of her. "You can't know how many nights I've lain awake thinking about this moment."

He kissed her, endlessly, until she was mindless, sweet kisses, hot kisses, deep kisses that went on forever.

Everything else between them today had been foreplay. This was the main event. When he kissed her, he devoured her. When he touched her, he made her moan with pleasure. When he put his tongue on her center and licked her, he made her come with abandon. She clutched her fingers in his hair until she knew it had to hurt. She held him down, reveled in her climax until the moment her body could no longer take it and she had to crawl away.

Marshall followed, pinned her with his big body, kissed her with all the flavor of their sex.

When he pulled back, she begged. "I need it now. I can't wait another moment. I need you inside me."

"You don't have to beg. I'm more than willing."

He left her only long enough to grab a condom packet out of his pocket. They'd stopped at a shop on the way back to the hotel earlier this afternoon, and he'd bought the necessities.

He knelt on the bed, rolling on the condom with expertise and ease, and she refused to think about the other women he'd been with, probably younger than her, their bodies taut, their skin supple.

Then she threw all the comparisons away because she was

the one with Marshall now, the one he wanted so badly his hands shook.

His eyes glittered. "Do you like watching me touch myself?"

"It's sexy." Of course, he couldn't know the other thoughts that had been crowding themselves into her head.

"Maybe you'll do it for me sometime." The thought of doing that for him was sexy, tantalizing. "But not right now," he said as he slipped between her legs, pushing them wide. "Right now, I just want to feel you take me."

She waited for him to plunge hard and deep, but he entered her with only the very tip.

And yet it was glorious. The feel of a man inside her, the weight of him on top of her. He flexed his buttocks, easing in and out in a slow, mesmerizing rhythm.

"Just like that," he murmured, seducing her. "Right there. How does it feel?"

He held her gaze, compelled her to look at him when she wanted to close her eyes and feel the sensations.

She could barely breathe, barely speak. "It's... I don't know... crazy and scary and good." She arched, pushed her head into the pillow. "Oh my God." Then he held her face between his hands and made her meet his gaze.

"It's better when it's slow at first." And it was, so good, so right.

"I can feel you clamping down on me."

It was involuntary, her body tightening all on its own.

There was something about looking in his eyes as they burned dark and wild, while he took her with that slow, gentle rhythm, never going deep, but riding that spot just inside, making her skin heat and her body tense around him.

"This will be even better." He braced himself on one elbow and reached between their bodies, caressing the heartbeat of her sex.

Dana wanted to scream. There'd never been anything like it. She pulled her legs around his waist, opened herself fully, her toes pointing, flexing. Then her limbs began to quake. She couldn't breathe, she couldn't keep her eyes open anymore. There was only sensation, only his body, her body, his voice whispering, seducing, the mind-altering rhythm of his finger on her. Something was building inside her, unstoppable, like a tsunami on the horizon. Coming. Coming. Closer, until finally it exploded over her, dragging her under as she cried out.

It was only then that Marshall took her hard, took her fast, slamming into her, intensifying everything, forcing her to ride the glorious crest of bliss.

She clung to him, crying out her pleasure, crying out his name, riding wave after wave with him. Until his body began to tremble and his thrusts became frantic and she plummeted into ecstasy all over again.

This time she took him with her.

❁

She lay wrapped in his arms as their hearts slowed and their breaths returned to normal.

"Now that was out of this world." Marshall could truly say he'd never felt anything like it. He enjoyed sex, it was always pretty damn good. He gave the lady a nice time and took a good time for himself, too. But the way he lost himself in Dana was something he'd never known. "But," he added, "I was supposed to make you come a thousand times before I came inside you."

"It felt like a thousand times." Her voice was low, soft, dreamy. As if she hadn't quite come back to her body.

"I wanted to make it better."

She laughed softly, buried her face against his chest. "You

make it sound like that wasn't the best never-ending orgasm I've ever had."

"The best *and* never-ending?" He chuckled. "I've never had that happen before."

"The first one hadn't even ended when you filled me up and it happened all over again. Like you knew just what to do, just how hard and how fast to make it go on and on, then I came again, with you."

He smiled even though she couldn't see it. "I've never had a woman rehash exactly what she felt." He realized immediately how crass that sounded, as if she were just another woman he'd fallen into bed with, no one special, simply a lady who'd scratch an itch. He tightened his arms around her. "I've never heard anything so special. And here I was, afraid I didn't spend enough time kissing you between the legs." He could have gotten raunchier, but Dana deserved something softer.

She tipped her head back on his shoulder, looking at him, a mix of heat and satisfaction and joy and even melancholy. "No one has ever made me feel like that. You let me cry and scream and dig my fingernails into your skin. I loved it all."

He wondered if she knew how many glimpses into her marriage she'd given him. Her husband didn't like foreplay, he didn't like the glorious sounds she made. He'd kept her inhibited and worried about his reaction. Marshall had gathered all the small things she'd said and tied them together, how she'd supported the man through law school, raised his kids, been his doormat. Until he dumped her for a younger model. Thank God her friend Carol had made sure she got everything she deserved for all the years she'd wasted on him.

Marshall wanted to give her the thing she craved. The truth. His honest feelings. "I'm fifty-five. And I sure as hell haven't been a saint. But what we just did, I've never felt that with anyone. I've never wanted to just lie here for hours, holding onto what we did. I've never craved making love all night long." He kissed her, first a gentle kiss, then something deeper yet sweeter. Until they both came up for air and he said, "I want you to pack up your things and move into my room. I know I have meetings and sometimes I might be late getting back, but I want to come home to you every night for as long as I can."

Emotions flitted across her face, fear, need, desire, uncertainty, disbelief, and so many more he couldn't interpret.

He rushed on. "If you like this place better, we can stay here." It felt almost like begging. And he'd never begged a woman for anything. Not since he'd fallen for Pamela Plunkett that first day of his sophomore history class, and she'd used him to make a junior guy jealous. Not since his parents divorced, and he'd seen what marriage and relationships were actually like.

Maybe it was because they were in Rome. Because this was her memorial holiday, the one she should have taken with her friend. Maybe it was because they'd somehow created their own world here. Despite all his other obligations, he wanted to live in this world with her.

"What's the view from your window?" she asked.

"I don't know, I never looked."

"Do you have a balcony with French doors?"

"No. But it's got a big seating area and a table if I want to have a conference there."

"Does it have a huge marble tub?"

"Just a shower. But it's big."

She nodded her head, distractedly, as if only to herself. "Then you should move in here. Because my room is a hell of a lot better."

He felt his breath sigh out of him and his heart climb into his throat.

"I can do that." His nerve endings seemed to dance a jig all over his body.

He swore to himself he'd make their time together the most memorable she'd ever have. Certainly the most memorable he ever would.

❦

He'd had to work the following day, and Dana agreed to meet him at his hotel for dinner so they could collect his things.

She ordered a scrumptious meal of grilled fish, sautéed vegetables, and a pesto couscous with raisins. The vegetables were crisp tender just the way she liked them and the fish was melt-in-your-mouth fresh. The large dining room was filled with mostly tourist types, the buzz of conversation rising around them.

They were picking up his luggage, closing out his bill, moving him over. They'd discussed payment because his company was covering his hotel cost, but her room was twice the price, and it didn't seem fair to charge the company the whole cost when it was her room. They agreed on half and half. "What about your sister's room?" she asked, only just thinking of it.

"If they don't have anything at your hotel, I'll put her up here."

"If they have a room at the Palazzo Roma, it's going to cost you more."

"It doesn't matter." He shrugged. "And I don't even know if she's coming."

Dana couldn't believe she was doing this, letting a man she barely knew move into her hotel room. Except that it was Marshall and she felt like she'd known him forever.

It was the wildest, craziest thing she'd ever done.

Her daughters would freak at the growing number of photos of Marshall on her phone.

But this was her life, not her daughters'. Not her husband's. Just hers alone.

Carol would approve wholeheartedly.

"It'll all work out with Laura," he said.

"It'll be fine," she agreed.

He smiled then. "It seems my fickle business partners need even more time to go over my proposal after the changes we made today." He picked up her hand, kissed her fingers. "And now I have another day off tomorrow. Will you spend the day with me?"

"That would be nice," she said mildly while what she really wanted to do was punch the air.

"We could go to the Villa Borghese. There's an art gallery and some beautiful gardens."

"Lovely."

Then his phone rang. Marshall was never without it. There were always questions to answer, comments to make. And naughty texts he needed to send her.

The restaurant was crowded enough that she couldn't hear the other end of the conversation, only Marshall's replies. "Yeah, I'm having dinner, and it's kind of loud." He looked straight at Dana. "No, not a customer.... Yeah, that's great... Fine, I'll pick you up." Dana felt his gaze on her face as if his fingers caressed her. "Just send me the time.... I'll work it all out. I'm glad you're coming." Then he smiled. "There's someone I want you to meet."

Dana's stomach became a jumble, the fish, the vegetables, the couscous and pesto. His sister's arrival was imminent now. Two seconds ago, she'd been joyful about Marshall moving into her room, about their relationship, and not caring what her daughters thought, not caring what anyone thought.

Now suddenly it was topsy-turvy. His sister was coming.

He obviously wanted Dana to meet her. But they hadn't had enough time together, just the two of them, making love, touring the city, just being with each other.

His sister's arrival could ruin everything. No, correct that, Dana would ruin everything because she was nervous what his sister would think about a woman inviting a man to share her hotel room after knowing him only a few days. His sister would think Dana was the desperate type to fall in bed with any man who came along. And what if Marshall let it slip about all those dates she'd had? As if she were some middle-aged housewife trolling for sex? Her heart rate was rising rapidly, and her blood pressure had probably gone through the roof.

Marshall hung up and smiled as if nothing had changed.

But everything had changed. It had changed the moment she agreed to sleep with him. A self-fulfilling prophecy, she found herself censoring what she said to him.

"My sister says she can leave the kids for a week. She'll be here the day after tomorrow."

Dana didn't say a word, her emotions roiling inside. She sipped her water, afraid another gulp of champagne would go to her head. And finally she said, "Then we'll need to figure out the room situation. Maybe it's better if you just stay here."

He waved her off with a hand. "It's a shoulder season. There'll be something at your hotel. In fact, let me check now." He tapped on his phone, obviously searching her hotel. Then he pushed a button and put it to his ear. "Hello? Do you speak English? Yes, thank you."

She let the conversation drone around her.

It would all end after tomorrow night. He'd have to be back at work, and when he wasn't, he'd need to spend time with his sister.

She was absolutely crazy for having agreed to any of this in the first place.

Marshall set the phone on the table, his smile as wide as Niagara Falls. "You won't believe this, but they had a room on the same floor as ours." The room had now become 'ours,' not hers. "Just a few doors down. She'll have the same view. It'll be perfect."

"That sounds absolutely marvelous." As much as she tried, she couldn't keep the strain out of her voice.

"What's wrong?" His gaze was know-all, see-all. "I promise you'll like Laura."

Said by a loving brother, she wasn't sure how much it counted. "It's fine. It's great. I know I'll like her."

"But," he said for her.

"No but." But she knew he wouldn't let her get away with a white lie. "I'm just a little nervous." Then she blurted out, "What's she going to think of me, that I'm sharing a room with you?"

He reached across the small table, squeezed her fingers. "She's fifty years old. She's been through a nasty divorce. She's learned a lot, and she's not judgmental. She's going to think you're a lovely woman and that you make me happy."

It was as if they were talking about marriage. But this was a holiday fling that would end the moment she headed home.

He hadn't found happiness. He found flexibility.

"Give it a chance," he said, the words coming out louder to combat the noise in the restaurant.

She'd known his sister was coming, but in the last twenty-four hours, she'd pretended the woman would flake on the trip and Marshall would be all hers. She looked at him, really looked. He was so beautiful, the silver hair, the coffee-colored eyes, the sooty lashes, the strong lines of his face. He was movie-star handsome, the picture they put on the cover of AARP Magazine as the perfect example of a man in his prime. And somehow he'd found *her* in a crowd of thousands at the Colosseum.

Now she had two nights and a day before she had to share him.

She heard Carol's voice stern in her head. *Don't you dare ruin your last thirty-six hours with this gorgeous man.*

She needed to make the most of every moment. And they damn well better be good ones.

His hand was still around hers, and she returned the squeeze he'd given her. "I'm going to love her." She would give it a chance. "I'll take her shopping at all those fabulous designer stores." Leaning close, she smiled. "I'm so glad you got her a room because I really do love my hotel better than this one."

"So do I. Now finish your dinner because I need to take you back there and have you all to myself in that big bed."

That's what she needed, to be the sole focus of his attention.

Until his sister arrived.

21

He made love to her for long, luxurious hours. Marshall lost count of the number of times he'd made her cry out in pleasure as her body trembled. He used his skills with his mouth, his tongue, his fingers until she lay in an exhausted puddle in his arms. Then he made her come once more. The moment she hit her peak, he thrust home deep and high inside her. When she came again, they came together. An explosion that knocked his world off its axis.

The night air cooled the sweat on their bodies. They lay against the pillows wrapped in each other, body and soul. He felt her muscles relax, her breathing even out, and he knew she was asleep.

He understood that she was worried about Laura. And he'd wanted more time with Dana all to himself. But he also wanted them to meet. Dana could have no real idea that Laura would be ecstatic. Because this, what he was doing with Dana, moving into her hotel room, spending every waking moment he could with her, this was out of character. His female friends were good for dinners and events and customer parties and in his bed. Laura rarely met any of them, and only if she happened to come across him at some charity event.

Laura would know how different this was. And she would love Dana for it.

Dana murmured softly in her sleep and snuggled closer. He pulled the sheet over them.

This was different, the way she made him feel, the extreme pleasure he received from her pleasure, the way he could just look at her and feel his heart race.

For the first time he started to think about what it would be like to see her after they got back to San Francisco.

❦

Dana took him in her mouth, loving the taste of him.

He'd made love to her for hours last night, waking her in the middle of the night, his fingers on her, inside her, and finally his body filling her.

He'd made love to her again as the sun rose, but he hadn't come. He wouldn't let her give him the pleasure she so badly wanted to. This morning he'd ordered breakfast, then they'd showered, and he'd gone to his knees before her and made her come as the water pounded her.

Now, finally, he lay back on the bed and let her do dirty things to him. He tasted like ambrosia, sweet and salty and creamy and delicious. She'd never thought she'd say that, let alone feel it deep inside. She worked him with her tongue, her lips, her hand, until his body trembled, and he whispered dirty words to her.

Then she grabbed a condom, rolled it on his thick, hard length, and climbed over him.

"God, yes," he muttered as she slid down, seating him deeply inside her.

Riding him was an adventure. He gave her total control, and she thrilled as he groaned louder and clamped his hands on her hips.

She rocked on him, her breasts bouncing, and he begged, "Touch yourself. I want to see it, I need it, God, please."

Marshall made her lose all her inhibitions, made her want everything he wanted. While he guided her hips, she put her finger between her legs, rubbed herself with all the moisture building inside her.

Then Marshall reached up, pinched her nipple, hard enough to shoot a sharp pleasure straight through her. It was exquisite, and in the next moment, she contracted around him, her orgasm starting as a throb, then a pulse, then a wave rolling over them both. He slammed her down on him, reared up, going as deep as he could, fusing their bodies together, their orgasms simultaneous, turning them into one unit, one being, one body.

And she completely lost her mind.

The day was glorious in every way, from its beginnings in her bed to the beautiful gardens of the Villa Borghese. Every woman should start the day by making love. It altered her perspective, relaxing her, opening her eyes to the beauty of every bloom and the sweetness of every touch.

They wandered the galleries hand in hand, viewed sculptures by Bernini and Canova, paintings by Caravaggio and Raphael, classics everyone knew but also magnificent works by artists she'd never heard of. There was something amazing about seeing them up close, the perfectly formed fingers of a man pressing a woman's buttocks, the individual brushstrokes of a painting defined.

Discussing the perspectives with Marshall was illuminating. They didn't always like the same thing, but they could each point out elements they found inspiring, awesome, even dazzling.

She'd never been one for art galleries or museums, but Marshall opened her eyes to the beauty.

After the galleries, they picnicked on the grounds surrounded by the glory of flowers, and dined on takeout meatballs and pasta. "I told you takeout spaghetti would be good."

He laughed. "I should never have doubted you."

"It's so serene and beautiful here." Her smile felt serene on her face.

He reached out, touched her hair. "All the beauty I see is you."

She wondered how many women he'd said that to, scolding herself as soon as the thought came to her. He'd never said it to anyone in that same way. Marshall wasn't false, he wasn't playing her. It was just her insecurities.

Dana leaned back on the bench, the sun lulling her, as Marshall scrolled through his messages. "Laura's flight comes in at three-thirty tomorrow," he said, then continued scrolling, typing occasionally, until finally he held his phone out for her to see. "What do you think about dinner and dancing on the Tiber this evening?"

She'd thought he was reading work messages, but he'd been searching for tonight's entertainment. "That would be lovely."

"I'll make a reservation. The boat boards at eight-thirty. Is that too late for you to eat?"

"I might need a snack beforehand." She rubbed her stomach. "Although the spaghetti was filling. More than I normally eat for lunch."

"We'll have appetizers." He waggled his eyebrows lecherously. "Or you can be my appetizer."

She tried to waggle back, unsuccessfully. "And you can be mine."

He chuckled and started scrolling again. When he frowned, she knew he'd finally gotten to work emails. "Damn, they're ready for me tomorrow. I have to go in. I was hoping for another free day."

"I'm sorry." Then she thought. "What about Laura?"

He shrugged. "By the time she lands and gets through customs, it'll be closer to five. I should be done by then."

Sometimes he'd worked well after the dinner hour. "I can meet her."

"You don't need to bother. She's capable of taking a cab if I can't get there in time."

Should she just let it go and save the first meeting for when Marshall could make the introductions? "I really want to do it."

"Are you sure?"

He was remembering her expression last night after Laura called. She hated that she'd been so transparent. "Really," she insisted. "I want to."

Slipping his arm around her, he hugged her close. "Thank you. She'll love that."

Dana wasn't so sure. Maybe the sister wouldn't like the idea that her vacation would suddenly be spent with a stranger tagging along. But she'd committed herself. "Can you send me a picture so I'll recognize her?"

"Sure. I'll send her a picture of you, too."

It was their last night alone together, and she wasn't about to let anything ruin it.

Before their dinner cruise, there was time for a little delicious nooky. Marshall ordered stuffed mushroom caps and champagne, eating a mushroom off her naked body and licking away the garlic butter. She laughed, licked the seafood stuffing out of a mushroom, set the cap on his crown, and went down on him. He gasped and she sucked off the cap, chewing it, and saying with her mouth full, "Now that's the most delicious stuffed mushroom I've ever had."

The play moved into the shower, and they swapped garlic taste. Even that was delicious. Then finally they dressed for dinner.

"Wear that sexy new jumpsuit." He hauled her in, skin to skin, kissed her sweetly. "When I walked into the lobby that night and saw your bare shoulders, I almost begged you right then."

He always knew the perfect thing to say. And he was gorgeous in his three-piece suit.

They boarded the boat and had drinks as all the passengers arrived, and Marshall requested a table by the railing so they could see the sites. "We'll pass by Santangelo Castle."

The evening was cool on the water, and she had to cover up her bare shoulders with a sweater, but the candlelit dinner was scrumptious and romantic. For dessert, the waiter said the tiramisu was their specialty. Probably for the tourists, she thought, but they ordered it anyway, and it was as divine as the man claimed.

While the band had played softly during dinner, afterward they cranked up the volume for dancing. The dinner patrons were mostly older, and the music was more suited to ballroom dancing.

Marshall stood and held out his hand, "May I have this dance?" he asked formally.

She put her hand in his, feeling the center of attention as this delectable man led her out to the dance floor.

All she cared about was Marshall's arms around her as

they danced, his body flush against her, his tantalizing male scent surrounding her. All she wanted to do was melt into him, hold tight, and never let go.

Even she knew how dangerous the thought was.

She should have changed her wish at the very end, changed it to a wish for Marshall to stay in her life.

But then she needed Carol just as much.

Couldn't a person have two wishes?

They danced the cruise away. With all the champagne before dinner, during dinner, after dinner, Dana was tipsy on sparkling wine and desire. She looped her arms around his shoulders and went up on tiptoe to whisper in his ear, "Take me home and make love with me all night long." His arms tightened, holding her close as the song's last strains died away. "Your wish—"

"—is my command," she finished for him.

And Marshall took her home to fulfill every promise.

※

DANA FELT MARSHALL RISE EARLY IN THE MORNING TO GET ready for his meetings. He'd ordered coffee and Italian *cornetti* as he looked over spreadsheets on his laptop.

The scent of coffee and sweets calling to her, she joined him, wrapped in the fluffy hotel robe.

"I'm sorry I woke you up." He patted the sofa beside him.

"I just need coffee." Sitting, her thigh pressed to his, she took her first sip, eyes closed, savoring the aroma as well as the taste. "Oh God, that's good. Thank you."

He pushed the plate of *cornetti* closer. "I ordered extra."

"You think of everything."

He grinned. "I hope so."

"Is this the day you sign off on the contract?"

He laughed. "Hardly. Now begins the real wheeling and dealing."

"I wish you all the luck."

He saluted her with his coffee cup. "Thank you. I need it." Leaning forward, he rested his elbows on his knees. "What I really needed was last night. Every moment. You'll be in my thoughts all day long."

She flushed with the pleasure of his words, but made a joke. "Don't get distracted and give away the whole store."

"I'll try not to." Then he slid his hand beneath her hair, his palm warm against her nape, and kissed her with the delicious taste of *cornetti* and coffee and him. "I'm glad you woke up before I left, just so I could do that."

Finally it was time for him to go. He shut down his laptop and packed it away, then gave her a final delicious kiss to carry her through the day.

When he was gone, she felt alone, bereft in a way she hadn't before Marshall made love to her. Normally, she would have gone about her day, enjoyed the sights, snapped pictures, bought mementos, called the girls, told them everything she'd been doing. Except about Marshall and those misbegotten dates.

Now she barely knew what to do without him.

And wasn't that the most pathetic thing.

There was only one way to combat it, force of will. She picked up her guidebook and chose her destinations for the day.

Yet even as she wandered through the Piazza Venezia and stood in awe of the Altare della Patria, Altar of the Fatherland, with its Corinthian columns and magnificent statues, she couldn't help feeling that everything was better with Marshall. It was as if she'd come right back to the place Natalie had said she was in when she first broached the idea of this holiday, that she couldn't do anything on her own.

What did that say about her life when she flew back home?

She was doing it again, making her life all about someone else, placing her happiness and her self-worth in another person's hands. She was proving her daughters were right, that she needed someone to take care of her, that she couldn't be alone.

Are you really going to let yourself be this way for the rest of your life?

She heard the words in Carol's voice. Carol had always known her best. And it came to Dana that this trip wasn't about finding a sexy Italian lover or making a wish in a fountain. Carol had sent her to Rome to find herself. To show her that she was perfectly fine on her own, that she could arrange everything, dine alone, walk the ancient sites on her own, shop without needing someone else's approval. That she could enjoy herself *by* herself.

She ended up at the bottom of the Spanish Steps. She'd walked the streets of Rome so much in the last couple of weeks, it was if she knew them all. The steps were crowded with people, families, toddlers, teenagers, elderly men and women, walking up, walking down, taking pictures. A policeman shooed away a couple who sat on the steps to eat their gelato.

With all the voices filling the air, the laughter, the shouting, the cars, the horns, she felt a need deep inside her. She didn't just walk the steps, she ran them, clutching her purse and her water bottle, weaving through clusters, around groups, fast enough to make her breath saw in her chest.

Finally, standing at the top, she told herself the kind of woman she wanted to be. The kind of woman she *was*. She was capable. She had raised two wonderful girls, put her husband through law school, started her own bookkeeping business. She'd run charity events at her daughters' schools.

She'd organized and arranged and herded and controlled and made other parents do exactly what she told them to. She'd come on this trip all alone, she'd attracted three different Italian men, inspired them to ask her on a date.

And she'd made beautiful love with Marshall.

She was not incapable, and she could be alone. She liked Marshall, no, she more than liked him, but she would still need to be a whole woman without him. What she needed was her own backbone. No matter what Anthony thought, no matter what her daughters believed, she had to believe she was capable.

It was a pep talk, of course, and she'd backslide. But she would remind herself of this moment at the top of the Spanish Steps, even if she had to do that over and over.

When it came time to pick up Marshall's sister at the airport, Dana grabbed a taxi without rushing back to the hotel to change. She'd had a good day on her own. She didn't need to get all crazy making herself look perfect for Marshall's sister. If Laura didn't like her, so be it.

At least she didn't smell bad. The thought made her laugh. She texted Marshall, telling him she was on her way to the airport, and he texted back a quick thank-you and another apology for not being there.

At the airport, she brought up Laura's photo on her phone. There was a definite resemblance, same eyes, same nose, maybe even the same mouth. Marshall was gorgeous, and of course his sister was a pretty woman. Her smile was sweet, and her arms around the two boys in the picture were motherly. Her hair was a rich auburn, and she'd probably dyed the gray from it. Dana was glad Marshall hadn't. She loved running her fingers through the distinguished silver.

She loved how he made her feel when he touched her.

She scanned the faces of the passengers coming out, families throwing themselves at their relatives, squealing and crying with joy, couples, probably tourists, moms and dads with kids, lone business travelers with computer cases.

Then finally there was Laura. She wore a loose blouse, black skinny jeans, and high-heeled boots. She'd pulled back her shoulder-length hair with a scrunchie. Taller than Dana by a couple of inches, she had the statuesque figure of a runway model, the kind of woman people did a doubletake on, wondering if she was that famous movie star or that rich celebrity.

Dana was tempted to feel dowdy in walking shoes and white Capri pants, her hair probably a rat's nest after walking around all day.

She was so tempted.

But she remembered her pep talk on the Spanish steps. She channeled those thoughts all over again. Laura was no different than she was, a woman who had gone through a messy divorce, a woman who needed a holiday. Two peas in a pod.

Waving her hand, she called out Laura's name.

22

An hour later, they were sitting on the balcony of Dana's room and finally able to relax with the inspiring view of the Colosseum.

"Oh my God," Laura moaned. "I never knew how long that transatlantic flight could feel when you're alone. Especially when you realize you've seen almost all the movies they have on streaming."

Missing Carol, Dana had been lonely on the flight, too. Even after her wishes, she still missed Carol. She craved someone with whom she could discuss her feelings about Marshall.

"You're settled now." She handed Laura a glass of champagne.

"Marshall's told me so much about you." Dana wondered how much. But she liked the idea of him mentioning her to his sister. "It's amazing," Laura went on, "that you're from the Bay Area, too." She reached over to pat Dana's hand. "You are an absolute angel. Thank you so much for suggesting this." Laura closed her eyes as she took a long sip of bubbly.

They'd managed to get Laura's two massive suitcases into

the taxi, thank God. That's just how Carol had traveled, too, with far too much, but she claimed she needed choices. Laura had checked into her room, which was three doors down from Dana's, and had the bellboy dump the huge bags there while Dana texted Marshall to say they were safe and sound at the hotel. He sent back a brief text with a kissy face. Then she'd ordered champagne and canapés.

"This view is just what I needed." Laura relaxed deeply into her chair, slouching down to rest her head on the back. Having removed her boots, she propped her feet on the balustrade

Dana slouched, toed off her shoes, and propped her feet next to Laura's.

In this position they could see only the top of the Colosseum, puffy clouds scudding across the blue sky. The sun would dip soon, and there were enough clouds for a lovely sunset.

"Thank you again for picking me up. I could have taken a taxi."

"It was my pleasure. It's nice to have someone meet you, especially since you were expecting Marshall to be there." Dana reached over to squeeze Laura's hand, then she pointed to the small table where she'd set the champagne and canapés. "You really have to try these stuffed mushrooms. They're the best." She couldn't help the flush when she thought about what she and Marshall had done with them.

Laura marveled at the appetizers, then settled once more. "It's wonderful to have you to unwind with since I picked the wrong day to fly in with Marshall having that big meeting."

Dana was glad to have had Marshall all to herself yesterday.

"The truth is, I really, really needed to get away." Laura glanced at her. "I suppose Marshall told you about my divorce."

Dana rolled her head on the chair and nodded. "He mentioned it, no dirty details, though." She wondered how much Marshall had told his sister about her divorce.

"The boys have been impossible." Laura sighed. "One minute they want to live with their dad. The next minute they want to live with me. Then one of them wants to do one thing and the other wants to do something else. My husband talks about splitting them up and having one live with him and one live with me." She was expressive, her hands documenting everything she said. "I don't know what the right thing is. And your friends get totally sick of hearing about it and advising you and then getting angry when you don't do what they tell you to. Even though I suppose I really should have done what they said." She shrugged. "Then, because I don't know how to handle the boys, they start acting up at school."

"I'm so sorry. My girls are in college, so my divorce was a completely different situation. But they're still messed up about it."

Laura looked at her, laughed. "See, that's why my friends don't want to talk to me. Because it's all me-me-me. But I'm sorry for you, too. Was it a midlife crisis with your husband?"

It was Dana's turn to sigh, but she didn't close her eyes, not wanting to miss a moment of the sunset. "He fell in love with his paralegal. He's a lawyer."

"Mine fell in love with the secretary. Such a cliché, aren't they?" Laura laughed softly, bitterly.

Dana joined her in the laugh and tried not to sound bitter. "My ex married her and is about to have another baby."

Laura covered her mouth in shock. "Oh my God. That's totally beyond the pale."

Dana nodded, gazing out at the Colosseum and the beauty of the setting sun as colors washed across the smattering of clouds. "Wow. Will you look at that?"

"It's divine," Laura murmured, as entranced as Dana.

"But I'm not sure I care that much anymore," Dana went on as if there'd been no interruption. "About the new baby, I mean." She missed Carol so much more." I just want the girls to feel settled." She looked at Laura. "I'm sorry your boys are having trouble with the divorce." Marshall hadn't said a lot, just that the boys were acting out.

Laura sighed. "Okay, here's the worst, which is why I didn't make the previous flight." Then Laura gave her the scoop as if they'd been friends for years. "My ex dumped the secretary. He found her a job at another company, just got rid of her in other words. Then—" She snorted as sharply as an angry horse. "—he has the nerve to tell the boys he's rethought the divorce and wants to get back together. And he sends *them* to tell me." She waved a hand widely. "Can you believe it?"

Glancing at Laura, Dana found her staring at the sky, her features rigid. She tapped her foot in solidarity. "What a dick."

Laura looked at her, too. Then they laughed. This time it wasn't angry or bitter or fearful. It was almost a release.

"Oh my God, he's so totally a dick," Laura said between giggles. Then she sobered. "But it really messed up the boys when I had to tell them it wasn't going to happen." She closed her eyes as if she saw the scene all over again. "I mean, they're just kids, early teens like Marshall was when our parents went off the rails." She made a face. "Not that they weren't off the rails a long time before that with all the arguing." She flapped a hand. "Anyway, the boys were just so hopeful that everything was solved and life would go back to normal so they could stop worrying about how Mom was coping and they could just be with their friends again." She flattened her lips into something that could hold in the momentous feelings wanting to spew out. "Lon was so angry. And Kyle, he just clammed up. You know, I thought it would've been Lon who acted up. But it was Kyle. He barely said a word but two days later he cut school and went out drinking with his friends. Someone told the school counselor that he talked about suicide. They actually brought in helicopters to search for him in the woods near the school." She shrugged at Dana. "I don't know how a helicopter is even supposed to see a kid in the woods." She sighed again. "They finally found him, and he was so horrified that all the helicopters were because of him that he continued the lie about suicidal thoughts." She shook her head. "He finally admitted that to the family counselor we saw."

"Oh my God. You must've been going crazy."

Laura shook her head slowly, then gulped her champagne, finishing half. "I didn't know what the heck was going on, except one thing, that Kyle wasn't suicidal. That's not him at all. And my dick—" She smiled at Dana as she used the word. "—of an ex-husband kept saying that I was minimizing everything. He said it was all my fault. And I said it was all his fault for leaving in the first place, then telling the *boys* instead of *me* that he wanted to come back."

"He wanted them to do his dirty work for him."

Laura shot her with a pistol finger. "Exactly. He wanted to use them to wheedle his way back into the house. He really just wanted out of the alimony and child support. Divorce is expensive."

She thought of Anthony. "My ex resents every penny he has to give me. Isn't that always the way? They find something new and better, or they just plain want out. But they sure don't want to pay the price."

"I know." Laura leaned over to clink her glass to Dana's. "Here's to dickhead assholes that we're absolutely better off without."

"I totally second that." She reached for the bottle and

topped off their glasses. They'd probably be drunk by the time Marshall finished his meetings. "My friend Carol, she was my divorce lawyer, she really stuck it to him." Dana smiled, feeling gratification all over again.

Laura gasped. "Carol? Are you talking about Carol Hunt?"

"Yes. She was my best friend and my lawyer."

"Oh my God." She put her hand to her chest. "Carol was my lawyer, too. She was the best." Then she laid her fingers on Dana's arm, her dark chocolate eyes just like Marshall's. "I am so sorry. Marshall told me you just lost your friend, that you were even planning to take this trip with her. But I had no idea that was Carol Hunt. She was amazing. I'm sorry I didn't make it to her memorial."

There was a wild hiccup in Dana's heart, that she was somehow connected to Marshall even before she came to Rome. Could it be more than coincidence? Could it be fate? "That's so crazy you went to Carol, too. But she was the absolute best, and I'm glad she got you a great settlement. And thank you, but I'll tell you the truth. I miss Carol more than I miss my ex-husband. I suppose that's a terrible thing to say."

"Of course it isn't. He treated you like crap, cheated with his paralegal. And now you see how much better your life is without him." She patted Dana's arm. "But it's not better without Carol. She was a smart, caring, incredible woman."

Dana was silent for a long, long moment, then she said softly, "I met her when we were eight years old. We were like sisters. We went through everything."

"She's irreplaceable." Laura nodded as if she truly knew how Dana felt.

"She understood me completely. Sometimes we didn't even need to say anything." She felt tears prick her eyes.

"I've never had a friend like that. Except maybe Marshall."

"I'm so sorry you've never known that. Carol never got

tired of listening to me talk about what Anthony did." Dana shrugged. "Maybe it was because she was my lawyer, too."

"It was because she was your friend. And maybe I never had a friend like that because I was never a good friend myself."

Dana tsked. "I'm sure that's not true."

Laura snorted softly with a cluck of her tongue. "Of course it is. You probably already recognize that I'm all me-me-me."

"It's understandable right now. Your ex-husband tried to screw with you all over again. Your son acted like he was suicidal, and you had to attend family counseling. *And* you had to cancel the fabulous trip you'd planned with Marshall." She glanced at Laura. "Where are the boys now? With their father?"

Laura shook her head. "No. The principal recommended I take them out of school for the rest of the term since there's only a few weeks left. They can do their studies and tests remotely." She rolled her eyes. "He was suggesting one of those military-style camps. But I sent them to Yosemite. My ex's sister lives out there. She adores the boys and they adore her. There's all sorts of fun things to do. And she won't let them shirk their classwork. I'd planned to go, too, but my sister-in-law said it would be better if she had some time alone with them first before I came out. Can you imagine that?"

"She's your sister-in-law? Aren't you afraid she'll take your husband's side and try to make you into the bad guy?"

She pressed her lips together, humming a negative in her throat. "She doesn't have kids and she loves the boys. I really think she's going to help them. The only side she's taking is the boys' side."

"That's amazing. See, you do have a friend."

Laura smiled. "I'm just a drama queen. Didn't Marshall tell you that?"

"He's only ever said the sweetest things about you. He loves you very much."

Laura tipped her head, smiled. "He really is a good guy. He never once said I told you so even though he didn't think I should have married the dickhead in the first place."

"He's a good listener," Dana agreed.

"Yeah, he was always a good big brother." She leaned forward to tap Dana's knee. "I'm glad he met you. You make him happy."

This wasn't the place she wanted to go. She didn't want to explain their relationship or talk about the holiday fling or admit how badly she wished it could go on. Then again, she itched to know exactly what Marshall had said about her and why Laura would think that she made him happy, as if she were different from any other woman he'd ever slept with.

She was caught in a trap of her own making. She could tell herself all she wanted that she'd be okay— and she would, she really would, eventually— but it would hurt when their fling was over. Things had gone too far for it not to. And she didn't want any false hope from Laura.

Though God knew, she was dying to ask questions, about what he was like when he was young, about that girl in high school he'd fallen in love with— Pamela, wasn't it?— the one who'd trashed his heart so that he never wanted to try again, about how many women he'd dated, and if Laura thought there was ever a chance he'd change his mind about marriage.

But she didn't want her desperation to show through.

"Tell me more about yourself," she said instead. "Do you work? Outside the home, I mean."

"I'm a realtor. I always loved looking at other people's homes. A fun day for me was going to open houses." Laura laughed. "I know, weird. But I really like people. Sure," she shrugged, "like any other job, there's things you don't like. But I love matching people up with the perfect home." She let out a moan. "It's usually the other realtors that are a pain in the butt." She looked at Dana. "And you're an accountant?"

"I have a small bookkeeping business. I don't do taxes. I hate taxes. But I'm a real nitpicker, and I love reconciling down to the last penny."

Laura grabbed her hand. "Oh my God, I need you. I hate QuickBooks. And I'm always so far behind."

"I'd be happy to help."

Dana wanted to grab on. It would be a link to Marshall, though that sounded pathetic. She liked Laura for herself. The woman was open and funny and aware of her own faults.

Her cell phone rang, Marshall's name flashing on her screen where she'd left it on the table. She'd even moved his number into her favorites.

"The Eagle has landed," she told him without even saying hello. "I'm already plying her with champagne. And we're eating those wonderful stuffed mushroom caps that you and I enjoyed so much."

"Oh that's cruel, reminding me of all the ways we enjoyed those mushrooms."

She laughed, hoping Laura couldn't overhear him. "Your sister wonders when you'll be here."

Laura tapped her arm. "Tell him I love the hotel you picked. It's so much better than the one he picked."

"Laura said," she started but Marshall cut her off. "I heard. Tell her she's so picky." He lowered his voice. "But I do adore your bed." Then he added, "I've got another hour here then I can take you both out for a nice dinner. Unless Laura needs to sleep."

"He asks if you're sleepy or if you want to go out for dinner. He'll be here in an hour."

"I just got my second wind," Laura said loudly enough for

him to hear. "I'm dying to go out for some good Italian food, fashionably late like they do here in Rome."

"Great," he said. "I'll get there as quick as I can." Then he dropped his voice to a whisper. "We'll have dinner and then we'll get rid of her."

Dana laughed. "Don't be too long. Or we'll both be tipsy on champagne."

One brief conversation and her heart was beating faster in her chest, her excitement to see him bubbling over.

After she'd hung up, Laura said, "Okay, tell me everything."

Dana gathered a moment to think by playing dumb and asking, "About what?"

Laura rolled her eyes.

"You look just like my daughter, Natalie." Dana laughed. "If I had a penny for every time she rolled her eyes at me, I'd be a very rich woman."

Laura's laughter was soft and sweet, her eyes suddenly bright. "I totally know it's none of my business. It's just that, Marshall, you know." And Dana thought, no, she didn't know. "He's very closemouthed," Laura said. "I have to drag every little detail out of him." She demonstrated like she was pulling a rope. "He never talks about any woman seriously. But he told me about you, about your daughters, your friend. And he said he wanted me to meet you. He's never done that before."

Dana laughed. "That's because he wants me to take you shopping so he doesn't have to."

Laura gave her that soft, pretty chuckle again. "That's not how it sounded to me."

Dana tried to change the subject. "By the way, I found a marvelous shopping district by the Spanish Steps. We can go there on a day when Marshall has a meeting."

Laura wagged her finger. "Oh no," she said with a little

lilt. "I'm embarrassing you. I apologize. But I can't say I'm *really* sorry because I really *really* want to know."

Dana's cheeks felt hot, and it wasn't from the champagne. "You're just like Carol. She always nagged me until I told her." She felt the same pain that hit her every time she thought about Carol being gone forever. But somehow it was good to share with another woman.

"That's me, a nag." Laura laughed to show the comment hadn't stung. "But I get it. It's too new with Marshall. You don't want to jinx it. At least I hope it's good. It's just that my brother is being very uncharacteristic, but he won't admit it either." She leaned over to tap her glass once more to Dana's. "I'll just figure it out myself tonight when I watch the two of you together."

23

"I like her a lot," Laura said over after-dinner drinks in the hotel restaurant.

Dana had gone back up to her room, *their* room, to call her girls. She liked to do it when she was on her own. It didn't bother him, of course. She had a life separate from his. Just as his life at work back in the U.S. was his own world. They each respected that about the other. But when they came together, it was so goddamn amazing.

"I like her, too." It was such a simple statement for the emotions he had about Dana, some he couldn't even define. And didn't want to.

He'd been hoping Laura would crash early, leaving them alone. Because he did so want his alone time with Dana. He wanted to bury his face in her lush hair, smooth his hands over her warm skin, thrust deep inside her while she quaked with pleasure.

But Laura had slept most of the way on the plane, and she wasn't tired yet.

"I know you like her, but do you *like* her?" She stressed the word in different ways, pushing her agenda.

"I enjoy being with her. She's pleasant company." Christ, wasn't that an understatement.

Then his sister got blunt. "She's crazy about you. Are you crazy about her?"

Yes, he was crazy about her. The emotions invaded his entire body. And he liked it. "What are you getting at, Laura?"

"So, like, is she the one? You know, the one you've been saving yourself for all these years."

He sighed. "I would have thought your divorce had cured you of all that romanticism."

She smirked at him. "It hasn't. I found the right man for a long time. Until he wasn't the right man anymore. But somewhere out there *is* the right man who will stick around and not cheat. Just like there's a right woman for you."

He snorted softly, furrowed his brow. "You grew up in our parents' marriage. Then you were dumped by your husband for another woman. And now that he was dumped by her, he's trying to screw with your life by begging to come back. I don't know what that says about marriage, but it certainly isn't anything good."

"It's not just marriage, Marshall. It's about relationships. About dating a woman for more than a month and knowing her inside and out and caring about her anyway."

They'd had this discussion every time Laura learned he was seeing a new woman. "Relationships are messy."

"And you don't like mess," she said, her lips pursed.

"Why is that so bad?" He certainly didn't want what his parents had, or many of his friends, or even Laura.

But there hadn't been a single moment of mess with Dana. And he knew her inside and out. He knew about her marriage, her daughters, her disappointments, her losses. In the past, as soon as a woman got too personal and started sharing whatever was going on in her life, he backed away.

Maybe the difference was that Dana had shared all that before they became lovers. He liked her and *knew* her before he'd admitted to himself that he couldn't live without getting his hands on her.

"I can see you're thinking too much with that male pea brain of yours."

He laughed. "I'm not thinking. I'm simply ignoring you. And my brain is at least the size of two peas."

She struggled not to laugh, glaring at him. "Your problem is that you're afraid to take a risk."

He snorted. "I take risks every day. Over my lifetime, I've taken thousands of risks."

She did that pursed-lip thing again. "That's business. I'm talking about your heart." She reached over to tap his chest.

"I don't have a heart." He crossed his arms. "That's why I make a good businessman."

"I just can't win with you. We've been arguing about this for thirty years." She crossed her arms, imitating him. Or mocking him. "I have only one question for you. Are you going to see her when you get back home?"

"I haven't thought about the future. I'm too busy enjoying the moment." But he had wondered what it would be like to watch her get on a plane and know he'd never see her again. Despite the fact that he didn't have heart, it seemed to ache at the thought.

"This is what you have to understand about Dana," he said. "She just went through a bad divorce."

Laura interrupted, "I know all that. Her husband cheated on her, he married the bimbo he was cheating with, now that bimbo is about to have a baby."

Had he told Laura all that? He couldn't remember. "She just lost her best friend. I think that's even worse than the divorce."

"I know," Laura whispered. "She talked about her. She

misses her." Then she stabbed her finger at him. "Why didn't you tell me her friend was my divorce lawyer?"

He felt his face screw up in astonishment. "What?"

She nodded. "Yeah. Carol Hunt. Didn't you even connect the name?"

He stared into the distance, considering the coincidence. Or maybe the inevitability. "I didn't even remember your lawyer's name. You were always saying 'my lawyer said this, my lawyer did that.'"

"Well, now you know. I liked Carol a lot. She was a good lawyer, but she also understood how I was feeling."

"Then you understand that Dana needs fun right now, a companionable relationship."

She arched an eyebrow. "So that's why you're staying in her room?"

He felt a momentary stab of guilt straight through his heart. A part of him wondered if he'd done the wrong thing, if he should have stayed Dana's friend and never become her lover. He didn't want to discuss his sexual relationship, but there was one thing he needed to understand from a female perspective. "When the asshole cheated on you, did that make you feel undesirable and unwanted?"

She shut her mouth. A shiver ran through her body, and he saw how stupid and insensitive he was. "I'm sorry. I shouldn't have said it that way."

"Yes," she said softly, almost like a child. "I kept thinking there was something wrong with me instead of realizing there was something wrong with him."

"I'm so sorry, Laura. I should have been more supportive."

She looked at him again, crossing her eyes and smiling. "Don't be stupid. You were the only one who listened to me." Her smile turned soft. "Except Carol."

He thought again of how much Dana had lost. How much Laura had.

Then she asked the hard question. "Are you just pandering to her need to feel desirable?"

He closed his eyes, stared at his own lids, the flash of Laura's silhouette against the black. "I'm not pandering to her. I'm trying to give her what I think she needs." He didn't say that she might have had an affair with a sexy young Italian, and after that she would have felt even worse about herself, if she didn't get physically hurt as well. But Dana wouldn't want Laura to know.

"I think what she needs is a man who will show her that not all men are dickheads." She raised her eyebrows, laughed. "By the way, that's Dana's word. I'm making it mine." Then she let the smile fade. "But I'm afraid when this trip is over and you go your separate ways, she might end up lumping you in the same dickhead category."

Her words knifed him.

She pushed back her chair and stood. "Really, I'm getting tired now and you know when I get tired, I just get bitchy. But I love you and I'll never think you're a dickhead no matter what my dickhead ex-husband says." Her lips curved in a smile.

"I love you, too," he said.

She rounded the table and kissed him on the cheek.

She was a beautiful woman, and as he watched her walk away, he saw heads turn. Not the young men, because sometimes young men could be stupid, but the older ones, the ones who understood that a woman really did get better as she got older.

His mind turned to Dana. And when they got home. The thought hung like a specter in the air. He didn't want it all to go to hell. He wanted this brief time together to be the best memory she ever had. For him, the problem was that when relationships went south, as they always did, he couldn't remember the good things anymore. Just like he had a hard time remembering that his childhood hadn't been completely awful. It only turned to shit once his parents started fighting. Now those bitter arguments were all he remembered. The bad always expunged the good.

He didn't want that for Dana. He wanted her to remember how much he desired her, that he couldn't get enough of her.

He signaled the waiter, paid the bill, and went upstairs to Dana to make another good memory neither of them would ever forget.

❦

He knocked on Dana's door instead of walking in.

When she opened it, she stood with one hand on the doorknob, the other planted on a cocked hip. "You don't have to knock. You have a key." She was still dressed in her capris, with a sweater she'd put on to ward off the night's chill.

"I didn't want to just walk in. What if you were naked?"

She fluttered her eyelashes at him. "That's exactly why you should walk right in."

The moment the door was closed, he hauled her up in his arms, kissing her deeply, tasting her, his body absorbing her heat.

"God, I've missed you," he whispered. "I could barely concentrate on my meetings."

She laughed sweetly, took his hand and led him to the French doors, the two chairs waiting for them. He wanted the night sky, the lights of the Colosseum, and the sweetness of simply sitting next to her.

She'd already opened the champagne. Then she reached for his necktie, pulled it off. "You look far too buttoned up. You need to relax." She took her time, leaned close, drawing his jacket down his arms. "I'll go hang this up while you pour the champagne."

She hung them in the bedroom closet, and he realized his suitcase was gone, too.

"You unpacked for me?" he asked, pouring two glasses.

"Yes." She smiled as she returned. "It's all put away."

"Thank you. But you didn't have to do that."

He'd never been taken care of. He had a housekeeper and a gardener because he wasn't home enough to take care of all that, but he picked up after himself, cooked his own meals if he left work early enough, planted new flowers in the yard. But he never came home to anyone waiting for him, especially not with a bottle of champagne. No one with whom he could just sit down and talk about the day.

He'd never known it was something he missed.

"I had a lovely talk with your sister this evening." She settled into the chair beside him.

"I knew you two would get along."

"She's nice. I like her. How was your day?"

They acted like an old married couple, a drink before dinner, a chat, checking in with each other.

"It was long," he said. "Thanks for the texts keeping me informed. It was hard to break away to get to you."

"That's okay." She gave him all her attention, as if she cared about what he said.

"We're getting somewhat closer to an agreement. But these guys are tough."

"Just remember, the sooner you get through it, the sooner you can spend time with me and Laura." She leaned an elbow on the chair, propped her chin on her hand, and gazed at him as if everything he said was totally fascinating.

"I apologize for making you take care of her."

She smiled. "It's fine. Like I said at dinner, I'll take Laura to all the fabulous stores near the Spanish Steps. And after a relaxing day shopping, we can hit all the long lines at the Colosseum and the Vatican."

"I'll buy tickets for the tours, so you can avoid the lines." He reached into his pocket for his phone. The sites were already bookmarked.

She waved him off. "You don't have to do that. We can take care of it."

"Dana."

"Marshall," she singsonged at him. "I don't want to talk about money or you paying for everything," she whispered.

Neither did he. At least not right now. He'd order the tickets later. Bringing her hand to his lips, he kissed her fingers. "Thank you for taking my sister to all the places you've already seen."

"Oh my God, are you kidding? We can take different tours, see entirely different things. And honestly, I didn't spend enough time at the Roman Forum or Palatine Hill."

Looking at her, something moved inside him. She was so beautiful, so caring, so sweet, so lacking in an agenda. He was used to women who wanted something from him, be it a fancy dinner or a night on the town followed by a raucous time in his bed. He was an open wallet to them. Some might have had plans for his whole portfolio, but they never got there.

Laura said he never had relationships. But he did. They were just disposable. He'd never seen anything wrong with that.

Dana was anything but disposable. What was between them had started as a friendship, then it became a holiday fling, but what was it now? And how could he let it end?

"Come here," he said as he set both their champagne glasses on the table. Then he hauled her into his lap and brought her down for a kiss that filled him up.

"More," she whispered, needing every bit of him.

They made it to the bed where she stripped him down and he tore off her clothes.

He bent to her pleasure, his body between her legs, his mouth on her, his fingers inside her. It was all too delicious, too perfect.

He was so good, knowing exactly what she needed, just the way she wanted it. "Don't stop, oh God, don't stop," she begged. "Please, you need to do this forever and ever."

Everything intensified, the depth of his fingers, the swirl of his tongue, the rush of her breath, and the pulse of her body. Then she went off like fireworks on the Fourth of July, crying out his name and words even she didn't understand.

When she opened her eyes, he was inside her. She wanted to ask how he could do that without her being aware, but she was beyond words. It was exquisite, and she was rising to the pinnacle all over again. It was so good, so hard, so fast, even a little rough, and yet so perfect. She dug her fingers into his butt cheeks, pulling him hard and tight against her. Until she lost her mind completely.

Only to find herself cradled in his arms moments later, their bodies deliciously sweaty, their breaths fast, their hearts racing. He was still inside her, filling her with one last pulse.

"Jesus," he muttered into her hair. "That was so damn good."

How was she supposed to live without this now that he'd shown her how perfect they could be together?

She couldn't live without him.

But this was a holiday fling. He hadn't wanted anything more.

She was the one who'd changed. And she didn't know how to tell him.

"Are you okay?" Laura asked.

Dana snapped out of it. "I'm fine. Why?"

They'd stopped for a light lunch and a latte, both of them parched and hungry after a morning of shopping.

"You just seem a little subdued."

Dana touched the shopping bags at her feet. "I bought a bunch of stuff when I first got here, and I feel like I spent a little too much today." She wasn't a spendthrift. Some might even call her cheap. But her thoughts had nothing to do with the money she'd spent.

"Everything you bought was classic. It will last forever."

Dana laughed, even if she didn't feel it. "Not if I get fat."

Laura snorted at her. "You're eating a salad."

Dana leaned forward. "You haven't seen everything I've had since I got here, all the pasta, the rich sauces, the delicious treats and desserts."

"You're on holiday." Laura waved away the calories like she had a magic wand. "You deserve to treat yourself."

Oh yes, she was on holiday. And she was treating herself to a holiday fling with Marshall. Whatever she ate during the day, she worked off with him during the night.

But she didn't want to talk about Marshall with his sister. She knew all she'd hear was that Marshall was different with her, that Laura had never seen him so happy. Then Dana would start believing she could have more. The thought was far too dangerous. Marshall didn't believe in relationships. He believed in sexual liaisons with women who didn't want a man sleeping in their bed night after night. No matter how good it was between them, it was still just sex.

"Let's make a pact right now," Laura said. "I'm going to tell you that you deserve all the best. And you're going to tell me the same thing. Not because of what we've been through in the past few months. But because we're good people. We treat others nicely. We're sympathetic. We haven't even trashed our husbands to our children." Laura spread her palms in a get-a-load-of-that gesture.

"How do you know I haven't trashed my ex to the girls?"

Laura gave her a wide-eyed look of disgust, her mouth slightly open. "I just know. I never want my kids to hate their dad. And I know you don't either, because it's not good for the kids." She laughed. "Although screw their dad, I'm not playing nice for his sake, but for the boys." She tipped her head slightly, as if she were asking Dana a question.

"I've gone out of my way not to trash Anthony. I would never hurt my girls with what he did. They have to make up their own minds about him." She nodded, not at Laura but at herself. "But I think he actually treats them well. It's the only thing I'm grateful for."

Laura held up a hand and Dana high-fived her. "That's what I'm talking about, girlfriend. We've gone out of our way to be nice. And while we're on this holiday, we deserve the best of everything." She waved at their waiter who raced over the moment Laura raised her hand. "We'd like to share your caramel flan."

He rushed away to do Laura's bidding.

"If we really want to treat ourselves the way we deserve," Dana said, slyness in her tone, "shouldn't we each have a whole one?"

Laura laughed, a big laugh, like Marshall's. Like Carol's.

In fact, everything Laura said was reminiscent of Carol, especially that Dana needed to treat herself the way she deserved.

Laura leaned in to whisper conspiratorially, "I know that we *say* we deserve the very best, but we'll both feel terribly guilty in about two hours. If we share..." She raised an eyebrow, smiled. "Then we only have half the guilt."

"You are so right. Why didn't I think of that?" She felt so comfortable with Laura. Just the way she had with Marshall those first few days when she'd info-dumped everything about herself. Before they made love and she'd become self-conscious.

"I like you," Laura said. "I'm serious about having you take a look at my accounting books when we're back home. Is that okay with you? I don't want to force you if you're not interested."

"It's great. Honestly." In fact, it was an honor. "I don't have more clients than I can handle. But I'd take you even if I did."

Laura's smile was wide. "Thank you." Then she stuck out her hand. "It's a deal. But if it gets to be too much, you tell me."

They shook, and Dana added, "I will."

Their flan arrived, and it was creamy and smooth and delicious. They each took tiny bites, savoring every spoonful.

"Marshall gets a whole one," Dana groused.

"He doesn't have approaching menopause to worry about." Then Laura pointed her spoon. "Mother Nature was really unfair to women's bodies."

"Totally unfair." Dana relished another bite. "But then men never get to feel the glory of carrying a child for nine months."

Laura scrunched her nose. "Except those first three or four months."

"Yes, but those last five months are amazing."

"Except the last month where you have to pee all the time and you literally waddle like a duck."

They laughed so hard together.

Then Dana added, her hand over her full mouth, "Plus we get to pick from a slew of gorgeous sexy older men. Right?"

"You're a genius," Laura agreed, her eyes twinkling like

Marshall's. "I never thought of it that way. I really need to start looking."

"What about some of the other realtors you work with?"

Laura rolled her eyes. "Oh my God, no. First, that kind of thing bites you in the butt later if it doesn't work. Second." She groaned. "Oh my God, male realtors." Her tone said it all.

"Doesn't Marshall have any business friends or associates?"

Laura shivered. "I wouldn't want to be a fly on the wall listening to what they say about me."

"Your brother would never talk about you like that. And if someone else did, he'd shut them down. If they treated you badly, he'd punch them in the nose," she added with enthusiasm.

"I'll admit he's a pretty good guy." Laura's features softened. It was obvious she adored her brother. "He wanted to go after my ex, but I held him back. A woman has to fight her own battles."

"I fought mine with Carol's help."

"Carol was the best listener." Laura gave a gratified sigh.

"I still hear her in my head sometimes. The things she would have said if she were here. It helps me be stronger." Dana smiled despite the ache in her heart.

Laura squeezed her arm. "We just have to carry on for Carol, bolstering each other the way she did." She shuddered. "Because sometimes I really do feel weak."

"I will be your voice of reason. You are not weak. You're an amazing realtor. You find people their perfect home with the perfect deal."

"Thank you," Laura said. "And that means fighting right down to the very last dollar. Like playing rock, scissors, paper."

Dana laughed, in fact, she laughed so hard she cried as she

imagined Laura playing rock, scissors, paper with some horrible old male realtor. And winning every time.

She hadn't laughed this much since that day in the park just before she lost Carol.

Except with Marshall.

24

The very early morning traffic out on the avenue was like a backdrop to the music they were making in Dana's bed.

"Oh my God." She arched her neck, wrapped her hands around the backs of his thighs and pulled him deeper, forcing him to the harder, faster rhythm she craved. "Don't stop, don't stop," she chanted over and over.

"I'm not stopping until you come again."

The sound of his voice, the feel of him against her palms, the pulse of him inside her, his beautiful face above hers. That was all she needed. She erupted like Mount Vesuvius. Marshall followed her only moments later.

She loved the sounds he made, the animal grunts, the beastly growls. Until he fused their bodies together and held tight against her. As if they were one.

If the ash of Vesuvius had covered them in Pompeii, they would be one together forever.

Marshall sighed, taking her with him until he was on his back and she lay flush on top of him, her head nestled on his shoulder, his body still throbbing inside her.

"Am I too heavy?" she asked dreamily.

He ran his hand down her flank. "You feel so damn good, I can't let you go."

But their time together was dwindling.

He'd worked four of the last five days, and Dana had gone everywhere with Laura, including the Roman Forum and Palatine Hill, where Dana hadn't spent enough time. She and Laura had done Pompeii today, but instead of climbing Mt. Vesuvius, they'd toured Naples. And Dana had seen things she hadn't seen the first time. Pompeii was like a gift, as if around every corner there was a new box to open with a different treasure inside.

Returning from the long day, Laura had gone to her room, and Marshall had arrived in time to shower with Dana. What should have taken ten minutes lasted half an hour.

They made love again after dinner. In fact, they'd made love every night no matter what time Marshall finished his meetings. He never seemed to tire of her.

Maybe there was a chance this didn't have to end.

"You're so beautiful." He stroked her arm. "At work, I want to pick up my phone and send you a dirty text. Tell you everything I want to do to you in the night."

"You should." She tipped her head to look at him. "In fact, I insist. Tomorrow, I want a dirty, filthy, naughty text. It'll be like foreplay."

He pulled her down, hugged her tight, "I am so crazy for you. We think exactly alike."

But was he thinking that he couldn't go on without her once they were home?

THE DAY BEFORE SHE WAS SUPPOSED TO FLY OUT, DANA FELT sick. Marshall had tried to get out of his meetings, but they were signing papers today, pledging millions of dollars.

"I must have eaten something bad yesterday," she told Laura, though it was her heart that ached. "I'm so sorry, but if you don't mind, I just want to lay by the pool and not move."

Marshall told her over and over that he couldn't get enough of her.

But he hadn't mentioned the future or San Francisco or the end of her holiday.

Laura was so understanding. "We've been rushing around so much, I'd like a day by the pool, too. We'll get those frothy drinks with umbrellas and lots of fruit and soak all our ills away." Laura hugged her, tightly, almost too tightly, as if she knew all the fears wreaking havoc on Dana's insides.

Her stomach was too upset for fruity concoctions with umbrellas. But as they lay on their lounge chairs, the warmth was good. They sat under umbrellas so they wouldn't burn and ordered salads and laughed and talked and read and swam.

Dana ticked down the minutes in her mind until Marshall would be back. It was their last night. Would he say he couldn't get enough of her and had to see her when they were home?

Just tell him what you want.

It was Carol's voice. Since Laura had arrived, maybe even since Dana had started sleeping with Marshall, she'd rarely heard Carol's voice in her head.

She remembered that day all those weeks ago when she'd told the girls about this trip. Even she had wondered why she'd go alone when she had no one to share the experience with. And yet now, she'd experienced so much with Marshall, the beautiful sunsets, the amazing food, the ancient sites they'd visited. Even that moment in the Colosseum when she'd thought about Livia's speech to the gladiators in *I, Claudius*.

There was so much more to share. If she could ask for it.

In a daze, almost asleep, Dana enumerated all the reasons why she couldn't, as if Carol were sitting beside her. Because it could spoil everything, because she couldn't stand rejection, because she didn't want to start something only to have it hurt even worse if he got tired of her after a few months. Because he wasn't the relationship kind and she was the marrying kind. She wanted a man in her life, a good man who wouldn't cheat on her.

"Marshall will never cheat on you."

Dana jerked. She'd fallen asleep. She'd thought Carol was talking to her. And she turned her head.

"He cares about you," Laura said.

Good Lord. She hadn't been sleeping, she'd actually said all that aloud as if Laura were Carol.

"He's a good man," Laura added. "I'm biased because he's my brother." She fluttered her hand. "But if you don't ask him, he might not ask you. Because he thinks you're on the rebound from your divorce, especially after losing Carol so suddenly. But if neither of you say anything, then you both go your separate ways and you'll never know." She stared at Dana, her gaze penetrating even through her sunglasses. "And that would be a tragedy."

Dana opened her mouth, but nothing came out.

"It's just a few little words," Laura said, her voice barely loud enough to be heard above the childish squeals in the pool. "It could mean a lifetime of happiness."

"Or a world of heartache."

"But what if it's not?" she asked, softly, sincerely.

Laura sounded like Carol in the park all those months ago, urging her to take a chance.

But like a child, she wanted to stamp her foot. "Why can't he do the asking?"

Laura threw her head back and laughed loud enough for everyone in the vicinity to turn their heads. "You sound like Kyle when I told him that if he needed a date for his first homecoming dance he could ask any pretty girl he wanted and she would probably say yes."

"Did he ask someone?"

"No. And the girl he wanted to ask went with another boy. Now they're a couple and Kyle missed out."

"Are you going to remind him about that when the next dance rolls around?"

"I sure as hell will." They laughed together, then Laura ended by saying, "Just think about it."

This time it really was Carol's voice in her head. *If you don't ask, I'm going to haunt you for the rest of your life.*

<hr />

"I'M GOING TO MISS THIS SIGHT," DANA SAID. SHE WAS going to miss him.

Marshall wrapped his fingers around hers, stroking the back of her hand with his thumb. "Why don't you change your flight and stay a few extra days? You can fly home with us."

Dana was dumbfounded. They'd had a fabulous goodbye dinner at an exclusive restaurant one of Marshall's customers had recommended. When they got back to the hotel, even though it wasn't late, Laura had begged off another drink down in the bar and gone to her room.

Dana and Marshall had skipped the nightcap and gone straight to making beautiful love. Now they sat in their hotel robes in their usual spot on her balcony, looking at the Colosseum and Rome's skyline for the last time.

"There'll be a huge fee if I make a change." She didn't think her heart would be any less broken a few days from now.

"I'll pay the change fee," he said.

Did he want more time with her now because he expected it to be over once they were home?

"No, I can't let you do that." She stared at the familiar outline of the Colosseum, wondering if she'd ever see it again.

He gave her fingers the slightest pressure. "I don't want you to leave yet."

"Why?" The question was out before she let herself be afraid of his answer.

"Aren't you enjoying yourself?" He blithely turned it back on her.

"I am. What about you?"

"Absolutely. That's why I want you to stay."

He hadn't said he didn't want their relationship to end. He just didn't want it to end now.

Her pain was her own fault. Neither of them was supposed to get attached. He was filling in for her sexy young Italian lover. And she was just coming off a wrenching divorce, reacting to the first man who desired her.

But what if they'd found something special, something real, something lasting? She needed to know if he felt the same way, even the tiniest bit.

In her silence, he added, "I'll have more free time now. Not just at night. And there's still so much more to see here in Rome."

He could have been begging, but what was he begging for?

Tell him what you want. Be the mature woman you are and just tell him. The voice in her head wasn't Carol's. It wasn't even Laura's. It was her own inner longings screaming their way out.

She was tired of subjugating her needs to other people's

desires. First it had been Anthony, then her girls, and as the years passed, she kept on doing it because she didn't know any other way.

That's what Carol had been trying to tell her, that she needed to start asking for what she wanted, not what she thought everybody else wanted.

What she really wanted was a man to desire her, a man who could be her friend *and* her lover. A man who wouldn't leave. She didn't want it because her life couldn't be full without it. She wanted it because she deserved happiness.

"It's been good." He tugged on her hand until she looked at him. "I can't get enough of your company."

She remembered running the Spanish Steps, the pep talk about how capable she was. Well, she could be capable and courageous right now.

And finally, she leaped. "Then let's make a date for when you get back."

He simply stared at her, his eyes like dark, unfathomable pools at midnight. She heard everything he didn't say, and she made it worse by asking, "This doesn't have to be just a holiday fling." She took a deep breath. "It doesn't have to end."

He dropped her hand to reach for the champagne bottle, refilling her glass, then his. It was an act meant to cover up the fact that he couldn't touch her, that she'd broken the rules, that she'd stepped outside acceptable boundaries.

Her heart broke in all that silence.

But now that she'd started, there was no reason to stop. She had nothing left to lose.

※

"Is that what you really want?" Even to Marshall, it sounded like a cheap-ass way to get out of answering.

"What's the difference if we have a few extra days here when we can have a date back home?" Her voice was infinitesimally harder, sharper.

The difference. Jesus. The difference was in watching something simply end, versus watching it end badly.

"I know you're afraid." Her voice rang out clearly, but not loudly, as if she knew the truth could cut him.

"I'm not afraid." But he sounded defensive. "I just know how things usually turn out." His denial was too fast, too adamant. Not out of fear, but because he was a realist. "Remember how you were afraid that going to bed with me would change things between us? That you wouldn't be as open as you had been?"

"I remember." She looked out at a skyline made bright with the Colosseum's lights as if she were memorizing it.

"And that's exactly what happened." He kept his voice low, cajoling, willing her to see. "We're amazing in bed. But you don't tell me everything the way you used to."

She closed her eyes. As if she needed to shut out the truth of his words. "That's exactly right. I have been holding back. I've done all my talking with your sister. I treated her like she's Carol, my BFF."

"She could be a friend to you like Carol was."

She slashed a hand in the air, her anger showing through. "What I'm telling you is that I treated *you* like you were Carol, like *you* were my best friend. And when we started making love—"

He almost corrected her, almost said they'd been having sex. But even he knew that was a lie.

"—I stopped being able to talk to you just the way I thought I would. But that's my problem." She fisted her hand in the robe. "It's something I need to get over." She sighed, a long, lonely sound. "It's taken me days to get up the courage to tell you that I don't want our relationship to end." She held up her hand when he opened his mouth. "It *is* a relationship no matter what you say. We connected on a deeper level than any of those gigolos I went out with. You know it and I know it. But I let our new level of relationship get in the way." She meant the sex got in the way. "I've done that all my adult life, closed up, put on the pretty façade so that everyone would be happy and everyone would like me. The only person I was ever real with was Carol. So now, I could let you off the hook, and say you're right, Marshall, we shouldn't go on. There's nothing to fight for. I could stop making you feel uncomfortable."

"You don't make me uncomfortable," he managed to get in.

He would have said more, except that she put two fingers over his lips. "If we were still friends and not lovers, and if I was talking to you about some other man, I'd tell you that I'm afraid, too. I'd say that I was hurt in my marriage, but it hasn't made me stop wanting another relationship. I would tell you that I've met a man who makes me feel wonderful and that I'm not willing to walk away without finding out if things could work out between us."

She was so beautiful, so honest, so sincere. But she didn't understand. "I'm not willing to let you get hurt in the end. I watched my parents' marriage dissolve. I've seen it happen to countless friends over the past thirty years. I've watched a bad marriage tear apart my own sister. It makes my heart sore. And I absolutely do not want that for you." He flung out his hand. "Look at your own marriage, it didn't survive. Nothing survives." She winced at the brutal truth, but he had to be ruthless to make her see. "Do you know any good marriages, even one?"

"Yes, Carol and her husband Thomas. They were loving and caring. Just because my marriage wasn't like that doesn't mean all marriages are bad. Are you telling me not one friend or acquaintance is still married?" she challenged.

He shrugged off her words. "Sure, I've seen a few marriages that are seemingly decent from the outside. But who knows what it's like on the inside? Just because they're still married doesn't mean it's still good."

"God, you're cynical," she whispered, her eyes pale and sad.

They'd made love so beautifully. He wanted to gather her in his arms, sleep the night away with her, make love to her in the morning before she left. He should never have asked her to stay those extra days. Things would have been good if he hadn't opened his mouth. But that's exactly what happened when you asked for too much. That's what he wanted her to see.

Didn't she know that if he could really have more, he'd grab it?

"The kind of relationship you're talking about is a fantasy," he said. "Like one of the wishes you made in the fountain."

She turned on him. "You told me to wish for the impossible. And I'm willing to try for the impossible. I'm willing to tell you everything that's in my heart." She thumped a fist to her chest. "I care about you so much. It's teetering on the edge of love, Marshall."

He couldn't breathe he was so afraid for her. He couldn't hurt her. He'd do anything not to. And that meant making her see the truth. "You've known me for what, three weeks? You can't be in love with me."

"Only a person who doesn't know how to love could say that. I know what I feel. You can call it whatever you want. But I love you." Pain and anguish burned in her gaze.

He knew how much it cost her to say those words. He

knew about her husband, her daughters, her best friend, he knew about her fears, her troubles, her desires.

He apologized because she was right. "I'm sorry. You do know me. And I know you. That's why I'm not willing to get to a place where I'll hurt you."

"Or a place where I'll hurt you," she said so very softly.

"It's really not about me."

She called him on that, too. "You don't know what it's like because you've never let yourself be hurt. I'm actually sorry for you, Marshall. You're fifty-five years old, and you've never let yourself really experience life and love."

"Oh, I've experienced life." He tried to give her a smug smile, knew he failed.

"All you know is business. Anthony may have hurt me. He may have made me feel undesirable and cheated on. But I did know love, and I want that feeling again. You simply don't know what you're missing."

He knew what he'd be missing, her in his bed. She was special. They had a connection he'd never experienced before. "But everything dies, Dana."

She winced, and he felt the callousness of his words. "I'm sorry, I didn't mean Carol."

"You're right, Marshall." She blinked away tears. "I wished for the impossible. And now I see that it really is impossible."

"I wasn't talking about Carol. That was a special wish and you needed to make it."

She looked at him, her pretty green eyes tracing his brow, his cheeks, his nose, his lips. Almost as if she were touching him. "I don't see how the same man who walked me from fountain to fountain telling me to make my impossible wish could actually say that our relationship isn't possible." She sniffed softly, but there wasn't a single tear on her cheek. "I thought I was the one who was scared of life. But I see that you're worse than I ever was."

He wasn't afraid. He wanted to protect her.

She stood then, held out her hand. "You need to make love to me one more time, Marshall, before I leave. I want to remember it. I want you to remember it."

Her words reached inside his chest like a fist closing around his heart, squeezing until he thought it might burst.

But he took her hand. And swore he would give them both one last memory neither would ever forget.

25

Dana didn't cry. She had opened her heart to him, given him every last ounce of emotion she had in her.

He hadn't wanted any of it.

She would cry over that later.

Now she gave herself over to the physical, to the way he smiled, to the sounds he made, to how his body caressed hers, to the sensations only he could elicit.

She pushed him down onto the rumpled sheets, untied his robe, and spread it wide open across the sheets. Then she crawled down his glorious body to take him in her mouth. She didn't want to create a memory he would never forget. She wanted to create one she never would.

He tasted sweet and salty and delicious, and she gave him all the pleasure she could, with her lips and tongue, with her hands and fingers, squeezing him, stroking him, licking and sucking until he reared deeper in her throat and groaned. She didn't stop until his legs began to quiver. She knew that sensation intimately, knew his climax was imminent.

But she wasn't letting him go there without her.

Pulling back, holding him lightly, she gazed down at the beauty of him in her hand, the rapid rise and fall of his chest, the dazed look in his eyes as he waited for her.

"Make me come," she whispered, smoothing a finger over his tip, finding the droplets, licking them off her fingers. "And then I'll let you have me."

For a man who'd seemed dazed by pleasure only moments before, he moved fast, rolling her beneath him. "I'll make you come until you scream, until you beg me to stop."

Since they'd gone from friends to lovers, they'd always been good at sex talk. She was wet and ready for him, and she pushed him down between her legs. "Use your mouth on me."

Then he was on her, his fingers in her, his tongue and his lips driving her wild. She fisted her hands in the sheet, arched against him. He knew just how slow, how fast, how hard or gentle and sweet she wanted it. He let her tremble on the edge, only to back off and drive her up again, over and over, until she became a wild thing, writhing beneath him, crying out his name, holding him close as she reached the crest, rode the wave, and crashed down on the other side.

Just like every beautiful, amazing, wonderful, perfect time, he was inside her before she knew how he got there.

"I will make it so good," he whispered.

This time he took it slow, didn't pound the way she sometimes needed. He simply rode that spot inside her until she was trembling, gliding along the razor-sharp edge, ready to fall. The moment her body clenched around him and all her cells exploded, the moment she screamed his name, he thrust home, hard and deep, matching the explosions inside her.

And the shockwaves dragged them both under.

He fell asleep with her in his arms, sated, boneless, mindless. He didn't remember the fight out on the balcony. He didn't remember the pain on her face or the hurt in her words. He didn't remember the fear in his heart.

Not until he woke to the morning light spilling across the bed, igniting her hair with red-gold fire.

Then he remembered everything as if it were a dagger straight through his heart, spilling every last drop of blood.

He eased off the bed without waking her, closed the bathroom door, climbed beneath the hot shower spray.

Her flight was today. He had to get her to the airport by eleven.

He wanted to ask again, to beg for a few extra days.

And then what? An airport goodbye when they got back home?

She was right. She couldn't stay. It was best to end it now.

Except that's not what she'd said at all.

He wanted to throw open the shower door, march into the bedroom, make love to her, and *make* her stay. He would promise they'd work it out. He would have his few more days.

And then break his promise?

He would never forget their nights together, their mornings and afternoons, their showers, their talks on her balcony, their walks, the places they'd visited, her hand in his.

Laura had accused him of not being a risk-taker. Dana had accused him of being afraid.

It was none of those things. It was the deep inner knowing that wishes never came true.

Then why had he insisted that Dana make her wish to bring her friend back?

If he could make a wish, he'd wish that she would stay.

She'd packed her bags yesterday. All she had to do this morning was add the last few items, cosmetics bag, the clothes she'd worn yesterday, the dress and high heels for last night's dinner, her walking shoes, her hopes, her dreams.

Marshall showered without her, waking up before she did. She heard the water running, and she could have joined him. But she didn't think she could stand one more touch, one more kiss, one more look.

Last night had taken everything out of her.

They had breakfast with Laura, who did all the talking and begged Dana to stay, entreating Marshall to do the same.

Dana smiled and said, "No, I really need to get home." Without looking at Marshall, she added, "Be sure to call me about your bookkeeping when you get back."

Laura slapped her hand playfully. "The bookkeeping is the least important thing. I just want a nice coffee chat. Or maybe a wine chat. Or a good dinner. We are absolutely not going to let this friendship fade into the sunset just because you're flying home today."

The silence stretched long and uncomfortable around the table.

Until Dana broke it. "I'm so glad we met." She squeezed Laura's hand. "You know I have a shortage of friends now." She smiled, even if it felt like her cheeks would crack and her heart would break wide open.

"Good." Then Laura began a discussion, with very little input from Marshall, of the things they would do in their last few days in Rome. "And I don't care if you've visited all those places with Dana, you have to see them all over again." She reached across to pat Dana's hand as if she were sending a message. "If Dana were staying, I might be willing to see some other things, but since she's not, you have to take me." She stabbed a finger into Marshall's shoulder. He reacted like stone, as if she couldn't move him.

Just like Dana couldn't move him.

Breakfast ended, Laura unhooked her purse from the back of her chair. "Now, I'm going up to my room, put on a bathing suit, and get a little sun by the pool. And I'm letting you—" She eyed Marshall. "—take Dana to the airport. You'll find me drinking cocktails on a lounge chair under an umbrella when you get back."

She bent down to hug Dana tightly. "I'm so glad you came into my life. And you will be staying in my life, I guarantee," she said softly, too softly for Marshall to hear.

What she wouldn't give to hear those words from Marshall's lips.

But as Laura walked away, he signed the bill and thanked the waiter.

Looking at Marshall's beautiful profile, she ached in every organ, every muscle, every cell of her body. Yet there was a kernel of self-esteem growing inside her. She'd asked for what she wanted. She didn't get the right answer, but she had been brave.

Maybe that was the difference between her and Marshall. He lacked the courage.

※

"You don't have to take me to the airport." Her voice wasn't harsh, but she didn't look at him either.

"I want to take you." He gave her bags to the valet to put in the trunk of the taxi.

Jesus, where had it all gone wrong? Maybe it was Laura's arrival, because they had so little time together after that. The work had consumed his time, stripping away all the daylight hours. But they'd had the nights, had sex every moment they could.

But that's not what they'd done. They'd made love. No

matter whether it was permanent or whether it was a relationship, they had made beautiful love together.

As they sat silently in the backseat, the driver wended his way through the city, their last few minutes together ticking away in the smell of exhaust and the blare of car horns. For the first time since he'd found her in the Colosseum, the silence between them was unbearable.

This was never how he'd wanted it to end.

"Dana." He took her hand, raised it to his lips, kissed her knuckles. Even that felt awkward, as if he no longer had a right.

"It's all right, Marshall," she said softly, forcing him to lean close enough to smell the fragrance of her hair, the perfume of her skin. "I understood the rules from the beginning. But I'm glad I asked you. I wanted to give us a chance. Everything we did together, I loved. And thank you..." She trailed off as if she didn't know what to thank him for.

The only ineffectual thing he could say was, "You don't have to thank me." He wanted to say he'd treasure every moment, but it sounded so freaking final.

And isn't that what he'd made it? Final?

They arrived at the airport, and he'd squandered all the time they had left.

He helped her with a hand on her elbow. When her bags were on the sidewalk, he paid the driver.

"You don't have to walk me in."

He waved the taxi away. "I want to."

Grabbing the handles of her two suitcases, one large, one small, he rolled them into the arrivals lobby. They found her ticket counter and checked in her bags.

He'd needed those extra days. He wasn't ready to let her go. He felt frantic, a sensation he hadn't known in years, if ever. He was always calm, cool, and collected in business meetings. Associates called him unflappable. Yet now he was out of words, out of time.

"We could have a cup of coffee before you go." He wanted to take her hand the way he'd done so many times as they'd walked the streets of Rome. But she was so far away now.

"I'd really like to get through security. I'll find a seat in the lounge."

He longed for the days when you could walk someone all the way to the gate, sit with them until it was time to board. But he couldn't follow her in there.

"Just one cup. I won't keep you long. I'll get you to the security gate in plenty of time."

He heard how desperate he sounded. How pathetic. But he wanted to grab her, holding on until her plane was in the air and she had to stay.

"No, really." She didn't look at him. "I'm all jittery until I get settled in the lounge."

He recognized the excuse. She was done with him. He'd ignored her question about seeing her again when they got home. He hadn't actually denied it, he simply hadn't answered it, saying things about how relationships could hurt, they couldn't work.

She pulled up the handle of her carry-on, hitched her purse higher on her shoulder.

Then he wondered why they couldn't see each other again? It didn't make a difference. It would hurt later, sure, but it hurt now. At least he would have more time with her.

And he said it, finally. "I'll call you when I get back."

She stopped, half turned away from him, and stared far too long, her features almost hard, and so unlike her. Then she asked, "Why?"

She was going to force him to say it. "Because we're not done yet."

"Why do we have to be done at all?" she said very softly,

and with all the passengers streaming by them, he had to move closer to hear.

He'd tried last night but he could never make her understand. Because she'd been married. Because she'd had a relationship that worked, at least for a few years. Because she still believed in love.

"I know you don't think the way I do. But I know—"

She cut him off. "You don't know anything, Marshall. All you've ever done is watch other people's relationships. You've watched other people's mistakes. You need to make your own mistakes, then you can tell me what you know." She put her hand under his chin, and he realized he'd been looking at her feet. "Look at *me*," she demanded. "My marriage didn't work. But I'm not afraid to try again."

He wanted to say he wasn't afraid, but the words stuck in his throat.

She turned, the wheels of her case gliding smoothly over the floor as she walked away.

He'd call her when he got home. She'd see things differently then.

He watched her join the security line to show her passport and ticket. She didn't look back so he could wave.

In that moment, as if someone had suddenly hit him on the head with a brick, he knew she would never answer his call when he got home. She'd given him his chance last night, then again just now.

He'd failed both times.

There wouldn't be a third chance.

He recognized the emotion welling up in his throat. Fear. Fear that he would never see her again. That he'd just made the biggest mistake of his life. Laura was right, he wasn't a risk-taker. He was a fearful man who'd never put his heart on the line.

And if he didn't do that now, the very heart he was afraid of having broken, would shrivel up in his chest and die.

Marshall broke into a run.

❀

She heard feet pounding even over the sound of her own heartbreak.

She heard shouting, but she couldn't understand the words. She shuffled forward in the line. She just wanted to get to the gate.

Yet the next shout sounded like her name. "Dana." And the voice sounded like Marshall's.

Five passengers ahead, the agent held out his hand for a passport and boarding pass.

"Who on earth is Dana?" the elderly lady behind her said in a very American accent.

Dana turned and Marshall was standing at the edge of the barrier.

"Is he shouting at you?" the woman asked, the lights overhead shining on her glasses.

"Yes, I think he is."

The lady frowned, pursed her lips. And she called out, "You better make this good, sonny." Then she pointed at the queue, which had grown exponentially behind them. "Because she'll have to wait in this line all over again."

"I'll make it good, I swear," Marshall called right back.

They were now a spectacle, everyone in front and behind, including the security guards, leaning close to take in the action.

With everyone listening, he said what she'd wanted to hear. "I don't want this to end."

She waited for him to add a qualifier. When he didn't, she

pushed her way through the queue and ducked under the barrier belt to stand in front of him.

"You're right about everything, Dana."

"What exactly does that mean?" She needed him to spell it out.

The elderly woman in line gave Dana a thumbs up, and seeing that, a fortyish man with thick black hair and a mustache gave Marshall a thumbs down.

But Marshall didn't seem to care, drawing her away from the crowd as another agent stepped in to help move the line faster.

"I'm a complete idiot," Marshall said. "You've just given me the best three weeks of my life. When I saw you that day in the Colosseum with your eyes closed and your head tipped back, I just had to know you. And when you talked about *I, Claudius*, I knew there was something about us that was fated. But I've been in denial ever since. I don't know why I'm letting you leave now. Maybe it's because I'm a fearful, fifty-five-year-old man who doesn't know how to change." He cupped her cheek, his hand big and warm and beautiful. "But I want to change for you, Dana."

She felt the cold, hard knot around her heart begin to melt. "Are you sure?"

"You're worth any risk." He slipped a hand behind her nape, drawing her close enough to smell that manly scent she so loved. "I will call you when I get back. I don't want just a date with you." He leaned in, brushing his lips against hers. "Or to have sex with you." He opened his mouth, kissed her. "I want to make love with you." Then he whispered, "I want all your days, all your nights. I want to fall asleep with you and wake up beside you in the morning. I want a relationship. I want everything." He leaned his forehead against hers. "Take a risk with me, Dana. Help me make it work. Because I do love you."

She did what her heart wanted most, throwing her arms around him and whispering, "Yes, yes, yes."

Applause erupted in the line, from people inside and outside the security gate.

Marshall held her face in his hands. "I'm not going ask you to stay. I already did that and I screwed it up."

"My bags are probably on the plane." She waved a hand behind her as if they were back there somewhere in the airport ether.

"Don't get me wrong, I want you to stay, but I'm also looking forward to an amazing reunion when I get home."

"I'll be waiting for you at the airport. And I'll throw myself in your arms."

"Even with my sister beside me?"

She laughed. "Especially with your sister beside you."

He kissed her openmouthed to another round of applause and a voice calling out, "See, romance is alive and well." The voice was female and rusty with age. "Even in your fifties. There's hope for us all."

"She is so right." Marshall's voice was rough with emotion.

"I have enough time for coffee." She didn't even look at her watch.

If she didn't make the flight, it was meant to be.

EPILOGUE

In the end, Dana had made her flight, and Marshall stayed another week in Rome with Laura. Every night he'd called her at nine-thirty before she went to bed, six-thirty in the morning Rome time. And he taught her the delicious art of phone sex. Sometimes during her day, before he went to bed, he'd sent her a few sexts. It was fun, it was sexy, it was something most fifty-year-old people didn't do, and she loved it.

Even once he was back, she'd often pick up her phone during the day to find a naughty text telling her what he planned to do to her that very night.

A month after Marshall returned, Dana hadn't exactly moved into his house. And he hadn't exactly moved into hers. They split their time between the two. Sunday through Thursday, she stayed at his house in Hillsborough because it was closer to his office right near the San Mateo Bridge. On the weekends, they were at her place farther down the Peninsula because she had the pool and hot tub in the backyard. At his house, they binged *Game of Thrones* because he'd subscribed to the channel, and at hers, she brought out *Buffy the Vampire Slayer*. She thought she had a convert for both shows, though Marshall preferred *Game of Thrones*, less teenage angst, he said.

But all that had changed this week when the girls came home from college for the summer. Since it was their first week home, it hadn't felt right to leave them. And today they were visiting their father and Kimberly and the new baby.

Dana could only hope it went well, but she still wasn't sure about Natalie's feelings.

It was Friday afternoon, and Marshall would drive down after work. The girls knew about their relationship, and they'd met him last Sunday. Tonight would be the first night he stayed over with the girls in the house.

Thankfully, Laura was stopping by, ostensibly for some work on her realty books, but they'd also have a good chat. Dana had baked a coffee cake and brewed a fresh pot. Maybe she would get one of those single-cup machines that Marshall had.

As usual, Laura blew in like a tornado. She was always a presence. She already referred to Dana as her sister-in-law. "It's too difficult to say my fifty-five-year-old brother's girlfriend." Then she would nudge Dana's shoulder. "I feel like we're sisters."

A week after her return from Italy, Laura had brought over all her paperwork, saying, "I fully admit things are a mess. I leave everything till the last minute and input it all right before I need to give it to the tax man." Laura had moaned and Dana groaned with her. "But that makes me totally crazy."

"I promise to stay on top of it, and you'll never have to worry again," Dana assured her.

"Oh, thank God."

This afternoon they planned to go over what Dana had put together so far.

"You look marvelous," Laura said. "And this coffee cake." She patted her stomach. "You're going to ruin my diet, but I can't resist one piece."

Dana waved a hand. "You don't need to worry about coffee cake. You always look amazing."

That's what they did, built each other up.

Just like she and Carol had done. And since going through Laura's books, Dana could assure her that her business was doing well.

"Bless you," Laura said, looking at the year-to-date profit-and-loss statement on Dana's computer screen. "During the year, I figure that if I have enough cash, it's all good, but it's still this huge cloud hanging over me." She waved her fingers around her head. Then she reached for Dana in a spontaneous, heartfelt hug. "I feel free."

"That makes me very happy." Dana meant every word.

"How's Thomas doing?" Laura knew Dana saw Thomas once a week for lunch.

Dana shook her head, sadness creeping over her. "He still misses Carol. He will for a long, long time. But spending time with me gives him a chance to talk about her. Everyone else just thinks he needs to move on."

Laura tsked.

"Yeah," Dana added. "Some friends are even trying to set him up on dates."

"Oh my God. That's just crazy."

Dana shrugged. "He needs time right now. At some point he'll have to get out more, but he's still grieving. And he's agreed to see a counselor. It'll be good for him."

Laura squeezed her hand. "You're a good friend." Then she glanced at her watch. "I better get out of here if I don't want to get stuck in the commute traffic." They'd whiled away the afternoon looking at the numbers and talking. It felt like the old days with Carol.

"Why don't you to stay to dinner?" Dana asked.

Laura raised a brow. "Well, the boys are with their father this weekend, so I have the evening free." She smiled. "I'd love to."

Her ex-husband had stopped bugging her about a reconciliation, there was a man at the title company she found very interesting, and things had settled down with the boys. They'd returned from their time with their aunt, which seemed to have done them a world of good. Though Laura swore she didn't try to pry out of them what had been said or done or revealed. That was for them alone, unless they wanted to tell her.

Dana thought that was a very good strategy.

"We're just having hamburgers. I bought those new veggie burgers that are supposed to taste like meat because Olivia says she's trying to go vegan."

"If you're sure I'm not horning in. I know you're using this time to get the girls used to Marshall."

"I want them to get to know you, too."

"I could never replace Carol."

Dana touched her shoulder. "There's always room in a woman's life for another really good friend." Dana had room for Laura, plenty of it. "And the girls need to have room in their hearts for another auntie."

She thought of how seamlessly Laura fitted into her world.

She'd had a long talk with Carol about it. She would always have long talks with Carol. Her BFF was irreplaceable, but her friendship with Laura was growing like spring bulbs in the garden.

"How are the girls really doing with Marshall?"

Dana shoved down the tiny knot of tension. Honestly, that was about herself, not the girls and not Marshall. She was always looking for signs that they were unhappy. After all, they'd come home from college for the summer to find their mother had a boyfriend. It was something to get used to, even though Dana had told them about Marshall as soon as she returned from Rome. But it was quite another matter when they were faced with a man sleeping over.

"They were exceptionally polite with him last week when they got home. They laughed, they told jokes, and they talked about college." She sighed. "But there's still that sense of..." She looked out the window trying to find the right word. "I guess it's standoffishness." She rubbed her temple. "I thought about having him sleep in the guest room tonight. But that's not fair to Marshall. Or me. And I don't want to get into some weird routine with the girls of hiding what I'm doing whenever they come home from school."

"They're big girls," Laura said. "They need to know you have a life. You can't treat them like kids where you have to have silent sex because they might overhear."

Dana reflected back on her marriage and was honest enough with herself to wonder if that might have been part of their problem. "I was always the one shushing Anthony. He used to say I took the fun out of sex." She shrugged. "And maybe I did."

"That's only natural. Everybody does it. You don't want to be wailing away in the night when kids with big ears are in the next room hearing everything."

Dana laughed. And Laura went on. "But you shouldn't have to hide exactly what your relationship is with Marshall. You're in love. The girls should celebrate that with you."

She nodded, still thinking. "You're right. Absolutely."

Laura leaned in. "Be wild and crazy tonight," she whispered as if someone might overhear them. "And make the bedsprings squeak and the headboard hit the wall."

Dana couldn't help tumbling into hysterical laughter right

along with Laura. When she could finally speak again, she said, "And I really do like to be loud."

Laura put her hands over her ears. "Please, he's my brother, I don't want to hear."

When their peals of laughter died away, Laura said, "If you walk around on eggshells with the girls, they're going to walk around on eggshells, too, and they'll never get used to Mom having a love life. It's not like they don't know you're a complete slut." She crowed with glee, and they fell into fits of laughter all over again.

Then the front door opened, and she knew by the footsteps in the hall that it wasn't one of the girls. She'd given Marshall his own key, just as she had a key to his house. And she was glad he'd used it even if the girls were home from school. She'd given him every right to.

"We're in the office," she called out.

"Hey." He stood there a moment, framed in the doorway. Big, beautiful, and brave. Then he swooped in and kissed her openmouthed. "God, I missed you this week." After one more sweet kiss, he added. "I love you." She'd never get tired of hearing it.

"Love you, too," she whispered.

"Get a room," Laura groused with a laugh laced beneath it.

Dana smiled. "He's already got a room right here."

In her house, in her life, in her heart.

"So, Marshall," Laura asked. "What did you think of the veggie burgers?"

He was surrounded by women. And he loved it. The June evening was warm, and they were all dressed in summer tops, Laura, Natalie and Olivia, Dana's two girls, beautiful women like their mother. But the most beautiful woman of all was seated next to him. Dana. They were all his family now. Even if the girls didn't know it yet.

"Well, they barbecue like regular burgers." They'd even sizzled like real burgers, dripping fat onto the flames. "But why are you all looking at me?"

Natalie, the older one, smiled with a glint in her eye. "Because men are the carnivores."

It was almost like a challenge. And he understood that. He'd walked into their mother's life, practically out of nowhere, and they were protective. He approved of that. "I'd have to say they're pretty darn good." He looked at Dana's younger daughter, the one thinking about going vegan. "What do you think, Olivia?"

She smiled. "I've got nothing against carnivores." She lifted her burger. "But these are tasty."

Beneath the table, Dana took his hand in hers. Her skin was warm, her scent sweet and motherly and sexy as well.

"I think they're amazing," Laura said. "But they're expensive. I hope the boys don't decide to go vegan or they'll eat me out of house and home."

Her laughter broke all the tension. Or maybe he'd imagined the tension in the first place.

Dana picked up her burger, asking, "So how was the baby?"

She took a bite to hide her feelings. He knew her so well, the slight crinkle at her eyes, which right now had nothing to do with laughter.

"Oh my God." Natalie groaned. "I have to admit he's the cutest little thing. And Dad." She clucked her tongue. "It was like he'd never even seen a baby before and this was the most amazing thing." She rolled her eyes. "And what's with naming the kid Damien? Isn't that like a devil name or something?"

Marshall rubbed his hand on Dana's thigh, just a little

connection. She'd known the girls were going to see their new baby brother who'd been born a couple of weeks ago. Dana wanted her daughters to have a relationship with their half brother. And it wasn't the baby's fault his dad was an asshole who couldn't appreciate the woman he'd married. His loss, Marshall's gain.

"He was pretty amazing," Olivia said, her voice softer than her sister's. She smiled. "Five fingers and five toes, what more could you ask for?"

Dana smiled just like her daughter. "They do all have them. I hope you go see them again."

Olivia bit her lip. "Dad wants to have a special Sunday dinner once a month." She looked at her mother almost shyly, gauging her reaction. "What do you think?"

With a gentle, understanding smile, Dana said, "That would be wonderful."

She was a generous, forgiving woman. She wanted the best for her daughters, and the best did not include a feud with their father over his mistakes and his newborn.

Seeing Laura's almost empty glass, Marshall picked up the champagne bottle, but she put her hand over it. "Remember I have to drive, big brother."

"Why don't you spend the night?" Dana offered. "We've got plenty of room."

Laura's gaze flicked to him. He gave a slight nod.

"Yeah," Natalie said. "I can bunk with Liv, and you can have my bed."

He knew where this was heading.

"No," Dana said without even a hesitation. "You can have the guestroom, Laura." Then, before either girl could say anything, she added, "Marshall will stay with me."

They'd talked about this, whether she wanted to downplay their true relationship. There was a big difference between being their mother's boyfriend and being her lover. But it was obvious Dana had made her stand.

For a moment, neither girl spoke. Then it was Olivia. "That sounds fine." She gave Natalie a light shove. "She's a bed hog anyway."

Natalie laughed. "Hah, look who's talking."

He didn't know her well enough to determine whether the laugh was brittle or acquiescent or completely accepting. Yet it broke any tension at the table.

They chatted about the girls' summer jobs, about Laura's realty and Dana taking over her bookkeeping. They had a light fruit salad for dessert, and when Dana started to rise to clear the table, Natalie waved her down. "We'll do the dishes, Mom." Then she pierced him with a look. "Marshall's going to help us."

He wondered if Dana's daughters had planned this all along, knowing he was going to be here. Whatever they wanted to dish out, he was up for the challenge. He would show them he was the best thing for their mother.

Natalie started the moment they were in the kitchen. "So, you met Mom in Italy."

He turned to the sink to rinse a dish, hiding a smile. "Yes. I saw her on her very first day, at the Colosseum."

"What, exactly, are your intentions?" Natalie asked, an edge to her voice. She sounded like the father of a teenage girl grilling her prom date before he let them leave the house.

He stacked a plate in the dishwasher. "She's an amazing woman," he started.

But Olivia interjected smoothly, "What Natalie means is that we love our mother, and she's had a hard time this past year, with my dad leaving and Carol passing away. We're just worried about her."

He turned then, leaning against the sink, and folded his arms over his chest. "The first thing your mother said to me was that she was reliving the scene from *I, Claudius* where Livia lectures the gladiators about putting on a good show." He didn't care whether the girls knew of their mother's love for all things Roman, he had a point to make.

Natalie snorted and Olivia laughed. "That is *so* Mom."

"I fell for her right then. I knew any woman who loved *I, Claudius* had to be the woman for me." Of course, it hadn't been that easy, they'd both been fighting the attraction all the way. Until the night Aureliano had tried to spike her drink. "But we were friends first, touring together, getting to know each and just enjoying the company. I learned a lot about her. And I understand completely how much Carol's loss affected her." Then he laid it out for them. "I love your mother very much."

"But it's all so fast." Natalie said, and he saw the love they both had for their mother, the caring, the worry.

"We just don't want her to get hurt. She's vulnerable right now," Olivia added.

"I don't want to see her get hurt either. I want to be the best thing for her. I know it seems fast to you, but I don't have kids and I've never been married. That's why I know we're meant to be together. Because I've never felt like this before. I will never hurt your mother." He looked at them both a long moment. "It's the nicest thing I've ever seen, the way you both want to look out for her. And I'm sure you'll read me the riot act with the first misstep I take. She loves you both very much." He could tell them how she worried about their feelings for their father, Natalie's anger and hesitancy, Olivia's acceptance that could mask more complex feelings underneath. But that was for Dana to discuss with them if she wanted. This was about him. "I'll do anything for her. She's my life now." He smiled. "She's even got me binging *Buffy the Vampire Slayer*."

Dana's beautiful girls laughed.

"Oh my God," Natalie said with an eye roll.

"Well, do you like it?" Olivia asked.

He grinned. "Truthfully, I like *Game of Thrones* better."

They looked at each other, smiled. And he knew he'd said the right thing. After all, honesty was the best policy.

It was late, and the house had grown quiet. Laura had borrowed a nightgown and toiletries from Dana. The girls had gone to their rooms, probably not to sleep but to look at their social media.

He held Dana in his arms, the only place he wanted to be for the rest of his life.

"So, what were they saying to you in the kitchen?" she whispered, her naked body pressed to his.

Marshall smiled. "They wanted to know my intentions."

She put her hand over her mouth, stifling a laugh. "What did you say?"

"I told them that for you, I even watched *Buffy the Vampire Slayer*."

She laughed, and he loved her laugh. "Did you tell them about *Game of Thrones*, too?"

He nodded his head. "I told them I preferred *Thrones*."

She nuzzled his neck. "How do you always know just the right thing to say?"

He rolled her beneath him. "I just tell the truth." He turned serious. "It's taken me a long time to find the right woman. And now that I have, I'm never letting you go. I'll just have to win your daughters over."

She pulled him down for sweet, gentle kiss. "Do you want to know my last wish at the Trevi Fountain?"

"Only if it won't jinx it."

Smiling, she said, "It's already come true. I wished to have my friend back. And here you are, my best friend as well as the love of my life." Her kiss was longer this time, deeper, their bodies and minds melding. But when she spoke again, her smile was cheeky. "We can have friendship *and* hot sex."

"Let me show you just how hot it can be."

With her, he finally had it all.

※

Once Again, a later-in-life series that will whisk you away to fabulous foreign locales where love always gets a second chance.

Look for the next **Once Again** novel, **Dancing in Ireland**.

ABOUT THE AUTHOR

NY Times and USA Today bestselling author Jennifer Skully is a lover of contemporary romance, bringing you poignant tales peopled with hilarious characters that will make you laugh and make you cry. Look for Jennifer's series written with Bella Andre, starting with *Breathless in Love*, The Maverick Billionaires Book 1. Writing as Jasmine Haynes, Jennifer authors classy, sensual romance tales about real issues such as growing older, facing divorce, starting over. Her books have passion and heart and humor and happy endings, even if they aren't always traditional. She also writes gritty, paranormal mysteries in the Max Starr series. Having penned stories since the moment she learned to write, Jennifer now lives in the Redwoods of Northern California with her husband and their adorable nuisance of a cat who totally runs the household.

Learn more about Jennifer/Jasmine and join her newsletter for free books, exclusive contests and excerpts, plus updates on sales and new releases at **http://bit.ly/SkullyNews**

ALSO BY JENNIFER SKULLY/JASMINE HAYNES

Books by Jennifer Skully
The Maverick Billionaires by Jennifer Skully & Bella Andre

Breathless in Love | Reckless in Love

Fearless in Love | Irresistible in Love

Wild In Love | Captivating In Love

Unforgettable in Love

Once Again

Dreaming of Provence | Wishing in Rome

Dancing in Ireland | Under the Northern Lights

Stargazing on the Orient Express

Memories of Santorini

Mystery of Love

Drop Dead Gorgeous | Sheer Dynamite

It Must be Magic | One Crazy Kiss

You Make Me Crazy | One Crazy Fling

Crazy for Baby

Return to Love

She's Gotta Be Mine | Fool's Gold | Can't Forget You

Return to Love: 3-Book Bundle

Love After Hours

Desire Actually | Love Affair To Remember

Pretty In Pink Slip

Stand-alone

Baby, I'll Find You | Twisted by Love

Be My Other Valentine

Books by Jasmine Haynes

Naughty After Hours

Revenge | Submitting to the Boss

The Boss's Daughter

The Only One for Her | Pleasing Mr. Sutton

Any Way She Wants It

More than a Night

A Very Naughty Christmas

Show Me How to Leave You

Show Me How to Love You

Show Me How to Tempt You

The Max Starr Series

Dead to the Max | Evil to the Max

Desperate to the Max

Power to the Max | Vengeance to the Max

Courtesans Tales

The Girlfriend Experience | Payback | Triple Play

Three's a Crowd | The Stand In | Surrender to Me

The Only Way Out | The Wrong Kind of Man

No Second Chances

The Jackson Brothers

Somebody's Lover | Somebody's Ex

Somebody's Wife
The Jackson Brothers: 3-Book Bundle

Castle Inc

The Fortune Hunter | Show and Tell
Fair Game

Open Invitation

Invitation to Seduction | Invitation to Pleasure
Invitation to Passion
Open Invitation: 3-Book Bundle

Wives & Neighbors

Wives & Neighbors: The Complete Story

Prescott Twins

Double the Pleasure | Skin Deep
Prescott Twins Complete Set

Lessons After Hours

Past Midnight | What Happens After Dark
The Principal's Office | The Naughty Corner
The Lesson Plan

Stand-alone

Take Your Pleasure | Take Your Pick
Take Your Pleasure Take Your Pick Duo
Anthology: Beauty or the Bitch & Free Fall